The Boss's Boy

A Mafia Mayhem Romance

~ *Dmitri* ~
I was intrigued by Eiji the first time I saw him dancing in my club. I became obsessed with him when the ink was still wet on our marriage certificate. I wanted to give Eiji the life he should have had until I realized I had taken something from him I had no right to take, and then I knew I had lost him forever.

~ *Eiji* ~
My life became uncomfortable the moment my father married my stepmother. It became a living hell when he died, leaving me in her cruel hands. At least, that' what I used to think, but then I discovered what true hell was, a brutal assault leaving me without a voice. When my stepmother married me off to a mob boss to pay her gambling debts, I realized that I had been wrong once again. My hell had just started...So why was he so gentle with me?

Warning: *Gay erotic romance. The material in this book contains explicit sexual content that is intended for mature audiences only. All characters involved are adults capable of consent, are over the age of eighteen, and are willing participants.*

Warning: *sensitive topics include violence, post trauma, depression, and anxiety attacks. Please read with caution.*

Copyright

The Boss's Boy
Copyright © Aja Foxx, 2023
ALL RIGHTS RESERVED

Cover Design by Sinfully Sweet Designs
All art and logo copyright © 2023 by Aja Foxx

First Electronic Edition June 2023

All rights reserved under the International and Pan-American Conventions. No part of this book may be reproduced or transmitted in any form or by any means, electronic or mechanical including photocopying, recording or by any information storage or retrieval system, without permission in writing from the author.

No part of this book may be scanned, uploaded or distributed via the internet or any other means, electronic or print, without permission from the authors. **Warning:** The unauthorized reproduction or distribution of this copyrighted work is illegal. Criminal copyright infringement, including infringement without monetary gain, is investigated by the FBI and is punishable by up to **5 years in federal prison and a fine of $250,000.** Please purchase only authorized electronic or print editions and do not participate in or encourage the electronic piracy of copyrighted material. Your support of the author's rights and livelihood is appreciated.

This book is a work of fiction. The names, characters, places, and incidents are products of the writer's imagination or have been used fictitiously and are not to be construed as real. Any resemblance to persons, living or dead, actual events, locale or organizations is entirely coincidental.

Table of Contents
Copyright
Chapter One
Chapter Two
Chapter Three
Chapter Four
Chapter Five
Chapter Six
Chapter Seven
Chapter Eight
Chapter Nine
Chapter Ten
Chapter Eleven
Chapter Twelve
Chapter Thirteen
Chapter Fourteen
Chapter Fifteen
Chapter Sixteen
Chapter Seventeen
Chapter Eighteen
Chapter Nineteen
Chapter Twenty
Chapter Twenty-One
Chapter Twenty-Two
Chapter Twenty-Three
Chapter Twenty-Four
Chapter Twenty-Five
Chapter Twenty-Six
Chapter Twenty-Seven
Chapter Twenty-Eight
Chapter Twenty-Nine
Chapter Thirty
Chapter Thirty-One
Chapter Thirty-Two
Books by Aja Foxx
About the Author

The Boss's Boy

A Mafia Romance 2

AJA FOXX
Copyright © 2023

Chapter One

~ Dmitri ~

"Who is that man?"

"Which one, sir?" My second-in-command stepped over to stand next to me.

"The one on the dance floor with Parker Lane right now." Parker and his crew of dancers came to the Illumination Club quite often, and as the sole owner of that club I reaped the benefits of each and every visit. "The one in the pale blue sweater."

I didn't remember ever seeing him in here before, and believe me, I would have remembered. The man was simply stunning.

"Oh, that's Eiji Yamada," Yasha stated. "He comes in with Parker and Buffy and their crew sometimes. Not often, though. The others are here more frequently."

"I want to meet him."

"Uh, sir..."

I snapped my gaze to Yasha. "You have something to say?"

"Eiji is a mute, sir."

Interesting.

I slid my hands into the pockets of my slacks and turned back toward the floor-to-ceiling windows that allowed me to look out over the first floor of my club. "I still want to meet him."

Mute did not mean stupid.

"Yes, sir."

Yasha didn't question me more. He knew better. I wasn't the boss for nothing. I got what I wanted when I wanted it, and those that denied me paid for it painfully.

"Vasil," I said to one of my bodyguards, "find out what he's drinking and have it brought to my office." I wanted Eiji made comfortable while I got to know him.

When my phone rang, I reluctantly pulled my gaze from the attractive man on the dance floor and made my way over to my desk, picking up the phone.

"Petrov."

"I wanted to let you know that O'Donnell has been spotted going over the bridge into your territory. I don't know if he's up to something or—"

I recognized the voice immediately. Vincenzo Borelli, the head of the Italian mafia in New York City. He controlled Manhattan. I controlled the Bronx.

"If he's in my territory, then he's up to something." Michael O'Donnell had taken over the Irish mob for his father, and they were two peas in a pod. They both thought they had a right to territory in New York City that was not theirs. "I'll have someone look into it."

"You do that."

"Thank you for the call, Vinnie."

"Yeah."

I chuckled when Vinnie hung up without saying goodbye. Vinnie and I were not friends, but we had a healthy respect for each other. I appreciated him calling to give me a heads-up.

Maybe I'd send him a fruit basket or a case of vodka.

I walked over to the sideboard to pour myself a glass of that vodka. Yes, it was stereotypical of a Russian to drink vodka, but it was really good vodka. I had it imported all the way from Siberia. Due to the embargo set down on Russian items, when I say imported think smuggled.

It was worth every dime.

I had just set the top on the crystal decanter and grabbed my glass when Yasha entered.

Alone.

"Where is Eiji?"

"He left before I arrived downstairs, sir. I questioned a few of his friends and they said he had to return home."

My disappointment was like a rock in my stomach. I had been captivated by the vivaciousness on Eiji's face when he'd been out there on the dance floor. Yes, it had been a very sensual dance, but more than that, the smile on his face told the story of how much he had been enjoying himself.

It had been a long while since I'd had a smile like that on my face. I wasn't even sure I could remember the last time. Being the head of the Russian mob didn't leave a lot of time for joy in my life. I was usually mediating disputes, planning my next big crime, or trying not to be assassinated.

With my evening plans shot to hell, I sat down behind my desk and started working. I was always working so it was easy to slip into that mindset.

I'd been running my family's business for ever a decade. I knew what needed to be done, starting with finding out if O'Donnell was stepping foot in my territory.

"Yasha, send out word for our people on the streets to keep an eye out for any of the O'Donnells passing into our territory. Borelli called and said O'Donnell had been spotted heading our way."

"You got it, Boss."

"And get me the figures we have so far tonight." Might as well get started on the accounting side of things. I was into a lot of different businesses, not all of them legal.

This club was one of my legal ventures and I had to make sure everything stayed above board in case the authorities decided to stick their noses where they didn't belong.

I had one or two other legal businesses, but smuggling illegal items into the United States paid so much more. No drugs and no human trafficking. I didn't need to go those routes to make myself rich. I was more the smuggle-in-vodka type anyway.

I knew Vinnie Borelli felt much the same as I did, although his illegal wares tended to be guns and ammunition. O'Donnell on the other hand ran anything that would make him a quick buck, which was one of the reasons I wanted nothing to do with him.

The man was a lowlife thug.

"Boss!" Yasha shouted as he came running into my office with a tablet in his hands. "I just got this off the security tapes. You're going to want to see it."

"What now?" If there was a problem in the club, I needed to know about it. I did not need another headache.

Yasha set the tablet down in front of me and pressed play on the video. It took me a moment to figure out what I was looking at, and then rage boiled through me at an alarming rate.

"This was the side parking lot?"

"Yes, sir, the one closest to the alley. I'm pretty sure they didn't think there would be any cameras back there because of how close it was to the alley."

"Did you get a license plate?"

"I did, and I already have our tech guy tracking it down."

"Good." My fingers clenched tightly around the tablet screen as I hit play and watched the video again. It didn't lessen my anger one damn bit. "Get me every piece of video on Eiji from the time he walked into the club tonight until that car left."

"Right away, Boss."

I waited until Yasha left the room before hitting play for a third time. There was no way to mistake the fact that three men had grabbed Eiji as soon as he stepped out of the club and dragged him to a car or the fact that they had hit him so many times, even I winced in sympathy.

I simply needed to figure out who had grabbed Eiji so I could end their miserable lives.

I don't know where this fierceness I was feeling was coming from. Maybe it was the fact that Eiji had been grabbed right outside the doors to my club. I had a reputation to uphold here and if people learned someone had been kidnapped, it wouldn't go well.

And maybe it came from the fact that Eiji intrigued me. The man danced like a wet dream, but unlike the other dancers, he had been covered from the neck down. His clothes were not sexy or meant to entice, and that made what was under them all that more intriguing.

Even his head had been covered.

I owned a nightclub. I'd seen all manner of dress and undress. I'd seen girls wearing skimpy dresses so short I could tell the color of their pubic hair. I'd seen men wear pants tight enough to cut off circulation and mesh shirts that left nothing to the imagination.

I wanted to know what Eiji was hiding under that blue sweater, white dress shirt, and slacks. Was he as beautiful undressed as he was with his clothes on?

I was betting he was, and I did own a casino in Jersey after all. I was used to betting, and winning.

I planned to win this time as well.

* * * *

"Boss, I got that information you wanted."

I glanced away from my computer screen when Yasha walked into my office. This was my home office where I preferred conducting the day-to-day operations of my business. I only went into the club a few nights a week or to have meetings when I didn't want someone setting foot in my home.

I took the tablet Yasha held out to me and started flipping through the information he had found. There was a surprising amount, and not just on Eiji, but his family members, too.

"His father died when he was a child?"

"Mother died at his birth. Father died a few years later. Eiji was raised by his stepmother."

"Why wasn't he raised with other family members? It says here that Jiro Yamada and his new wife were only married a few short months when he died. They couldn't have been very close."

"Beverly Yamada was made trustee of Eiji's inheritance and the executor of his father's will."

I ground my teeth together for a moment before stating, "So, it was about the money for her then."

"I believe so, sir. As long as she retained custody of Eiji, she got to enjoy his wealth and live in the mansion he was set to inherit from his father when he turned twenty-five years old. There is also a sizeable trust fund that she draws seventy-five thousand dollars from every quarter for Eiji's upkeep."

I whistled low under my breath. "That'll pay for a lot of sports cars."

"Eiji doesn't drive, Boss. He also doesn't attend college, go on vacations, throw lavish parties, or attend social functions of any kind. In fact, the only thing he does is sneak out of the house once a month to go dancing with his friends."

I glanced up at Yasha to see if he was telling me the truth. "Really?"

Yasha nodded. "There's something else, Boss."

"Well, tell me," I said when Yasha winced and pressed his lips thin.

"Eiji was born able to speak. In fact, he spoke up until the time he turned fifteen. I haven't been able to find out what happened to him then, but he hasn't spoken a word since."

I didn't like the way that information made my stomach knot. "Could he have some sort of PTSD?" Had something bad enough happened to Eiji that he had lost the ability to speak?

"Again, I don't have that information. What I was able to find out is that one day he was in a private boarding school up-state and the next day he was living on the family estate, unable to speak. Except for those monthly trips to dance with his friends, he doesn't leave the estate, Boss. Ever. They even bring in a doctor to see him when he needs one."

I frowned. "Has he needed a doctor often?"

"The family physician is called to the house at least once a month, sir. I can't say he is seeing Eiji every time, but I suspect he is. Those visits seem to coincide with Eiji's monthly dancing trips."

What the fuck was going on in that house?

"Get me everything you can on Beverly Yamada."

"Already working on it, Boss." Yasha leaned over to flick his finger across the screen. "Beverly Barnes Yamada, married twice, widowed both times. Her first husband died in an auto accident five years and four kids after they married. Jiro Yamada died within six months of their wedding."

"She already had four kids when she married Yamada?"

"Yes, but they didn't officially move in with her until after Yamada died, so I am not sure he was aware of them. Before that, they lived with various relatives all over the city."

"How old are they now?"

"The three boys all range of age from twenty-five to thirty years old. The youngest is a girl and she just turned twenty-one. She currently attends the university and dorms there. Her older brothers all live at home with dear old mom."

"Do they have jobs?"

"Just the girl. She works part time in a coffee shop on the university campus. She also has a full-ride scholarship based on her grades."

"So, there's only one of them that has any smarts?"

"It certainly looks that way."

"I want to speak with her."

"Boss?"

"She seems like the only good one out of the bunch. Maybe she can tell me what's going on with Eiji." I held the tablet out to Yasha. "Don't scare her, but bring her in. Offer to pay her five thousand dollars for two hours of her time. That should make things a little easier for her."

One way or another, I was going to learn Eiji's story. I didn't care how much it cost me. The man had caught my interest and I wasn't going to let it go until that interest had been satisfied.

"Send that file to me."

"Doing it now, sir."

I waited until my email dinged and then waved Yasha away. "Go now."

"Yes, Boss."

Once the door closed behind Yasha, I started going through the file he had sent me again. Maybe there was something in here that would give me a clue into this mysterious man.

Chapter Two

~ Dmitri ~

"Caroline Barnes, sir."

I stood up when Yasha held the door open and a young brown-haired woman walked in. I already knew who she was. I'd read over her file extensively before she arrived.

I hoped she was willing to cooperate with me. I didn't know any more about Eiji now than I had three days ago when Yasha brought me the files. The man was an enigma.

"Good afternoon, Ms. Barnes. Thank you for meeting with me."

The nervous looking woman shot Yasha a small glare before shaking the hand I held out to her. "Your assistant didn't seem to think I had much choice in the matter."

I waved to her to have a seat in the chair in front of my desk before taking my own seat. "I'm sorry if he made you feel that way. That was not my intention. I merely wished to speak to you concerning a private matter that I felt should not be discussed in a public setting."

The woman frowned. "What private matter?"

"Your stepbrother, Eiji."

She stiffened instantly.

"Eiji and his friends frequently come to my club to dance."

"You own the Illumination Club?" she asked.

"I do."

She sat there for a moment, slack jawed. "You're Dmitri Petrov."

"I am."

"You're a mobster."

"I'm a businessman."

Mobster, businessman, same difference.

"What interest do you have in my brother?"

I was about to lie through my teeth because there was no way in hell I was going to tell her how much her brother intrigued me.

"The last time Eiji visited my club, he was accosted in my parking lot and tossed into a car before being driven off by three young men. I haven't been unable to locate a police reports pertaining to the incident or even anything saying that he is missing, and I am concerned about what happened to him."

"Eiji is fine," she replied. "I saw him a few days ago."

My eyebrows lifted in surprise. "He's fine?"

He certainly hadn't looked fine the last time I'd seen him.

She nodded.

"Ms. Barnes—"

"Carrie, please."

I smiled briefly. "Carrie, my security tapes clearly show Eiji being accosted in my parking lot. I'd much rather not involve the police in this matter, but—"

"No, don't!" Carrie's face went pale. "You can't call the police. That will just make things worse for Eiji."

My anger ignited. I slid my hand into my lap so that she wouldn't see me making clenching it into a fist. "What is that supposed to mean? I saw Eiji get beat up and kidnapped. How could it get any worse for him?"

"He wasn't kidnapped."

"He wasn't?" Sure as hell looked like it to me. "Then you tell me what happened."

Carrie's shoulders slumped. "My mother doesn't like it when Eiji leaves the house. Whenever he sneaks out, she sends my brothers to track him down and bring him back."

"He's a full-grown adult. What is it any business of hers?"

"Before I answer that, can you tell me what your interest in my brother is? If you're just worried about the reputation to your club, don't be. No one will be reporting what happened. I doubt Eiji will ever be back there, so you don't have to worry about it happening again either."

"Why wouldn't he be going back there? He seemed to be enjoying himself when he was there before, and his friends go there all the time. I've already upgraded the security around the area where he was taken, so it's perfectly safe."

"Not for Eiji. Now that my brothers know where he goes—"

"Is that who took him?"

Carrie nodded reluctantly. "Like I said, my mother always sends them after Eiji when he sneaks away."

"Why does she care?"

"Why do you care?" she countered.

I chuckled. "Fair enough." I had to think of my words carefully so I wouldn't offend her. If she got offended, she wouldn't tell me what I needed to know. "Your brother intrigues me."

Carrie's eyes widened for a moment. "Intrigues you how?"

I just stared at her, unwilling to go into specifics, especially considering I didn't know myself. Hard to explain something to someone when you didn't know what it was you were supposed to be explaining.

"Oh," Carrie whispered before wincing. "Eiji might not be the best person for something like that. You do know that my brother is mute, don't you?"

"I do, but I fail to see how that is relevant. Mute doesn't mean stupid."

"No, it doesn't, and I'm glad you know that, but I still think Eiji would be a bad bet for someone who might be interested in...uh...well, any type of relationship with him."

I wasn't sure that was what I was interested in, but I couldn't say I wasn't either. "Why?"

"Can I get some water, please?"

I leaned forward and pressed the intercom button. "Yasha, please bring Ms. Barnes some water."

"Right away, Boss."

"How is your schooling going?" I asked to pass the time until Yasha brought in some water for the young woman. "I hear computer science is your field of study?"

"Yes and no. I have to take computer science to get the training I need, but my real passion is graphic arts. I want to create graphic novels when I graduate and that takes training that I don't currently have." She shrugged. "Besides, computer science sounds better than graphic artist."

I couldn't say if that was true one way or another. I'd never had an interest in either area. "As long as you have a passion for what you are doing, does it matter?"

"It does to my mother. Computer science means I can get a high paying job in a bank or with some design firm. Graphic artist means I like to dabble in comic books."

"And that would be bad because?"

"It doesn't look good for Beverly Yamada's daughter to be obsessed with comics."

Right.

"How else is she supposed to marry me off to some handsome, rich bachelor if I don't have a good career that I would be willing to give up just as soon as the ink was dry on the marriage certificate so I could have two point five kids and become some rich stay-at-home trophy wife that spends her days shopping and going to the spa?"

Carrie had said that so fast, and without stopping to breathe once, that I could barely keep up, but I got the general idea. "I take it you don't want two point five kids?"

Carrie snorted. "Maybe, someday, but I want to live my life a little before that happens."

"I hope that five thousand dollars will help."

"I don't want your money, Mr. Petrov. I just want to know why you are so interested in my brother."

I smiled. "I wish I knew."

There. I'd admitted it.

"The first time I ever saw your brother, he was at my club dancing with his friends. I was intrigued. He moves like a dream and dresses like a nun. Considering the outfits his friends were wearing, it didn't fit, and anything that doesn't fit in my club makes me curious."

Carrie swallowed tightly, her eyes growing sad. "Eiji didn't always dress like that. When he was younger, he was full of light and laughter. He could brighten up a room just by walking into it, and make anyone's day better with a simple smile. It wasn't until...later, that he became what he is today."

"What happened?"

Carrie lifted her head and looked me straight in the eyes. "I'm not actually sure that it is my place to tell you that. Just know that there was an event that happened when he was fifteen that stole his voice from him and his joy from the rest of us."

"If that's the case, then surely hiding away on that estate isn't doing him any good."

"He's not there by choice, Mr. Petrov. My mother won't let him leave. As long as he remains under her thumb, she controls the money, and my mother is all about money."

My mind started racing, trying to find a solution to this problem. "What if I could find a way to free him from your mother? Do you think he could survive in the outside world?"

"Eventually maybe, but not right away. Besides being mute, Eiji has other...issues."

"What sort of issues?"

"He has debilitating social anxiety. He doesn't like being touched by anyone, not even me. He doesn't even like people looking at him. He usually has some sort of scarf covering his head and part of his face."

"Was he injured? Does he have scarring or something?"

"No." Carrie shook her head. "He just doesn't like people looking at him."

That might explain the conservative clothing, but it didn't explain the dancing.

"If he hates people looking at him so much, why does he dance?" I asked. "Why even come to a club?"

"Because he loves dancing even more than he hates people looking at him. For Eiji, dancing is an escape from the world. He can close his eyes, listen to the music, and free himself from whatever bonds are holding him down to the earth and he can just float away."

"You seem to know a lot about this."

Carrie smiled. "I asked him about it one time. That's how he explained it to me."

I sat forward quickly. "So, he can talk?"

"Not verbally, no, but he's really good at charades."

"Charades?"

"And finger gestures. If all else fails, he can write it down. Granted, his education ended when he was fifteen, but he still knows how to read and write."

"Why did his education end?"

"He flips out if strangers are around. After the first couple of times my mother tried to bring in tutors and he lost it, she gave up."

"So, no schooling past the age of fifteen?"

"No formal schooling. He has a Kindle, and he is a veracious reader. He probably reads thirty books a week on any subject that perks his interest."

"What?" I asked when she smiled again.

"He once got interested in a BL television series from Thailand, but it was all in Thai with English subtitles, and he hates subtitles, so he taught himself Thai so he wouldn't have to read them."

Okay, that was pretty damn impressive, but... "BL television series?"

"Boy Love television series. Eiji is addicted to them."

Maybe I needed to check these BL television series out.

There was a knock on the door and then it opened, and Yasha walked in. He set a bottled water down in front of Carrie and a cup of coffee down in front of me. "Will there be anything else, sir?"

"Not at the moment, Yasha. Thank you."

Yasha nodded once and then turned and walked out of the room, shutting the door behind him.

"Is it a prerequisite of working for the mafia for all your men to be lacking in personality?"

Really glad I hadn't taken a sip of my coffee yet when laughter sputtered out of me. "No, but Yasha is very good at his job and that means he needs to have some emotional distance from the things he does."

"Yeah, I guess I can see that. Kind of hard to be intimidating if you have hearts and flowers blooming in your eyes."

Something like that.

"What else can you tell me about your brother?"

Carrie's brow flickered and she took a long sip of her water before replying. "If you are truly interested in Eiji, you're going to have to get through my mother and my three brothers to get to him. He's their golden goose, and they won't let him go easily."

I was sure I could figure out a way.

"And if you make it to that point, I suggest you up your security."

"If I make it to that point, I will not be keeping Eiji a prisoner. I'd be trying to get him out of that situation."

"The increased security isn't to keep Eiji in. It's to keep others out. Just because Eiji would be free from my mother doesn't mean he would be free from his nightmares."

So, what did I need to do to free him from his nightmares?

Chapter Three

~ Eiji ~

I silently groaned as I rolled over and stared up at the ceiling. Pretty sure most of my body ached in some manner. The three stooges had worked me over pretty damn hard last night.

I had known the beat down was coming the moment I refused to sign some stupid document my stepmother had placed In front of me. I wasn't about to sign over more of my inheritance to her. She'd already taken most of it. I planned to use what was left to escape her and her evil spawns.

I just needed to find the right time to get out of the house and get to a lawyer's office so I could have my father's will processed and then get the money he had left me so I could escape.

Escape was the key word there. Ever since my stepbrothers had found me at the Illumination Club, they had been extra vigilant at keeping an eye on me.

I think it was because I was now twenty-five years old, and the terms of my father's will had been met on my birthday. They really didn't want me to escape. They liked their cushy lifestyle.

They could have it as far as I was concerned. I just wanted my mother's jewelry, my father's pocket watch, their wedding photo, and enough money to get me away from these sick freaks.

That wasn't too much to ask, was it?

I dreamed of a day when I could leave my room without being smacked around or berated or told I was worthless. Hell, I just dreamed of a day I could leave my room without fear.

Hadn't happened in years.

Well, except for those monthly dance nights. Stepping a single foot outside my bedroom door took more courage than I ever thought possible, but I had to. Those little trips were my only escape. The one solace in the dismal world I'd lived in for the last ten years.

Over those years, my room had been stripped of almost everything in the form of one punishment or another. I'd lost my radio, television, my computer, and even most of the furniture.

I had no access to the outside world except for my kindle, which didn't allow me to contact anyone. Everything that came in or went out was monitored. Every book and television program I downloaded had to be pre-approved, and I had to earn that.

I gritted my teeth and forced myself to roll to the side of the bed and sit up. The mattress was actually on the floor since I'd lost the bed frame somewhere around the time I'd been eighteen. I'd used it to anchor myself while I went out the second-floor window using a bed sheet.

I had since been moved to the third floor of the mansion and had every major piece of furniture removed.

Upside, Beverly and her lazy ass sons didn't like climbing to the third floor, so I was usually left alone.

Downside, they sometimes forgot to order the servants to feed me. I'd gone more than one day without food in the past. I probably would in the future, too.

Luckily, every time I was able to escape, I snuck food back in and hid it in various places around my room. Granted, we weren't talking five-star cuisine here, but it filled me up and kept me from going hungry, so I wasn't complaining.

I staggered a bit when I climbed to my feet and then made my way to the small bathroom off my room. I wish it had a bathtub because I could really go for a long soak right about now, but it didn't. Just a single person shower, a sink, and a toilet.

At least I could keep myself clean.

I stripped off my dirty clothes and stepped into the shower. It took me a little longer than normal to wash up simply because every movement I made hurt like hell. I could already see several bruises starting to turn some really interesting colors.

I was going to look like a rainbow come tomorrow.

At least they hadn't hit me in the face. They never touched my face. Everything else could be hidden with clothing, but not the face.

Once I finished my shower, I quickly dried off and then hurried over to the plastic laundry baskets in the corner of the bedroom where I kept my clean clothes. I grabbed what I needed and pulled it on before making my way back to the bathroom to clean up my mess.

I also set my dirty clothes in the hamper next to the door. While a maid did my laundry and someone cooked my food and delivered it to me, it was my responsibility to keep my room clean.

Not that there was that much to clean up.

A guard stood outside my door to keep me from leaving the bedroom and everyone else from entering. I was pretty sure he was there to listen in and make sure I wasn't doing anything I wasn't supposed to be doing.

What that might be I had no idea.

Once the bathroom was all cleaned up, I made my bed and then grabbed my Kindle and carried it over to the nest of blankets and pillows I had made in the corner of the room. It was the one place I could curl up and see every entry and exit in the entire room.

I made myself comfortable and then opened up the current book I was reading. I had recently gotten interested in Russian folklore and I was attempting to read them in Russian, which was not an easy language to understand. I was still learning it, which was why the books I was reading were pretty low-key.

Think children's fairy tales.

I don't know how long I'd been reading when I heard the key in the lock. I stiffened for a moment and then wished I hadn't when my muscles protested.

When the door started to open, I pulled my hooded scarf up over my face and grabbed the blanket to pull it over me. I had a strong aversion to people staring at me and I didn't really care who it was.

"I brought you your food, Eiji. You'd better eat it before Mother gets mad."

I pulled down the edge of the blanket and peeked around it. I was surprised to see my stepsister standing there with a tray in her hands. She tried not to come to the house unless she absolutely had to.

I couldn't say I blamed her.

She walked over and set the tray down on the floor in front of me. Her eyes briefly met mine and then she tapped the saucer where the teacup was sitting. "Make sure you drink your tea."

I gave a single nod and then waited for her to leave. As soon as the door closed behind her, I lifted the teacup and set it aside and then reached for the saucer.

Taped to the bottom of it was a small white circular piece of paper. When I turned it over, there was a note on the other side. It was in Thai.

Hang in there, bro. I'm working on a plan.

I smiled before picking up the note and tearing it into tiny pieces that I could easily chew. No matter how many notes Carrie slipped me, I always made sure they were disposed of so no one would know she'd left them for me.

Carrie had been the one bright spot in this entire ordeal, and I'd be devastated if anything ever happened to her. She might not be my sister by blood, but she was the sister of my heart.

But what did she mean by plan?

As much as I wanted to get out of here, I didn't want to do anything that might harm Carrie's chance at a future. I had none. I knew that. Even if the world suddenly changed and I was freed from my prison, I still had no future.

The outside world terrified me. Like, soul sucking terror. Black spots in front of my eyes terror. Pass out from fear terror. I would rather spend the rest of my life in this small little room than brave the outside world type of terror.

That didn't leave me a lot of hope and I'd given up on daydreams years ago. There was no point. Either locked in here with my fears or out in the big bad world with them, I still was in a prison.

I ate the food Carrie had brought to me simply because I needed the nutrients after the beat down I'd received the night before. I had no idea when my next meal would come. I never did.

Once I was all done eating, I carried the tray across the room and set it on the floor before knocking on the door. I quickly made my way back over to my nest of blankets and tucked myself in before the guard could open the door. If I stood too close when they entered, they got mean.

I'd rather avoid that scene right now. I don't think I could take another beat down so soon after the last one.

I waited until the guard entered and took the tray before lowering the blanket and reaching for my Kindle again. I still had a few chapters to go on my current book before moving on to the next one, and it wasn't like I had anything else to do while sitting in my room. I might as well read.

My life might be a snooze fest, but it was a safe snooze fest as long as I stayed in my room and didn't break any of the rules my stepmother had laid down for me.

I wasn't looking forward to when she'd try to get me to sign another document giving away my inheritance. I knew it was coming. There was no way she was going to give up that money now that I had turned twenty-five.

But I still had enough stubbornness to refuse to sign, even knowing what that meant. Unfortunately, my stubbornness was wearing thin, and I wasn't sure how many more beatings I could take before I broke.

Carrie better hurry the hell up with her plan.

Chapter Four

~ Dmitri ~

"I think we got her, Boss."

I glanced up from my computer screen when Yasha came running into the room. "Got who?"

It was an honest question.

"I think I figured out how to get Eiji away from his stepmother."

"How?" I'd been trying to figure it out for the last two days, ever since my little visit with Carrie, and so far, I'd come up with a big fat nothing.

Yasha set his tablet down in front of me and then pointed to a line on the accounting form displayed. "Beverly Yamada has a gambling problem. In fact, she's into your casino in Jersey to the tune of almost five million dollars."

"How?" We never let people run up that much on an account. It was bad for business.

"She used Eiji's inheritance as collateral, but since he turned twenty-five not long ago and can now legally access the funds, she doesn't have anything to guarantee her gambling debt."

"Is she still gambling?"

Yasha grinned and I knew the answer before he said anything. "She's at the casino right now."

I got up and grabbed my blazer, pulling it on before reaching for my cell phone. I already had my gun. It didn't leave my shoulder holster unless I was using it or sleeping.

"Have management hold her if she tries to leave," I ordered, "but don't interfere with any gambling she is doing. The farther into debt she is to me, the better."

"Do you want me to have management encourage her to join in one of the backroom poker games?"

I glanced at Yasha as I headed for the door. "Does she play poker?"

Yasha looked down at his tablet. "Poker, twenty-one, and blackjack, but she also likes to bet on the races. That seems to be where most of her money goes."

"Is she in debt to anyone else?"

"She owes a little money to a couple of other casinos, but nothing like what she owes you. They wouldn't accept the collateral because it technically belongs to Eiji."

Smart people.

"We need to have a little discussion with the management. They shouldn't have accepted it either."

"About that..."

I glanced at Yasha when he hesitated. "What?"

"It's nothing I can prove, but I think Beverly slept with someone on the management team. It's the only way to explain it."

"Explain what?"

Pretty sure I wasn't going to like his answer.

"Not only was Beverly given the loan, but the terms were exceptionally good for her, not so much for us. There's only five percent interest on what she owes."

My eyes narrowed. "Five percent on five million dollars?"

Standard interest on anything over fifty thousand dollars was twenty percent interest. That was one of the ways the casino made its money. Big spenders paid big bucks to spend big.

"Find out who wrote that damn contract. I want them in my office and waiting for me by the time I get there."

Someone's head was going to roll.

Once we were in the car and headed toward the Jersey tunnel, I pulled out my cell phone and called Carrie. She might have some insight into how to make her mother give in to my demands.

"Carrie, it's Dmitri Petrov. Do you have a minute?"

"I do."

"Did you know that your mother has a gambling addiction?"

Carrie snorted. "I'm not surprised. It would certainly explain a lot."

"How so?"

"When I was younger, it was either feast or famine at our house. We were either rolling in money or so poor the lights were being turned off. Mother had to get the money from somewhere. I figured she either sold herself or sold her soul."

"She owes my casino five million dollars and she used Eiji's trust fund as collateral."

"Oh shit!"

Pretty much.

"I'm on my way to the casino right now to make her a deal. Any suggestions before I do?"

"One, but I don't think you're going to like it."

I sighed heavily. "Tell me anyway."

"You need to marry Eiji."

I blinked, and then blinked again. "Could you repeat that?"

There was no way I had heard her right.

"If you simply take Eiji away from her, she could cause all sorts of issues for you with the authorities. She might even report you for kidnapping. She'd get her debt paid off and get her hands on Eiji again, and you'd go to jail. If you married him, then it's not kidnapping and there would be nothing my mother or the police could do."

That made sense, but... "Marriage?"

"I figure it's the fastest and safest way to get Eiji away from my mother. If you offer to wipe the slate clean on her gambling debt in exchange for marrying Eiji, she'd probably jump at the chance."

I had thought to simply take Eiji away from her. I had never considered marriage. "You really think she'd agree to a marriage between me and Eiji to pay off her gambling debt?"

Yasha's head snapped around so fast I heard his neck crack and he stared at me as if my head had just been removed from my shoulders.

I wasn't sure it hadn't.

"No, I actually think she'll fight the marriage. You'll have to insist on it." Carrie let out a little laugh. "Tell her you saw him dancing in the club and became infatuated with him or something."

It wouldn't be a lie.

"What about his inheritance?" I asked. "You know she'll try and keep it."

"Don't bring it up if you can help it."

"She used it for collateral. I kind of have to."

"Okay, well, even if you do have to bring it up, don't let her use it as a means to keep owing you money. She'll just force Eiji to sign something that gives her the money like she always does and then she'll be able to pay you off and still keep Eiji. You have to make the deal lucrative for her."

Lucrative, huh?

I could do that.

"So, if I was really infatuated with Eiji and agreed to forgive her debt of five million dollars plus toss in another five million if she let me marry him, do you think she'd do it?"

"In a heartbeat, but are you sure you want to give away that much money? We're talking ten million dollars here. That's a lot of money for a man that you've only seen on the dance floor."

"I know."

Losing that amount of money wouldn't be a huge hardship. I was worth a ten times that amount, maybe more. It was the blow to my ego that I had hard time dealing with. Losing ten million dollars for someone I had never spoken to before was kind of crazy.

Maybe I could get away with just settling her gambling debt to me.

"Is there any way you can check on Eiji and make sure he's okay?"

"Not for another couple of days. I only go home for Sunday dinner, and everyone knows that. If I show up before then, they are going to know something is up."

"Is there any way you can call him?"

That seemed like the easiest route to go.

"Eiji doesn't have a phone or internet," Carrie replied. "You have to understand, he's been totally cut off from the outside world whether by his choice or my mother's. He doesn't go out and no one goes in. Everything he does is monitored right down to the books he buys for his Kindle. There is no part of Eiji's life that is not a prison."

And that would be why I was willing to spend ten million dollars to get him away from his family. I might be the only person in the world that could do it.

"I'll let you know what happens, Carrie. Hopefully, you'll be getting a wedding invitation soon."

I was a little shocked that I was leaning in that direction. A marriage between me and Eiji didn't have to be forever, though. Just long enough to get him away from his stepmother and make sure he was safe.

"Don't make it too far away. The longer she has to think about it, the longer time she has to scheme and plot. You need to act fast if you want to save Eiji."

"I know a judge." Pretty sure every mafia man did. "I'm pretty sure I can arrange for a wedding sometime in the next couple of days as long as it doesn't have to be anything fancy."

"It doesn't have to be fancy. Just make sure it's legal."

"It will be." I hung up before Carrie could say more and turned to look at Yasha. "Call that judge we have on retainer and tell him I'm going to need him to perform a marriage ceremony tomorrow or the next day. He needs to bring the marriage certificate with him and then call my lawyer and have a standard pre-nup drawn up with mine and Eiji's name on them. You can also give Eiji's information to the judge so that the paperwork is all filled out by the time he arrives."

"You're seriously going to go through with this?" Yasha asked. "You're going to marry this guy."

"It might be the only way to save him, Yasha."

"Why do you care?"

I had no idea.

"Just do it, Yasha."

Yasha shook his head. "Your funeral, man."

I couldn't say he was wrong. Married life in the mafia did not go easy on anyone. The second the ink dried on the marriage certificate, Eiji would have a target on his back.

The thing was, after everything I had read and heard, I didn't think he would be in any more danger than he already was. He might actually be a bit safer behind the walls of my estate. At least there I could assign guards to keep him safe.

Speaking of which... "I need you to choose three guards to watch over Eiji once he's at the house. They'll be on eight-hour shifts. I want him to be able to come and go as he pleases, but I want someone there whose sole purpose is to keep him safe."

"Dmitri—"

"I also want a team of four guards on standby for any time he leaves the estate. He can leave whenever he wants as long as I am informed and he has all his guards with him."

Yasha's shoulders slumped. "Yes, sir."

I knew my friend was worried for me. Kiryanov Yakovich had been at my side more years than I cared to count. We'd come up in the ranks together. Despite what it might seem to the outside world, he was my best friend.

I reached over and placed my hand on his arm. "This feels right, Yasha."

Yasha sighed. "I think you're crazy, but you know I'll support your decision, whatever it is."

I released his arm and then started fiddling with the ring on my index finger, twisting it around and around. "I can't explain it, but there is something about Eiji. It's like his soul is crying out because he's drowning, and this is his one chance for someone to notice and throw him a life preserver and I need to be that someone."

"Just make sure you don't drown right along with him."

I wasn't planning on it.

Chapter Five

~ Dmitri ~

I strode into the casino like I owned the place because, well, I did. Granted, I had several foreign investors I had to report to, but this was my casino. I ran the whole operation right down to the last slot machine.

It didn't hurt that I was dressed in a twenty-thousand-dollar suit and had four armed guards following my every move.

I saw the doorman whispering into his earpiece when I walked in, so I was in no way surprised when the assistant manager came running up before I'd even made it halfway to the elevators, although, I had expected the general manager, not his assistant.

"Mr. Petrov, sir, we weren't expecting you tonight."

I merely raised an eyebrow.

"Mr. Petrov owns this casino," Yasha snapped. "He does not have to announce his arrival ahead of time. You should be ready to expect him at any time, on any day."

"Yes, of course." The man started ringing his hands together. "I just wasn't expecting him tonight."

I slowly panned to look at Yasha. Hadn't he just explained things to the assistant manager?

"Where is Grayson?" Yasha asked. "He should be greeting Mr. Petrov himself, not sending you."

"Yes, sir, Mr. Grayson is surveying some of the games in the back rooms. I can get him for you."

"Have him meet me in my office," I ordered.

"Your office, sir?"

Seriously?

How could this guy work here and not know that I had an office here? Granted, I only came to the casino about once a week to check on things, but I still had an office. It came complete with a secretary and everything.

Amazing how that worked.

I started walking. It was either that or I tossed this guy into a slot machine. Maybe I needed to talk to Grayson about the people he hired. This guy was a moron.

My casino was a very lucrative one. I employed over a thousand people here and we were open twenty-four hours a day. We catered to the rich and famous and down and out. If your money was green, you were welcome.

Not only did the place have a full casino floor, but there were also hotel rooms, various restaurants and bars, two event halls, a movie theater, and a runway of high-end boutiques.

This place was a veritable cash machine.

When we all walked into the elevator, the assistant manager tried to join us. One of my guards stepped in his way, blocking him.

"I believe you were supposed to be getting Grayson," Yasha said.

"Yes, sir." The man bowed his head several times. He looked like a yoyo. "Of course, sir. I'll get him right away, sir."

Oh, my god, if I heard one more *sir* out of him, I was going to strangle him with his own tie.

I rolled my eyes as the elevator doors slid closed. I knew employing so many people meant that I wouldn't always get the cream of the crop, but this guy better have the perfect resume, or he was out on his ass.

When the elevator doors slid open on the third floor, I followed my guards out. We were in standard formation. Me and Yasha in the middle with two guards in front of us and two guards behind us. Until we knew what we were headed into, that was the way it would stay.

"Mr. Petrov." My secretary jumped to her feet and hurried over to open the door to my office. "It's nice to see you, sir."

"Evening, Ms. Deena." She was one of the good ones, which was why she was my secretary here at the casino. She kept an eye on the place for me when I wasn't here. "Please join me in my office. We have a few things to discuss."

"Yes, sir." Deena grabbed her tablet and followed me into my office. Yasha joined as well. The rest of my guards would be waiting out in the outer room, just a small shout away if I needed them.

"Who is in charge of writing up the line of credit contracts?" I asked.

"That would be Mr. Clausen, sir."

"He writes all the contracts?"

"Yes, sir."

"What about contracts for high rollers? Is he in charge of those, too?"

"Yes, sir, but standard operating procedure dictates that anything over fifty thousand dollars has to be pre-approved by Mr. Grayson."

"I want both Clausen and Grayson in my office right now. I also need you to get me copies of every contract over fifty thousand dollars."

Deena's eyebrows lifted. "Every contract, sir?"

"Forgive me if I am wrong, but standard operating procedure also dictates that any line of credit over fifty thousand dollars has an automatic twenty percent interest rate. Is that correct?"

"Yes, sir."

"I recently came across a contract for five million dollars that only had a five percent interest rate."

Deena's jaw dropped for a moment before she started shaking her head. "Sir, that goes against casino policy."

"Which is why I am here."

"Do you want me to go through all the contracts and see if there are any other incidents like this one? It might help weed some of them out."

And this was why I liked employing this woman. She was smart as a whip and cut down on my workload.

"Yes, please do. Bring me anything that doesn't fit our policy. Call someone in from accounting if you need the extra help. As of right now, this is your only priority."

"Yes, sir." Deena twirled in her high heeled shoes and walked out of the office. One of the guards reached over and closed the door behind her.

I rubbed my hand over my face as I walked over to look out over the casino floor below. "What the hell is going on here, Yasha?"

"We don't know that there are more contracts like Beverly's. Let's not panic yet."

Too late.

I had come here with one thing in mind. Find a way to free Eiji from his stepmother. Now, I was beginning to wonder if that was just part of a bigger plot. Her contract could be an isolated incident, but I was starting to think it wasn't.

Still, even if it was, how in the hell had it happened. We had procedures in place to stop things like this from happening. There were rules that had to be followed and no one had the right to break those rules without consulting me first, and I had not been consulted.

There was a knock on the door. When it opened, Daniel Grayson, my general manager, walked in.

"Mr. Petrov, I wasn't expecting you tonight."

I just looked at Yasha.

He snorted.

"Can you explain this?" I took the tablet Yasha held out to me and handed it to Grayson.

Grayson stared down at it, but the longer he looked at it, the deeper his frown grew. "Is this some sort of joke?"

I scowled at the man. "Do you see me laughing?"

"Mr. Petrov, we don't give five percent interest on lines of credit this large. It's against casino policy."

"Then how did it happen?" I pointed to the bottom of the contract. "That is your signature, isn't it?"

"Well, yes, but..."

"But what?"

"Sir, I wasn't here on that day."

"What?"

"Remember that week I took to fly to Colorado for my father's sixtieth birthday? That was that week. I wasn't even in the state when this contract was signed."

I grit my teeth to keep from shouting. "Who was in charge?"

"The assistant manager, Fred Clausen."

I turned to look at Yasha. "Find him and get him to my office now."

Yasha pulled out his cell phone and started speaking to hotel security.

"Deena is currently going through the rest of the contracts to see if there are any more like this one. In the meantime, I need you to dig up everything you can find on Clausen. I want to know what he's been up to, if he's working with anyone else, and especially what his relationship with Beverly Yamada is."

"The woman on the contract?" Grayson asked.

"Yes." I nodded. "She is currently downstairs gambling. Once I deal with Clausen, I'll be dealing with her."

"She has a contract, sir. Is there anything you can do?"

"The contract is fraudulent, so yes, there is. I'll be canceling it and calling the loan due immediately." And if she didn't have the five million dollars, I knew of another way she could pay me back.

Didn't look like I'd need that extra five million dollars after all. I almost wanted to thank Clausen for being such an idiot. He was making this so much easier for me.

"Yasha, have Mrs. Yamada escorted up here. She can wait in the outer office until I'm done with Clausen."

Yasha was still on the phone, so he just nodded at me.

I returned my attention to Grayson. "From now on, no lines of credit over fifty thousand dollars are to happen unless you've approved them."

"Sir—"

"I know things are already set up that way, but you need to send out a companywide memo or something so that everyone knows you are the only one that can approve them. I don't care if you are out of the country for a month. If you do not personally approve a contract, it does not happen. I also expect you to stay on top of this. I want a report from you on my desk each week stating who has received a line of credit and for how much. Something like this cannot happen again."

"No, sir. It won't, sir."

"And stop calling me sir. It drives me insane. You sound like that ass kisser Clausen."

"Yes, si—Yes, Mr. Petrov."

Slightly better.

I walked over to the cabinet behind my desk and pulled out a bottle of vodka. I poured one for me and Yasha before glancing over my shoulder to Grayson. "Vodka?"

"No, thank you."

I lifted an eyebrow at his grimace.

"I'm a scotch man. Can't stand vodka."

"You don't know what you're missing." I grabbed a bottle of scotch and poured him a glass before handing all the drinks out. "My grandfather introduced me to vodka when I was twelve. A little young, but when you are freezing your balls off in the Siberian winter, anything to warm them up is like liquid gold."

"Never been to Siberia," Grayson said. "I hear it's cold."

That made me chuckle. "Pretty sure it's the counterpart to the fires of hell."

Grayson took a sip of his scotch before staring intently at me. "I get the feeling I'll be hiring a new assistant manager here real soon."

"I get the same feeling."

The man's shoulders slumped.

"Want my advice?"

Grayson nodded. "Please."

"Promote Deena." I'd hate to lose her as my secretary, but the woman was more than qualified for the position and she ran a very tight ship. "You'll have to give her a sweetheart of a deal before she'll agree, but she won't let you down."

"You'd give up Deena?"

I smirked. "No." Not a chance in hell. "She would just have a different position in my organization."

I took a sip of my vodka as I strolled over to look out the floor to ceiling windows again. "I know good people when I see them, and Deena is good people. She's been loyal to me for over five years, and I trust her to keep on top of things. You would be at an advantage if she was your assistant."

I turned to look at Grayson. "Just don't underestimate her because she's a beautiful woman. She'll use your intestines as a jump rope and laugh while doing it."

Grayson smiled as he glanced down at his glass of scotch. "I actually wanted to hire her on as my assistant a while ago, but she was firm that she worked for you. I didn't get the impression she was willing to work for anyone else."

"Like I said, you have to give her the incentive to want to be promoted. You could start by offering to double her current salary and giving her one of the suites here at the hotel. I know for a fact that she hates commuting to work every day. Having her own residence here would make it easier on her and you. She'd be on hand if there were any emergencies."

"After we deal with Clausen, I'd be more than happy to write her up a promotion proposal, especially if you think she'll consider it."

"I think she will. Deena was meant for bigger and better things than being my part-time secretary. She just needs someone that sees her potential and appreciates all the hard work she does. As long as you treat her right, she'll be loyal to a fault."

Grayson nodded. "I will, Mr. Petrov. I promise."

Loyalty came at a price. Not a monetary one, but a personal one. In my experience, if I treated my employees right, they were loyal.

I have no idea what the fuck had happened with Clausen.

Chapter Six

~ Dmitri ~

There was a knock at the door and then it opened, and Deena stuck her head in. "Mr. Clausen, sir."

I nodded to her.

A moment later, the nervous little man that had met us at the front doors walked in. "You wanted to see me, sir?"

I grabbed the tablet Yasha handed me and held it in front of Clausen's face. "Tell me about this."

Clausen swallowed tightly as he glanced over the contract. "It's a standard contract for a line of credit, sir."

"Standard?" I snapped. "This contract is for five million dollars. Casino policy states that anything over fifty thousand dollars is supposed to have twenty percent interest." I jabbed my finger at the screen. "Does that look like twenty percent interest to you?"

"I'm sure it's just an oversight, sir."

Oversight my hairy ass.

"The contract was signed by Mr. Grayson," I pointed out, curious to see just how far this guy would go with his lies.

"Yes, sir. All contracts for amounts like this have to be approved by the general manager."

"Funny thing about that. On the date that that contract was signed, Grayson was out of state, so how did he sign it?" I asked. Clausen paled, which gave me the biggest clue that this guy was full of shit. "It's pretty hard for him to be in Jersey and Colorado at the same time."

"Sir, I'm sure that—"

"How long have you been sleeping with Beverly Yamada?"

Clausen gasped and stumbled back. "Sir, I would never—"

"Cut the crap, Clausen. I already know about your little affair. I want to know how long it's been going on." Yeah, okay, I was lying through my teeth, but he didn't know that. "Who else have you been giving deals to for a little piece of ass? I have Deena going over all the contracts right now. I will find out. It's better that you just tell me the truth now instead of making me hunt for it."

Clausen started to sweat. "Sir, I swear, I didn't—"

I held up my hand. I was done talking to this guy. "Yasha, have two of our men take Clausen down to the basement the back way and then call in Konstantin. I want to know everything Clausen knows."

Konstantin Kirillovich had one very special skill. He was a master interrogator. He could get information out of a rock. He'd have no problem breaking this guy. Question was, would Clausen survive the interrogation?

Yasha walked over to the office door and pulled it open, gesturing to two of the guards. He quickly gave them their orders and then stood back as they walked in.

"No, you can't do this!" Clausen cried out as they grabbed. "I didn't do anything wrong. Ask Grayson. He knows. High rollers get special deals on their contracts. That's the way it's always been."

"Actually," Grayson said, "that's the exact opposite of the way it's always been. High rollers are our bread and butter. If we don't charge them a good amount of interest, we make no money." Grayson cocked his head. "Is that what you want? Do you want this casino to go under?"

My head swung around so fast my neck popped. "You're trying to take down my casino?" Was this bigger than Clausen trying to get a piece of ass? "Yasha."

"Sir?"

"Make sure Konstantin questions Clausen about who he is working for."

"Yes, sir."

Clausen's cries followed him out of my office.

I walked over to the cabinet behind my desk and grabbed the vodka again, refilling my glass. I grabbed the glass and shot back the entire contents before refilling it halfway.

"Grayson."

Grayson stepped forward. "Sir?"

"You've worked for me for a long time now?"

"Seven years, sir."

"I'm going to give you my trust and assume that you have nothing to do with this fiasco. If I find out differently, you won't make it to the basement. Is that understood?"

Grayson paled considerably. "Yes, Mr. Petrov, I understand. Your faith in me is not misplaced, sir. I did not have anything to do with this. However, I was the man in charge and that means I do have some responsibility for it. I should have known something was going on and reported it to you."

The man bent stiffly at the waist. "You have my profound apologies, sir. I will not let an oversight like this happen again."

"See that you don't." I heaved a heavy sigh. This was not how I thought my evening would be going. "You're dismissed."

"Thank you, Mr. Petrov."

My headache seemed to magnify when I spotted a woman sitting in the waiting area when Grayson opened the door and rushed out.

Beverly Yamada.

The other half of this mess.

"Yasha?"

"Sir?"

"You ever feel like you should have stayed in bed?"

Yasha chuckled. "All the time."

I held my glass to my forehead for a moment before walking around to sit behind my desk and waving a hand toward the door. "Go let her in."

Yasha didn't even bother nodding to me. He just walked over and opened the door. "Mrs. Yamada, Mr. Petrov is ready to see you now."

He stood back, holding the door open for the woman to enter the office. Once she did, he closed the door and walked over to stand just to my left.

"Please, have a seat." I waved to the chair on the other side of my desk. I waited until she sat down to hold out the tablet. "Is this the contract you signed with my casino?"

Beverly swallowed tightly as she glanced down at the table. "I believe so, yes."

"I'm afraid that this contract is null and void, Mrs. Yamada. It was not approved by my general manager. Instead, it was approved by Fred Clausen, who I believe you are currently sleeping with. Mr. Clausen does not have the authority to approve a credit account this large. As such, I am calling in your debt. I expect the full five million dollars to be paid by the end of the day."

Beverly gasped. "You can't do that."

"I can, actually. Clausen forged the general manager's signature, which is a crime, and he gave you an interest rate on your loan that is against casino policy. While that may not be a crime, sleeping with someone to get them to loan you money is. I could easily have you both thrown in jail right now."

"But...but...I don't have five million dollars right now. If you just give me a few weeks, I could—"

"Don't waste my time, Mrs. Yamada. I've been in this business for a very long time. If you don't have the money to repay your loan today, you won't have it after gambling a bit more. In fact, you'll probably end up owing me even more money."

"I can get the money," she said quickly. "I just need to move some funds around and—"

"If you are thinking of using your stepson's trust fund, don't. Legally, since he is twenty-five now, you no longer have access to that money, so you'll need to find another way to pay me back."

Her brow flickered. "How do you know about that?"

I dropped the tablet on my desk. "I make it a practice to know everything about my high rollers. Saves me the headache of tracking them down when they don't pay their debts."

I took a slow sip of my vodka to let her stew a little bit. I wanted her good and flustered before I gave her a way out. She needed to be desperate.

"Do you know who I am, Mrs. Yamada?"

She frowned before glancing at Yasha. "He called you Mr. Petrov."

"My name is Dmitri Petrov. I own this casino. I do not make a habit of giving people lines of credit in the millions of dollars without some sort of collateral. You used your stepson's trust fund, which you did not have a right to do as it does not belong to you. You were allowed to do this because the man you are sleeping with is an idiot, but not to worry. He is currently being dealt with."

"You...you..."

I raised an eyebrow. "Yes?"

"You're not going to hurt him, are you?"

Was this woman a complete idiot?

"Me? No, I don't do that." I smiled evilly. "I pay other people to do that for me."

Beverly gasped.

"So, Mrs. Yamada, how are you going to pay me back my money?" I leaned back in my chair trying to look as casual as possible when my heart was thundering in my chest. "I do own a few brothels in the city. I could put you to work in one of them, but that would take more time for you to pay off your debt than I'm willing to wait. What else can you offer me?"

"I don't have anything else," she cried out. "My late husband left the entire estate to my stepson, and now that he's twenty-five, he gets everything."

"Fine, then I'll take your stepson."

Her jaw dropped. "What?"

"You heard me. If your stepson is the only one with access to this money, I'll take him as collateral until you pay off the five million dollars."

"You can't," she whispered.

"I can, actually. I will take your stepson as collateral, allowing you to continue live on his estate while you gather the money together to pay me back. I will only extend your repayment time to one week, though. Not a second longer."

"Can't you just leave him where he is while I pay you back?"

"No."

"You don't understand," she said hurriedly. "Eiji is a sickly boy. He needs constant looking after."

"Not my concern."

"But I can't pay it all back that fast. It's too much money."

"Then you shouldn't have taken out a line of credit for five million dollars. Never borrow money you can't pay back."

Beverly's eyes dropped to her lap. She was quiet, but her brow kept wrinkling as if she was thinking hard. I gave her a few minutes to think things over.

"I'm waiting, Mrs. Yamada," I finally said. "What's your decision?"

"My son is worth a lot of money, Mr. Petrov."

"And?"

"I'll make you a deal."

Oh, this should be good.

"I'm listening."

"Wipe my slate clean and—"

"Seriously?" I both my eyebrows shot up at the balls on this woman. "You want me to simply dismiss a five-million-dollar debt like it never happened?"

"Like I said, my son is worth a lot of money. With a little encouragement from me, I could convince Eiji to marry you and then you would have access to all of his funds. It would be more than enough to recoup your losses from wiping my slate clean."

My jaw dropped. I slowly panned to Yasha only to find him staring at Beverly with the same stunned look I was pretty sure was on my face.

"The one stipulation is that I want to retain rights to my late husband's mansion, and I want a million dollars wired to my account when you get married."

Was she serious?

"Why would I want to marry someone I have never met when I can simply make you repay what you already owe me?"

"Because I don't have the money to repay you right now and if you kill me, you'll never get it."

Okay, that was true enough, but it still felt wrong that she was offering up her stepson on a silver platter. Granted, that had kind of been my goal tonight, but coming from her it felt wrong.

She was basically playing right into my hands, but was she really?

"If I agree to this, you won't be getting him back."

I saw the true Beverly Yamada come out when she rolled her eyes. "Like I want that sniveling little brat back. He's more trouble than he's worth. The only reason I've let him stick around this long is because the house and everything belongs to him."

"So, you want the house, a million dollars, and for your debt to me to be wiped out in exchange for a sniveling little brat? How does that benefit me?"

"He's worth easily ten times what I owe you. Once you are married to him, I am sure you could convince him to turn his trust fund over to you. That should easily compensate you for your troubles."

Man, this woman was a piece of work.

"I'll tell you what, Mrs. Yamada. I'll give your proposal some consideration and have an answer for you by morning. In the meantime, you can enjoy the hospitality of my fine hotel."

"Oh, but—"

"Is there a problem?"

"Well, no, but like I said, Eiji is a sickly boy. If I'm not there to check on him tonight, I don't know what will happen."

All this concern after she just offered him up to me in exchange for her gambling debt?

I wasn't buying it.

"You will stay where I can keep an eye on you until I've made decision."

"Can I at least call home and make sure someone checks on him?"

"Of course." I smiled, but I wasn't feeling it. "My secretary will see you to a room. Do not try and leave before we speak again. If you do, you will be stopped, and it won't be pleasant for you. Is that understood?"

"Yes."

"Yasha, please arrange a room for our guest."

"Already done, sir." Yasha walked over to the door and pulled it open. He spoke briefly with one of the guards before allowing the man to escort Beverly out of the room.

I waited until the door closed behind them before blowing a breath out. "That woman is a witch."

"Is it just me or do you have a slimy feeling even though she gave you exactly what you wanted?"

"It's not just you."

I was feeling the same dame thing.

Yasha shuddered. "If Eiji has been putting up with her for most of his life, no wonder he has issues."

"Now do you understand why I need to get him out of there?"

Yasha grimaced, but nodded. "I get it, but I can't help wondering what can of worms this is going to open up for you. That woman is bat shit crazy, and I don't see her giving up a cash cow like Eiji without a fight."

"She's the one that offered marriage, not me." Even if that had been my end goal.

"I think she's using that to stall for more time. If she gets you off her back and gets her slate wiped clean, it gives her a chance to figure out how to steal the rest of Eiji's money."

"So, we'll just have to ensure she doesn't get that chance."

"How?" Yasha asked.

"I have no fucking clue."

Chapter Seven

~ Eiji ~

My stomach had been one continuous knot since late last night. I don't know what had prompted my stepbrothers to come to my room and start in on me again. I hadn't broken any rules since the last time they'd beaten me up so there had been no cause for it.

What I did know was that every breath was painful. Every movement made me wish that I was in a coma and couldn't feel a thing. While they had avoided hitting me in the face like they usually did, they had pretty much gotten every other inch of my body.

They had been angered while doing it, but also a touch gleeful, which confused me. They were up to something. Whatever it was, it didn't bode well for me.

I jerked and then hissed when my bedroom door slammed open. I grabbed the edge of my blanket and pulled it over me as much as I could. I didn't even want to know who had come in.

I cried out silently when I was grabbed and dragged to the bathroom by two of the guards. When they pushed me inside, I stumbled to the far wall and then turned to look at them. There was no way to hide the fear I was feeling. I was shaking so bad I could barely stand.

"Mrs. Yamada wants you cleaned up and made presentable," one of the guards barked out. "Get to it or we'll come in and do it for you."

I knew what that meant, and it was very painful.

The door was slammed shut so at least I had some privacy, but I heard a lot of commotion from the other side of the door that worried me. Were they stripping something else from my room? Was I going to be left with nothing?

Was this my stepmother's way of punishing me because I wouldn't sign the title to the mansion over to her? I would have signed it in a heartbeat if she would have agreed to let me go, but I knew she never would, so why should I give her what she wanted most?

I knew I didn't have a lot of choices here, so I stripped off my clothes and climbed into the shower. Scrubbing myself was a form of torture. Every inch of skin the washcloth touched ached.

If I could have screamed, I would have.

By the time I climbed out of the shower and reached for a towel, I felt as if every inch of my body had been scraped with a Brillo pad. I wouldn't be surprised if I wasn't bleeding in a few places.

I dried off as quickly as I could, not knowing how long I had before the guards came for me again. I hadn't brought any clean clothes in with me. I hadn't been given time. I started to reach for my dirty clothes when the door was shoved open again.

I backed up to the wall on the far side of the bathroom, holding the towel firmly in front of me. It didn't cover nearly as much as I wanted.

The guard that walked in scoffed at me before tossing a stack of clothes onto the counter. "Get dressed."

I waited until he left before walking over to see what had been picked out of me. It would give me a good indication of what was going to happen. If they were just regular clothes, I probably had another face to face with my stepmother coming. If they were fancy clothes, she had something worse planned.

Damn it!

They were fancy clothes.

A tuxedo.

I did not want to wear a tuxedo. Not only did it mean she had something worse planned, but there would be other people there to witness it. Strangers most likely.

That knot that had been forming in my stomach turned as hard as a rock. I didn't do strangers real well. In fact, I hardly did them at all.

Strangers terrified me.

At least if I knew a person, I had half a chance of being able to read them and see what kind of danger might be headed my way. I couldn't read people I had never met before.

I jumped when someone banged on the door.

"Hurry up in there."

I grabbed the clothes and started pulling them on at a rapid pace. I no more wanted to be naked in front of the guards than I did my stepmother.

My hands shook as I buttoned up my shirt and then attempted to tie my bowtie. I liked bowties for the simple reason that they bound my shirt closed at the neckline. I'd wear them every single day if I could get away with it.

Once I was fully dressed, I ran a brush through my hair until I looked relatively presentable and then stepped over and opened the bathroom door.

The guard was waiting for me.

I barely had time to realize my room had been totally stripped of everything before I was dragged out of the room and down the hallway toward the back staircase.

Once we got downstairs, the two guards escorted me down the hallway to what used to be my father's study. As a child, I had loved being in here. I remember going in to sit on my father's lap and listen to him tell me stories of my mother and watching movies with him.

Now, it was a place I dreaded.

I was shoved in a chair in front of my father's desk and then the two guards walked over to take up positions by the door. They were clearly there to keep me from running.

I swallowed tightly and glanced across the desk to my stepmother. I couldn't exactly ask her why I had been dressed in a penguin suit and then made to leave my room, but I had no doubt I'd find out in the next few minutes. It just remained to be seen whether I'd survive whatever plan she had hatched up.

I had never liked my stepmother, not even back when I had been a child and she had been my father's new bride. I had seen the evil in her eyes back then. My poor father had been oblivious.

If it wasn't for the fact that he had died of a heart attack, I would have assumed she had had a hand in his death. She had married him for his money after all.

Bet she was surprised when the will was read.

"Sign these." Beverly slapped a pen and a couple pieces of paper down in front of me.

I shook my head without even looking at them.

Beverly smiled sweetly, which I had always taken to be her evil demoness look. "Sign these or I turn you over to the guards."

Fear spiked through me simply because it wouldn't be the first time she'd done something like that. Granted, it had been years, but I still lived with that memory firmly planted in my head.

She always threatened to give me to the guards to play with instead of just letting them knock me around, but it never happened. The threat still hung over my head with a very sharp blade.

I took the sheets of paper and pen she held out to me. My brow flickered as I started reading over the first one. At first, the words didn't make sense simply because they were so preposterous.

My head snapped up when they did make sense and I stared at my stepmother like she had grown horns out of her forehead.

"Just sign them, Eiji," she demanded. "Your future husband will be here soon, and you do not want to keep him waiting. Dmitri Petrov is the head of the Russian mafia. Pissing him off would be a really bad idea. The last guy that pissed him off disappeared, never to be seen again."

I shook my head and dropped the papers. There was no way in hell I was signing anything. I didn't care if she turned me over to the guards. My inheritance was my only leverage in staying alive.

Before Beverly could start shouting at me the door opened, and Carrie breezed in dressed in a full-length red evening gown. She walked over to stand next to the desk, her upper lip curling back when she looked down at me.

If I hadn't known she was playing a part, I might have been scared. But I did. She couldn't let on to anyone that she was not as evil as her mother or brothers.

"What's he doing out of his room?" Carrie asked. "I thought we were having a small cocktail party."

"Eiji is getting married."

Carrie turned to stare at her mother with wide yes. "You're not serious."

Beverly glanced at the delicate gold watch on her wrist before sighing. "I am, and I need him to sign the pre-nup and marriage certificate before his groom gets here. Dmitri Petrov does not like to be kept waiting."

"Dmitri Petrov." Carrie frowned. "Where have I heard that name before?"

"He's the head of the Russian mafia here in the city. They call him the Boss of the Bronx."

Carrie's lips parted. "Eiji is marrying a mobster?"

Beverly shrugged. "He made me an offer I couldn't refuse."

Carrie reached down and picked up one of the pieces of paper I had dropped. "Is this the pre-nup?"

"Yes, Petrov sent it over. It's a standard pre-nup, but the important part is that Petrov will have no rights to Eiji's inheritance."

Carrie snorted before holding the paper out to me. "Sign it."

I shook my head. I didn't know what she was playing at, but I hadn't agreed to marry anyone.

"Sign it before mother really gets angry."

My eyes darted to Beverly. The woman stared back at me with steely eyes, her arms crossed. "You have until the count of three," she started. "One..."

"Just sign it, Eiji." Carrie nudged me. "Sign it and I'll get you a cup of tea."

Tea?

"Two..."

I grabbed the pen and signed both pieces of paper before tossing them on the desk. I felt as if I had just signed my life away, but if I didn't sign, I wouldn't have a life, so...Not much of a choice.

"I'll get your tea," Carrie said as she started for the door.

"Forget the tea," Beverly snapped. "Help me hold him down."

As soon as I saw the syringe in Beverly's hand I jumped up and made a mad dash for the window. The doorway was blocked. I was grabbed and tossed down to the floor before I could take two steps.

"What is that?" Carrie asked.

I silently screamed when a needle was jabbed into my arm and then I felt a burning hot liquid shoot into my blood stream. The room became unfocused almost immediately and my head began to swim.

"It's just a little something to calm him down, that's all," Beverly said. "We can't have him going into one of his panic attacks in the middle of the wedding. Petrov would call off the deal for sure."

"What deal?" Carrie asked.

"We'll discuss it later."

Would I be here later?

I was pretty sure I was going to float away.

Chapter Eight

~ Dmitri ~

"Is this the place?"

I glanced up from my tablet and looked out the window of my limousine. "I believe so."

"It's actually a pretty nice place, Boss. Could use a few security upgrades, but other than that, it would work great as a home base."

"There's nothing wrong with our place."

"We're outgrowing it," Yasha stated. "With the new guards you want to hire, we're going to be crammed in as it is. Maybe once we get rid of the wicked witch, we can convince Eiji to let us move in here."

"We'll see how things go." I wasn't betting on it being that easy to get rid of Beverly. "Don't forget, she gets to continue to live here for right now."

"Yes, but you never put a time limit on that." Yasha wagged his eyebrows. "Once you are married, you could simply kick her out."

"I'm not saying that won't happen at some point, but I prefer knowing where she is for the time being. Speaking of which, once we go inside, have someone put trackers on all her vehicles."

Yasha grinned. "You got it, Boss."

Once my limousine came to a stop in front of the large stone mansion, I waited until my security detail got out and checked for signs of danger. I wouldn't put it past Beverly to try something.

When they gave the all clear, I climbed out and headed for the front steps. "Vasil, wait here for the judge. Let me know as soon as he arrives. And I want all of you to be on your toes. We're in enemy territory right now."

Vasil, another one of my bodyguards, gave a firm nod before going to stand next to the car.

"Lev, when we get inside, you are assigned Eiji's security until we can get him home. He is your only responsibility. Vasil will join you as soon as the judge arrives."

Lev gave me a head nod. "Yes, sir."

Lev was Vasil's brother and the two worked well together. I hated separating them even for a moment, but I needed Eiji protected right now.

I slid my hands into the pockets of my slacks and waited for someone to answer after Yasha knocked on the door. I knew I had to play this whole thing cool. It wasn't easy considering how anxious I felt.

If Beverly got wind of that, I had no doubt that she'd try to weasel more money out of me. I didn't mind that so much. I just worried about what she would try to get out of Eiji.

When the door opened, Yasha stepped forward, clicked his boots together, and said in a very haughty voice, "Dmitri Petrov to see Mrs. Beverly Yamada."

Got to love a man who knew how to make an announcement.

"Right this way, sir." The man at the door stood back so we could enter. Once we were inside, he gestured to a room just off to the left. "Your men can wait in here, sir."

Yeah, that wasn't happening.

"They go with me," I stated simply. I wasn't about to wander around in this house without my bodyguards. Besides, I wanted to get one assigned to Eiji just as fast as possible.

To give the guy some credit, he didn't even blink at my statement. "Of course, sir. If you'll follow me?" The butler led us into a living room before turning to look at us. "I'll let madam know you are here, sirs."

I didn't say anything after the butler left. I never knew when I might be under surveillance. It was better to keep my mouth shut and just wait to see what happened.

I did, however, stroll slowly around the room, checking out every nook and cranny. Two of my men had taken up standing positions by the entryway. The other two stood on the far side of the room by the fireplace. Yasha stood against the wall farthest from the windows, watching everything.

It was a large room as living rooms went. It even had two separate seating areas. I doubted I would ever be comfortable around white sofas, but they seem to fit the space well.

I did admire the large white marble fireplace. In fact, that is where I stopped, standing in front of it to survey the rest of the room. I didn't stop looking around until my eyes fell on a large portrait of a dark-haired man hanging above the fireplace.

Eiji's father, no doubt. I could see where Eiji got his good looks, but the eyes were a mystery. If I remember correctly from the information Yasha had gathered for me, Eiji's eyes were green. This man's eyes were dark brown. His mother maybe?

"Mr. Petrov."

I turned and then tried not to grimace at the white ruffled dress Beverly was wearing. It had a plunging neckline in the front showing off more of her cleavage than I ever wanted to see, and ruffles at the bottom.

A lot of ruffles.

I knew a many women her age that were stunning beauties. This woman, not so much. It was almost as if she was trying too hard to hold on to her youth.

Maybe she was hunting for another rich husband.

I gave her a simple nod. "Mrs. Yamada."

"Can I offer you a drink?"

"Not at the moment, thank you. Did you receive the papers I had sent over?"

"Yes." She turned to the younger man standing behind her. "Thomas, go get those papers Eiji signed."

"Yes, Mother." The young man turned and hurried out of the room.

"Eiji has signed them then?" I asked.

"He has." She smiled. "He was very excited to learn of your interest in him."

I doubted it.

"He's waiting in the study at the moment. As soon as the judge arrives, we can—"

"I'd like to see him."

Beverly's eyes widened. "Now? Before the ceremony?"

"Yes."

Beverly swallowed tightly before plastering what I knew was a fake smile on her face. "Well, I suppose that would be okay."

Like it was up to her.

"Where is he?"

"Oh, like I said, he's waiting in the study."

I started walking toward the entry way, but her next words stopped me.

"Why don't you wait here, and I'll go get him? The study is...Well, it was Eiji's father's study, and we don't usually allow anyone except family in there."

I arched an eyebrow. I was pretty sure me getting married to Eiji would make me family, but I wasn't going to argue that point right now. "I'll be waiting."

The moment she turned and started out of the room, I gestured to Lev. "Go with her."

After they had both left the room, I glanced at Yasha and gagged. He chuckled, but quickly wiped the grin off his face when the butler appeared in the entry.

"Can I offer you some coffee, sirs?"

"Not at the moment, thank you."

The man nodded once before leaving the room again.

I blew out a breath and turned to look at the portrait hanging above the fireplace again. If this was what Eiji would look like in the coming years, I was going to be a lucky, lucky man. Assuming I could convince him to stick around. That part was still up in the air.

I glanced toward the front windows when headlights shone through them. "I believe the judge is here."

"I'll go check, sir," Yasha said before rushing out of the room.

I really hoped it was the judge. I wanted to get this shit show over and done with so we could get out of here. I liked the house well enough, but there was something in the atmosphere that made my skin crawl.

I turned when I heard footsteps. A moment later, Beverly walked into the living room with some papers in her hand. Carrie was next and she was giving me a hard stare.

I had no idea what it meant.

It was the five men that walked in last that held my attention. Lev, Eiji, and three men that were obviously related to Beverly if their genetics were any indication.

I frowned when Eiji tripped just as he entered the room. I walked over and grabbed his arm when he swayed just a bit. I frowned as I looked him over. He was just as pretty as he had been when I'd seen him out on the dance floor, but something was off.

"What's wrong with him?"

Eiji's skin was flushed and there was a glossiness to his green eyes that unsettled me. It was almost as if he wasn't fully aware of his surroundings.

Was he drunk?

"He's been running a temperature," Beverly said. "I think he's got a stomach bug or something. You shouldn't worry about it. I'll get one of the maids to take him back to bed once the ceremony is over and give him something for it. He should be as good as new in a couple of days."

"My people will take care of it when we get home." There was no way in hell I was leaving him here alone once we were married. "Let's just get this over with."

"Oh, but..."

I raised an eyebrow as I glanced at the woman. "Eiji goes with me."

"That really isn't necessary, Mr. Petrov. He just needs a few days of bed rest and then he'll be fine. Once he's all better, I'll give you a call and you can come get him."

"Either he goes with me now or you can forget about our deal because there won't be a wedding."

"Mr. Petrov, surely—"

I raised an eyebrow. "Yes or no, Mrs. Yamada?"

"Fine, yes." Beverly heaved a sigh. "I'm just worried about Eiji. I told you he was a sickly boy." She waved a hand at Eiji. "Just look at him."

"He'll be fine." I held on tight to Eiji's arm as I glanced at Beverly. "Do you have those papers for me?"

"Oh, yes, right here."

I took them with my free hand and checked them over. I wouldn't put it past Beverly to try and put one over on me, so I wanted to make sure nothing had been changed in the pre-nup and that the marriage certificate had been filled out properly.

Everything looked in order.

Now we just needed a judge to marry us.

I pulled Eiji closer when Beverly walked over to us.

"Have you made the transfer yet?" she asked.

I had a fair idea why she was whispering. She didn't want anyone else to know that she had basically sold her stepson, although why the rest of her family would care I had no idea. Her sons gave off the same evil vibe that she did.

Carrie seemed like the only gem in the lot of them.

"I will make the transfer as soon as the judge officially marries us and not a moment sooner."

Beverly huffed as if that was the last answer she wanted. "What about my debt?"

"Same principal applies. Once the marriage is official, I will transfer the money into your account and then call my general manager and inform him that your debt is paid in full."

"And the house?"

"You are still here, aren't you?" Whether things remained that way was up to Eiji.

The front door opened, and Yasha walked in followed closely by the judge I had on retainer. I kept a tight grip on Eiji's arm as I held out my other hand to greet the man.

"Is this the groom?" the judge asked.

"Yes, this is Eiji Yamada." I smiled for the judge. "You'll have to forgive him. He took some cold medicine a little while ago and he's a little tired."

"Oh, well, we can plan this for another day if you prefer."

"No, today is good." I held out the paperwork to the judge. "He signed these before he took the medicine. We have several witnesses to the fact that he signed them under no duress if you care to speak to them."

"No, no, this is good enough." The judge glanced over the papers quickly before smiling. "Okay, so, let's get you two married."

Great.

Let the shit show begin.

Chapter Nine

~ Eiji ~

I woke in a bed that was not mine. I knew it wasn't mine because it was much softer than the one I had. This one made me feel as if I was floating on a cloud. Mine made me feel as if I was sleeping on a rock.

And there were sheets, real silk sheets. My bed only ever had a blanket. I'd lost the sheets the first time I had tried to use them to lower myself to the ground outside my bedroom window.

I also was not in my room.

I sat up and looked around, my confusion growing with every stick of furniture I laid my eyes on. There was this bed for one. A real bed with a bed frame and everything.

And then there was a small desk by one wall complete with a laptop, two cream-colored loveseats sitting in front of a large fireplace, nightstands on either side of the bed, and a large yellow printed wingback chair in the corner by the window.

This was so not my room.

I flipped back the soft downy comforter and started to slide off the bed when I noticed the silky green pajamas I was wearing. I had definitely not been wearing these the last time I was conscious because I had never seen them before in my life.

I didn't even own silk pajamas.

I forgot all about the silk pajamas when I felt a cool breeze coming in from somewhere. I got up and followed it to a set of curtains blowing around by the far wall. When I pushed them to the sides, I discovered a set of doors leading out onto a patio.

I pressed my fingers against the glass for a moment, too afraid to hope that I might be able to access the outside world from here.

Was I dreaming still?

My heart in my throat, I reached down and turned the door handle. More of that cool breeze blew in over me as the doors opened. I stood there in the entrance, afraid to step out, but afraid not to.

"It's okay," said a soft voice behind me. "You can go out if you want."

I jumped and swung around. When I saw the sheer size of the man standing just inside the bedroom by a door I had apparently missed, sheer terror filled every cell of my body.

I frantically scanned the room looking for a place to hide where he couldn't get me.

I saw none.

I ran to the corner of the room and crouched down, covering my head with my arms. Tears sprang to my eyes as I closed them and then they started trailing down my cheeks when I heard his heavy footsteps approach.

"I'm not going to hurt you, Eiji."

Like I believed that. People had been telling me that they wouldn't hurt me most of my life, and they always lied.

Even Carrie lied.

She tried not to, but there were times when she had to act a certain way in order to hide her true self from her mother. I didn't blame her for that. I would want to hide from that evil woman, too.

"My name is Dmitri Petrov. You can call me Dima if you want. It's short for Dmitri."

The man was very close. I was afraid to open my eyes and find out just how close.

"This is your new home."

That got my attention. I opened my eyes and raised my head just far enough to peek at the man over my arm. He was squatted down a few feet away. Close enough to touch me, although his arms were resting on his thighs.

"I bet you're pretty confused right about now."

I gave a single nod.

"Why don't I have Carrie come in and explain things to you?"

I lifted my head a little more.

Dmitri smiled as he stood. "Why don't you go get back in bed where you'll be warm? You don't have to if you don't want to, but I don't want you getting cold because we left the balcony doors open."

He was actually going to leave the doors open?

"If you prefer, I can bring a blanket over to you."

I nodded again.

Dmitri walked over to the bed and grabbed the big white comforter. When he carried it back over to me, he stopped a couple of feet away and just tossed it at me.

I immediately grabbed it and wrapped it around me, even taking a part of it and pulling it over my head so just my eyes showed.

"Are you warm enough now?"

I nodded.

"Okay, then I'm going to go get Carrie for you and then I'll arrange some breakfast. I imagine you're pretty hungry."

Not really, but what was I going to say?

No?

This man could crush me like a bug.

"If you want to clean up, the bathroom is through there." Dmitri pointed to a door on the far side of the room. "I've also laid out some new clothes for you on the counter that I think you'll like."

As good as that sounded, I was staying right where I was until I knew exactly what was going on.

Dmitri stood there for a moment, staring at me, before turning and walking out of the room. I watched every step he took until the door closed behind him and then blew out a breath.

What kind of mess had I gotten myself into this time?

I tensed when the door opened until I saw Carrie walk in. She looked around until she spotted me and then walked over to sit down on the floor next to me, her back against the wall.

"How are you?" she asked.

I shrugged.

"You're probably a little groggy still. Mother shot you up with some sort of tranquilizer. She said it was so you wouldn't have a panic attack, but we both know that was bullshit. She wanted to make you compliant so you wouldn't argue with her."

Yeah, I could see her doing that. I just wasn't sure what I was supposed to be arguing with her about. I tapped the floor with my hand and then shrugged when Carrie glanced at me again.

"So, that plan I was telling you I was working on? It got a bit complicated."

You don't say?

I stared at her.

"That man that was just in here. His name is Dmitri Petrov. He's kind of a Russian mobster."

A mobster?

How could someone kind of be a mobster?

I stared harder.

"Okay, so he owns the Illumination Club and he saw you and the others dancing one night and he wanted to meet you, only before that could happen, my bozo brothers grabbed you in the parking lot. Dmitri was worried you had been kidnapped until I explained to him what was really going on."

I narrowed my eyes.

"Dmitri came up with this plan to get you away from Mother. It seems he owns a casino and Mother is a gambling addict. She owed him about five million dollars."

My jaw dropped, but just as soon as it did, I snapped it closed. A very cold feeling began to spread across my chest. I pointed to myself and raised an eyebrow.

Carrie nodded. "She sold you to Dmitri to wipe out her debt."

Great, now I was some mobster's personal property.

"There's one more thing, Eiji."

Of course there was.

"Dmitri and I wanted to figure out a way to make sure that Mother couldn't come after you again. Being who he is, you can imagine the scrutiny he's under from the cops. With one phone call, Mother could bring the entire police force down on him and take you back. We wanted to prevent that, and we could think of only one way to do it."

Carrie grabbed my hand and held it up. "So, Dmitri married you."

Holy crap!

There was a diamond ring on my finger, and it wasn't just any diamond ring. That was a fucking rock. You could probably see it from the International Space Station.

I quickly pointed to myself, then the door, and then the ring.

Carried nodded again. "I was there when the judge married you."

My shoulders slumped in despair. I had just gone from one hell right into another.

"But don't worry. Dmitri insisted on a pre-nup. I'm not sure if you remember signing it, but you get to keep everything you came into the marriage with, and he gets to keep everything he came into the marriage with. He's not taking your inheritance away from you." Carrie grinned. "And now Mother can't take it either."

That was a plus, but marriage?

"Dmitri doesn't seem like a bad guy, Eiji, even if he is a mobster." Carrie waved her hand around to showcase the room. "He got you this nice room, a computer, and everything. You can even go outside if you want to. Being married to a rich mobster has its perks."

Name one.

Okay, a furnished room was nice. I was a little iffy on the computer since it had been so long since I'd used one, I wasn't sure I knew how. And the whole going outside thing was not the draw Carrie seemed to think it was. I liked being able to have that option, but I doubted it would happen.

Forcing myself to brave the outside world once a month to go dancing with my friends had pretty much been the limit of what I could handle.

Speaking of which...I made several hand gestures until Carrie chuckled. "Dmitri knows you go dancing with your friends once a month. He promised me that you could still go. You can even go more often if you want to. It doesn't have to be just once a month."

I shook my head. Once a month was plenty for me.

"Do you have any more questions?"

I tugged at my silk pajamas.

"Oh, I put you in those last night after we arrived here. I didn't think you would be comfortable having anyone else do it, and I knew you'd want out of that stupid monkey suit my mother made you wear."

She wasn't wrong.

Carrie pushed herself to her feet and then held out her hand to me. She was probably the only person on the planet that I allowed to touch me, so I took her hand and let her pull me to my feet.

"Why don't you go shower and change and I'll see about arranging breakfast for us on the balcony? It'll be close enough for you to come inside if you want, but still give you some clean fresh air to breathe."

I waved my hand back and forth between us.

"It can be just the two of us or you can let Dmitri join us so I can interpret for you if you have questions for him."

I did have questions, but I wasn't sure I was ready to be around anyone else at this point, so I shook my head.

"Okay, just you and me then."

I waited until Carrie left the room before carrying the comforter over to the bed and then heading for the bathroom. I was still pretty sore from the beating I'd taken a few days ago.

A few days ago?

A couple of days ago?

I wasn't sure.

I just knew I was still black and blue.

It took me a little longer than I would have liked to wash up, but I felt a lot more clear headed by the time I climbed out of the shower and reached for a towel to dry myself off.

I found the new clothes Dmitri had left for me and almost laughed when I started going through them. There was a pair of faded denim skinny jeans, underwear, socks, a set of low-rise deck shoes, a long sleeve white button-down shirt, a pale pink cardigan sweater, and a floral print bowtie.

And then there was the head scarf. It was the same floral print as the bowtie, but it wasn't just a long thin piece of material that could be wrapped around my throat. It was an actual hood that would fit over my head.

How had he known?

I dried off quickly and then pulled everything on including the hood. When I was all done, I looked at myself in the mirror. I was a bit astonished at what I saw.

My skin was a pale, but my eyes were bright. A slight smile curving up the corners of my lips was a surprise.

I couldn't remember the last time I smiled.

Chapter Ten

~ Dmitri ~

"How is he?"

"Scared, confused, uneasy." Carrie smiled sadly as she sat down in the chair across the desk from me. "Pretty much how he always is."

I sighed as I leaned back in my chair and picked up my coffee cup. My eyes strayed to the scene outside my window, but I wasn't really seeing it. All I could see was the frightened little creature that had been huddled in the corner of that bedroom.

I'd seen a lot of things in my life, and it had not been an easy life, but the rage I had felt as I stared at Eiji as he tried to make himself invisible was something I hadn't felt in years.

No one should ever be that scared, especially not Eiji.

I just didn't know quite how to fix that.

"I explained things to him as best as I could, but I know he's going to have a lot of questions. When he asks them, please try and be patient with him. Sometimes he has a hard time getting his words across."

I set my coffee cup down and reached into the top drawer of my desk. I grabbed the cell phone I'd placed in there earlier and held it out to Carrie.

"This has a special message app on it that allows him just to type when he's having a conversation with people. He can choose to have what he types turned into verbal communication or people can simply read what he types. It was initially developed for deaf people, but I suspect it will work much the same for Eiji."

Carrie smiled as she took it from me. "You got this for him?"

"I've already programmed your number into it so he can call you whenever he wants to. It also has his friend Parker's number in it. I figured he might want to talk to him, maybe arrange another dance night."

"Eiji's never been allowed to have a cell phone before."

My lips twisted with a mixture of sadness at what he had missed out on and anger that someone had forced him to miss out on those things. There was an entire world just waiting for him to explore, and he seemed too terrified to see it.

"When you talk to him, don't forget to tell him about the computer. He won't be monitored like he was at his old place. He can also call whoever he wants, have friends over, whatever. While he has to have protection, he is not a prisoner here."

Carrie stared at the cell phone for a moment, but I knew she had something to say. She just seemed to be having a hard time trying to figure out how to say it.

"Tell me," I said. When she looked up, I smiled to try and reassure her. "You obviously have something you want to say, so say it."

"Do you understand that Eiji isn't just a prisoner due to the things my mother did to him? He's a prisoner in his own mind as well. He's spent ten years living like this. That's a long time, Dmitri. Eiji might not know any other way to live."

"I'll teach him." I'd see a smile on his face if it was the last thing I ever did. "I know this isn't going to be easy, but he deserves a shot at having a normal life."

Assuming I could figure out what normal was. Being a mobster didn't exactly give me a level emotional guide to go by.

"I know it's not something that will happen overnight either. My first objective is to make him not frightened of me. That's going to take some time, but I have to do that before I can start introducing him to the outside world."

My gut was still in a clench from the frightened look Eiji had given me when he spotted me for the very first time. As a mobster, I wanted to instill fear in other people so they never crossed me. As Eiji's husband, I didn't ever want to see that look on his face again.

"Can I give you a few suggestions?"

"Of course." I'd take any and all suggestions.

"Get Eiji some extra blankets and pillows. He likes to build nests in the corner of the room where he can sit and read and still see all the exits. He doesn't like people coming up behind him."

That made sense. I didn't like people coming up behind me either. The mobster's creed was to always keep their backs to the wall, their guns fully loaded, and their wits about them.

Helped keep us alive.

"What else?"

"I know there are some things he wants from the house, things my mother took away from him. She says she put them away for safe keeping, but she really just doesn't want Eiji to have them. She's petty like that. I'll try and gather them together over the coming weeks. It won't be easy and I can't do it all at once, but—"

I grabbed a pad of paper and a pen and held it out to Carrie. "If you give me a list of what those items are and where you think she might be keeping them, I can have someone go get them."

I knew a few cat burglars who could do the job without getting caught. They could get in and out without anyone even knowing they had been there until someone went looking for the items, even if they were in a safe.

Carrie snickered as she started to write. "Must be nice to have that kind of power."

"It has its moments."

Some good, some not so good.

"There might be a few items I forgot," Carrie said. "I'll ask Eiji while we're eating breakfast."

"He's hungry?"

"I don't really think he is, but he'll pretend he is to make me happy. Right now, he's still reeling from learning he's married. I don't think he's had time to think about food."

I braced myself for the answer to my next question. "How did he take the news?"

Carrie snickered again, but this time there seemed to be a bit more amusement to it. "He was pretty stunned. He'll probably ask me a few more times if it's really true. I don't think he believes it quite yet."

There wasn't much I could do about that.

"There's a tray waiting for you in the kitchen," I said. "Just let Olav know when you're ready for it and he'll carry it upstairs for you."

Olav was in charge of my house. I was pretty sure there wasn't anything he couldn't do.

"He can carry it upstairs for me, but it would be best if I take it into the room myself. Eiji really has a problem with strangers entering his personal space."

"He's going to have to get used to me being in there." There was no way in hell I was shutting myself off from the man I had just married.

"I figured as much," Carried replied, "but everyone else needs to stay out until he gets used to things around here."

"I'll agree to that as long as there's no danger. I have three guards assigned to protect him around the clock. They won't be in the room with him unless there is a danger to him. They will just stand outside the door in case they are needed and to prevent anyone from going in that doesn't need to go in."

Carrie nodded as if she understood, but I doubted that she did. The life I led was not what Hollywood made mafia life out to be on the big screen. It was dangerous every single day, and if Eiji was in danger, he would be protected.

I waited until Carrie had left the room before picking up my cell phone and dialing Yasha. "Has there been any movement at the Yamada house?"

"Define movement," Yasha said. "If you mean are the three brothers still passed out cold, then no. They haven't moved. If you mean has the mother already headed to her favorite racetrack, then yes, there has been movement."

"Seriously?"

"She's got a million dollars to burn, Dmitri. Where did you expect her to go?"

I knew I shouldn't be surprised considering I owned a casino and dealt with people like Beverly all the time, but I honestly was. She had just gotten out from under a five-million-dollar debt and had gained an extra million dollars in the deal, and she was trying to burn through that, too?

"Call Grayson and let him know that she is not to be given another line of credit if she tries to gamble at the casino. She needs to pay up front for everything."

"You sure you want to do that, Boss? If she starts trouble for Eiji, having her in debt to you again might not be a bad thing."

I hated it when Yasha was right.

"Put a limit on her line of credit then. No more than a million dollars. I might be rich, but not even I have enough money to pay for her gambling addiction."

"Want me to drop a bug into the ears of a couple of the other casino bosses, let them know Beverly Yamada is on the short list?"

"Yes, do that." Maybe we could cut this woman off at the knees a little early, or at least before she tries to go after Eiji again. "Did Konstantin get anything out of Clausen?"

It had been a few days and I still hadn't heard from him.

"I think he's letting Clausen percolate a little."

That could be good or bad. Good because it meant Konstantin thought there might be more information to extract from the guy. Bad because that meant waiting even longer to find out what that information might be.

"Call Deena and find out if she's found any more suspicious contracts. Also have someone nose around the area. I want to know if anyone has been sniffing into the casino."

"I already have someone looking into that," Yasha replied, "but I'll give Deena a call and see what she's found."

"I'm really hoping this is just Clausen trying to get laid, but—"

"But you don't."

"No."

"Yeah, I got the same feeling, Boss. Clausen doesn't seem like the mastermind type. I mean, I'm sure his plan was to get Beverly Yamada into bed with him, but I don't see him coming up with an idea like this. Besides, if Konstantin is letting him percolate, there's something more going on."

"Send out a general alert to all our people. I don't want anyone causing any trouble, but it wouldn't hurt for them to stay extra vigilant. If something is going on, I want us to be prepared for it."

"I'll take care of it, Boss."

"I have some things to pick up for Eiji, so I'll be going out for awhile. I need you to keep an eye on things, especially Eiji. Call me if there is any trouble, I don't care how minor it is."

"Are you expecting trouble, Boss?"

"I'm always expecting trouble."

It was the life that I lived.

Chapter Eleven

~ Eiji ~

I stiffened when a door opened. It wasn't the main door that everyone seemed to go in and out of, or even the bathroom door. This door was on the far side of the room from the fireplace, over by the bed.

I hunkered down into my blanket, pulling the edges up around my face. For some reason, I wasn't surprised when the man calling himself Dmitri walked in.

I was surprised by the large bags he was carrying.

"Good evening, Eiji. Carrie said you might like some extra pillows and blankets for your corner." Dmitri set the bags down on the floor a few feet from me and then backed up, putting space between us. "I went out today and found some soft ones I think you'll like. I wasn't sure of the colors you preferred so I guessed. If there are any you don't like, just let me know and I'll replace them."

Was this man for real?

Dmitri walked through the door he'd come in, but he was back a moment later, a glass of clear liquid in one hand and a tablet in the other.

"I always like to have a drink at the end of my day while I go over my reports." Dmitri settled himself in the yellow wingback chair. He took a sip of whatever that clear liquid was and then set his glass down on the small table next to the chair. "If you have any questions for me, go ahead and ask them. You won't be interrupting me."

I watched him for the longest time, not moving, barely breathing. I expected him to jump up at any moment and rush me, beat me.

He didn't. He just sat there staring down at his tablet and occasionally moving his finger across the screen or taking a drink from his glass. He didn't even look in my direction.

After a while, my curiosity got the better of me. I dropped the blanket down and crept forward on my hands and knees far enough to grab the bags and pull them toward me.

Once all four of them were in front of me, I shot a look at Dmitri. He was still looking down at his tablet. I grabbed the first bag and pulled the contents out.

A frown flickered across my face. Pillows? He seriously got me pillows? And not just any pillows. Some were silky soft. Others were fuzzy. There were even a couple that felt like terrycloth. The next two bags held similar pillows in a multitude of colors. Some big, some small.

The last bag held two blankets. One bigger than the comforter that went on the bed. The other one was smaller, more my size. It was fuzzy and warm, and I wanted to roll myself up in it.

I shot Dmitri another look before dumping everything out of every bag. I stood up and grabbed the comforter I'd pulled off the bed and took it back to the bed. If I had new blankets, I didn't need this one.

I was almost gleeful as I took the other blanket and pillows and arranged them into a nest in the corner. Once I sat down in my new nest, I had a bit more arranging to do until it felt just right, and then I drew the fuzzy blanket over me and snuggled down.

"Do you need your tablet?"

I inhaled a swift breath. I had totally forgotten that Dmitri was there.

How stupid could I be?

"Eiji, do you want me to get your tablet for you?"

Dmitri didn't sound angry or upset so I slowly nodded my head. Dmitri got up and walked over to the nightstand where I had left my tablet. He picked it up and carried it over to me, holding it out.

I swallowed tightly as I stared at it, and then raised my eyes to look up at him. There didn't seem to be any anger on the man's handsome face, but I didn't know him. I didn't know what anger looked like on him.

After a moment, Dmitri sighed, set the tablet on the floor in front of me, and then walked back over to sit in his chair. He took another sip of his drink and then picked his tablet up again.

I almost felt bad.

Almost.

I picked up my tablet and opened it to my current book. I leaned back against the pillows, tucked the fuzzy blanket up around me, and started to read. I only glanced in Dmitri's direction a few times...maybe a few hundred times. It was hard to look away.

* * * *

"Good evening, Eiji," Dmitri said as he walked into the room with his usual drink and tablet. "How was your day?"

I didn't answer him because how could I?

But I didn't freeze up when he walked in this time, so I considered that a win. Dmitri had been coming to my room every night for the last week, always in the evening, and always with his drink and tablet. He'd greet me and then go sit in his chair to go over his daily reports.

He never said much, but I could feel him watching me every now and again. His presence had unnerved me at first, but after a week of him doing it, I'd actually started to look forward to his evening visits.

How weird was that?

Once Dmitri got settled in his chair, I slapped the floor. His eyebrows shot up as he turned to look at me. I gestured to the soft cushiony platform someone had placed under my nest so I wasn't sitting directly on the floor.

I wasn't sure how to thank him or show my appreciation, so I pressed my hands together and made a slight bow of my head.

"You're welcome, Eiji."

A small smile tugged at my lips as I grabbed my tablet and settled in to read some more. I'd worked my way up from Russian fairy tales to Russian classics. They were a little harder to read, but they were interesting.

I wonder what Dmitri liked to read?

* * * *

"Good evening, Eiji," Dmitri said as he walked into the room a few days later. "How was your day?"

This time when he walked in, he didn't have his usual drink and tablet. Instead, he had a white cup and a small stool in his hands. He carried them over and set them down near the edge of my nest.

"I thought you might like some hot chocolate. Winter is starting and there is a chill in the air. If you need a fire in the fireplace to help keep you warm, just let me know."

I nodded once.

Dmitri sent me a smile before going back into the other room to get his drink and tablet. I watched him for a moment as he settled into his chair and began going over his reports. He did the same thing every evening, almost to the letter.

The hot chocolate was new.

I smiled as I reached out and grabbed the cup. It had been so long since I'd had hot chocolate, I had almost forgotten what it tasted like.

When I took that first sip, I swear my eyes almost rolled back in my head. I would have groaned if I could have. This wasn't the pre-packaged stuff. This was real hot chocolate, rich and creamy and oh so good.

I drank down most of it very quickly. I didn't care how hot it was. It tasted that good.

When I heard Dmitri chuckle, I froze for a moment and then slowly turned to look at him. There was a smile on his face as he stood up, pulled a white handkerchief out of his pocket, and then carried it over and held it out to me.

"You have a whipped cream mustache."

Pretty sure my cheeks had gone fire engine red. I grabbed the handkerchief and quickly wiped at my mouth before holding it out to him.

Dmitri waved his hand at me before heading back to his chair. "You go ahead and keep it. You might need it."

Once Dmitri picked up his tablet, I brought the cup of hot chocolate back to my mouth and finished drinking it before placing the cup back on the stool. I wiped my mouth again and then tucked the handkerchief down beside me.

I picked up my tablet and started to read some more, but then stopped and glanced at Dmitri. I never really saw him during the day, so I didn't know much about what his life was like, but he was always going over reports in the evenings.

Did he ever rest or do anything for pleasure?

Was he always working?

I tucked my lips in and chewed on the bottom one for a moment as I glanced over at Dmitri. He seemed engrossed in whatever it was he was looking at, and I really didn't want to make him mad by interrupting him, but he said I could, so...

I swallowed down the lump of fear in my throat and crawled out of my nest. I made sure I had my fuzzy blanket wrapped around me and my hood over my head before padding across the floor. I stopped in front of Dmitri's chair, but not too close.

When he glanced up at me, I almost ran back to my nest. It was all I could do to stay right where I was and hold my tablet out to him.

Dmitri frowned as he took it and saw the book I had it opened to. When he glanced up at me, confusion covered his face.

I gestured to him, made a talking motion, and then gestured to the tablet before pointing to my ear...and then I prayed he understood charades.

"You're reading Russian classics."

I nodded before gesturing to him again.

His eyebrows lifted. "You want me to read it to you?"

I nodded again.

"Do you want to hear it in English or Russian?"

I held up two fingers, indicating the second choice.

Dmitri chuckled. "Okay, go get comfortable. I'll read you Russian classics in Russian."

So, he did understand charades.

Good to know.

I hurried over to get comfortable in my nest and then turned to look at Dmitri expectantly. He seemed to be waiting for that because as soon as I looked at him, he glanced down at the tablet and began reading.

I'd always seen Russian as a hard language, very cold and unemotional, but hearing it from Dmitri's lips gave me a whole new perspective. It wasn't a cold language at all. It was passionate, vibrant, and Dmitri's deep rich tone made it sound even better.

I didn't realize I had fallen asleep until someone lifted me up. I wanted to fight, but I was just too damn tired. I sighed happily a moment later when I was laid down on my soft bed and the comforter was pulled up over me.

A single finger stroked down the side of my face.

"Sleep well, *malen'kiy*."

A door clicked closed as I drifted off to sleep having dreams instead of nightmares for the first time in over a decade.

I obviously needed Dmitri to read to me more often.

Chapter Twelve
~ Dmitri ~

"It's O'Donnell."

My eyebrows lifted as I turned to look at Yasha. "What's O'Donnell?"

"Konstantin just called. He finally got the rest of the information out of Clausen. Michael O'Donnell is behind it all."

"Behind what exactly?" Not that I'd put anything past that lying Irish scumbag, but I needed specifics.

"O'Connell is trying to move in on our territory. Apparently, he needs easy access out of New York City. Borelli won't let him go through Manhattan, and he can't get through Brooklyn, so he's trying to go through the Bronx."

Logistically, that made sense, but it also didn't. We had an agreement with O'Donnell that allowed him access through our territory. Granted, he paid through the nose for that access, which might explain what the problem was. He wanted cheaper access, but to start an all-out war with me to get it?

That didn't make sense.

"Why doesn't he just go around?"

"That I don't know. I mean, it would make sense if he did, but for some reason he has his heart set on having a direct avenue from Queens to New Jersey."

"What's in Jersey?"

"I also don't have that information," Yasha replied, "but I am working on it."

"Get it. There's got to be some reason why O'Donnell is trying to get there. Queens is one of the biggest territories in New York. He should be satisfied with that and stop trying to home in on our territory."

"I'm not even sure if it's that, to be honest. From everything I gathered so far, it's not that O'Donnell wants the Bronx, but more that he wants access through it, but he doesn't want to have to pay for it."

That wasn't going to happen. If O'Donnell wanted access through my territory, he was going to pay through the nose.

"What did Konstantin do with Clausen?"

"He took him to one of our safe houses upstate. Konstantin wants to keep Clausen on the back burner for now. He's pretty sure he got everything out of him, but he doesn't want to get rid of him quite yet."

I wasn't sure if that reassured me or unsettled me.

"I trust Konstantin, so let him do whatever he thinks is best. I just don't want Clausen in my hair again."

"I'll let him know, Boss."

"Was Deena able to find any other contracts that were affected by this?"

"No, just the one, but she's still looking."

I nodded. "Tell her to keep looking. I want to make sure we didn't miss anything."

"She did ask me to pass on a message for her."

I raised an eyebrow. "What message?"

"She'll accept the promotion for now, but she's aiming for Grayson's position when he retires."

I chuckled with amusement at the balls on that woman. "If she proves to be a good assistant manager, she can have it."

Yasha grinned. "I told her."

"Have someone bring the car around. I need to make a trip to the bookstore."

"The bookstore, Boss?"

"Eiji likes me reading him Russian classics. I've been using his tablet to read to him every night, but I wanted to get him a set of actual Russian classics that he could hold in his hands."

"You're reading him Russian classics?"

"I am."

"Does he even know Russian?"

"He does," I said, although it had taken me a bit to figure that out. "He became interested in Russian folklore and decided to teach himself Russian so he could read them in their original language."

Yasha's jaw dropped. "He taught himself Russian?"

"And Thai. He hated reading English subtitles to his favorite BL series so he taught himself Thai so he could understand what people were saying without subtitles."

"I thought he wasn't allowed electronics?"

"I think they were used as a reward system. If he behaved like a trained puppy, he got to watch some TV."

Yasha frowned instantly. "Yeah, but those are two really random languages to learn."

I snorted out a laugh. "I know, but he seems to totally immerse himself in whatever catches his attention."

"Yeah, but Russian classics? I didn't even read those and I'm Russian."

I shrugged. I didn't know what about Russian classics had grabbed Eiji's interest, but whatever it was, it had given him the push he needed to approach me, and I didn't have a problem with that. If buying him the hardbound copies of the classics would further his interest in me reading to him, I'd buy out the whole damn bookstore.

"Make sure Olav has more of that hot chocolate on hand tonight. Eiji seems to really like it."

"Is he ever going to come out of his room, Boss?"

"I hope so." I just didn't think it would happen any time soon. "He needs to get used to things first. Once he's comfortable with me, he might be brave enough to venture out."

"Man, I'd love to just put a bullet in that woman's head. I don't know what she did to Eiji, but for him to be this scared..." Yasha shook his head. "I can't even imagine what he's gone through over the last ten years."

I didn't want to imagine it, but I had. From Eiji's reactions and the things Carrie shared with me, I had started to put together a picture of what Eiji's life had been like, and it wasn't good.

I'd seen stray dogs that had had better lives than him.

I frowned as that thought flittered across my brain. "Look into dogs for me, something that could act as both a pet and a protector."

"Dogs?"

"I doubt Eiji has ever had a pet. Maybe if we got him his very own dog, he'd be more inclined to go outside so the dog could run around. It would also give him someone to make him feel safer when he's in his room alone."

"So, like an attack dog?"

"Think more attack poodle."

Yasha stared. "An attack poodle?"

I chuckled as I grabbed my phone and walked out of the room. I heard Yasha repeat that phrase as I passed through the doorway, his voice tinged with confusion.

I wanted to get Eiji a dog, but I didn't want it to be a huge dog. He needed it to be a pet, a defender, and an emotional support animal. Something Eiji could take with him wherever he went.

I started for the front door when a thought hit me. Instead of heading out, I turned and went up the stairs to Eiji's room. I nodded to Lev and then knocked on the door and let myself in.

When I first stepped inside, I couldn't immediately spot him. A sliver of alarm shot through me. "Eiji?"

He stepped in through the balcony doors.

I smiled at him, relieved that he was okay and elated that he had been out on the balcony. "I was headed to the bookstore and wondered if you wanted to go." I couldn't say I was surprised when Eiji shook his head. "Is there anything you'd like me to pick up for you?"

Eiji chewed on his bottom lip for a moment before fishing his cell phone out of his pocket. He quickly typed something out and then hit a button on his phone that turned what he had typed into a verbal message.

"Crime and Punishment by Fyodor Dostoevsky."

"Oh, good choice. I read that in school." I smiled at him again to let him know I was okay with him actually asking for something. In fact, I was thrilled. "I'll see if I can find you a copy. Do you want the English version or the Russian version?"

"Russian please."

I nodded. "Russian it is."

"Thank you, Dima."

I couldn't keep the grin off my face when he called me by my nickname. "You're more than welcome, Eiji." God, he was communicating with me. I felt like dancing. "If there's anything else you want, just send me a text message."

"Can I get some more of that hot chocolate when you come to read to me tonight?"

"I already sent word to Olav to make you some."

Eiji gave me the first real smile I'd seen on his face since that night I watched him on the dance floor.

I didn't want to press my luck, so I nodded to Eiji and walked out of the room, quietly shutting the door behind me.

"Any problems?" I asked Lev.

"No, Boss, he's real quiet in there."

"I'm headed out for a bit. If there are any problems, let me know."

"Yes, Boss."

I'll admit that I had a bit of pep in my step as I went down the stairs, but I couldn't seem to help it. I didn't even mind the odd looks I got from several of my people.

I knew I was acting a bit strange. I wasn't usually a chipper type of guy, but I couldn't help it. Eiji had communicated with me of his own free will and he had smiled at me.

Who wouldn't be chipper?

When I got out to the car, four guards were already waiting for me. I climbed in and then ordered my driver to take me to a little-known bookstore on the east side of the Bronx.

It was a small place, somewhat dusty, but it had obscure books that the regular bookstores didn't tend to carry. I was hoping I could find what Eiji wanted plus a few other things.

It took us a bit to get there due to traffic. I occupied myself with going over the reports from the previous day. While I usually went over them at night, I'd been spending a lot of time reading to Eiji and hadn't had much chance to really look them over. Thankfully, Yasha had been taking up a lot of the slack for me.

When we finally pulled up in front of the old bookstore, I tucked my tablet away in the pocket of the door and then waited for my men to get out and check the area.

I sometimes hated the fact that I couldn't just walk around like everyday people. I always had to have bodyguards and be on the lookout for any signs of danger.

On the other hand, I couldn't really picture being anything other than a mob boss. In one fashion or another, I'd been a part of the Russian mafia since the day I was born.

My father had been the big boss before he "faked his death" and retired to Moscow. I'd simply taken over the position from him when he mysteriously died in an auto accident.

Once my bodyguards had given the all clear, I climbed out of the limo and walked into the store. I greeted the old man behind the counter with a wave of my hand and then went in search of the books I wanted.

I don't know how long I searched the aisles, but when I was done, I had an entire stack of books sitting next to the register.

"Getting in a little light reading?"

I chuckled because there was nothing light about any of the books I'd chosen. "Something like that."

The old man rang me up. I paid him in cash—giving him an extra couple of hundred dollars—knowing he preferred that, and then handed the stack of books to one of my bodyguards. "Go put these in the car."

I waited until the bodyguard left before leaning closer to the counter. "You hear anything about the O'Donnells moving into the area lately?"

The shop keeper had been here for so many years that I suspected the building had been built around him. And while his shop wasn't very popular, the man did know pretty much everything that was going on in his little area of town.

The old man glanced toward the front of the store before leaning closer. "Michael O'Donnell has been making a big stink over the agreement you had with his father. He's trying to make a name for himself, and he wants to use you to do it."

"That snot nosed kid?" If I remember correctly, Kirby O'Donnell's son was only in his early twenties. He wasn't experienced enough to run a newspaper route let alone a crime syndicate. He should have been taken out when his father got shot.

"He's old enough to shoot a gun, so don't discount him because he's stupid. He's been causing trouble all up and down the waterfront."

"Is his father aware of this?"

The old man snorted. "What do you think?"

I peeled a couple more hundred-dollar bills off the stack from my pocket and dropped them in his tip jar. "Thank you for your time. If you get any old Russian classics in, give me a call. I have a friend that is interested in them."

The old man waved before reaching in to dig the money out of the jar.

I shook my head as I headed outside to the car. I heard a loud pop just as I stepped out the door and then something slammed into my shoulder, sending me spinning back into the door.

"Boss!"

I was grabbed and tossed into the car before I could barely register the fact that I had been shot. The car took off at a high rate of speed and then someone pressed something to my shoulder.

"Yob tvou mat!" Fuck, that hurt. "Call Yasha," I panted out. "Double Eiji's guards."

If anything happened to him, no one in New York City would be safe.

Chapter Thirteen

~ Eiji ~

I padded over to the door when I heard raised voices outside in the hallway. Dmitri hadn't been in to see me tonight and I was growing worried. As much as I might protest him being there, I'd come to look forward to his nightly visits.

I pressed my ear against the door to hear what was being said on the other side. My heart started to thunder in my chest when the words became clear.

"The doctor said that there will be no lasting damage," Olav was saying. "Master Dmitri simply needs a few days rest and then he will be back on his feet. During that time, no one is to say a word to Master Eiji about what happened. Master Dmitri was very clear on this."

"Eiji isn't stupid," Yasha said. "He will figure something is wrong when Dmitri doesn't go to see him tonight."

"Master Dmitri asked me to inform Master Eiji that he had to suddenly go out of town on business for the next three days. While I do not agree with his decision to withhold this information from Master Eiji, I must abide by his order."

"Fine." Yasha sighed. "I'll assign some guards for Dmitri's room to keep Eiji out."

"That won't matter, sir. Master Eiji never leaves his room."

"I'd rather be safe than sorry."

"Of course, sir."

I waited until the voices faded before cracking open the door between my suite and Dmitri's. I stuck my head in and quickly peeked around the room. Once I found it empty, I stepped inside, shut the door behind me, and crept toward the man lying on the bed.

Dmitri was tucked under the blankets, but they were folded down to his waist and there was a small white bandage over his right shoulder. He had clearly been injured somehow, but how?

My heart pounded a little faster when I saw the blood drying on the outside of the bandage. It obviously needed to be changed. I glanced toward the door. If I went out there to inform someone Dmitri's bandage needed to be change, people would come in.

I didn't want that.

I hurried back to my room and then into the bathroom. I remember from my earlier exploration of the place that there was a first aid kit under the sink. I ran in and got it from the cupboard by the door and then carried it back to Dmitri's room.

I set the first aid kit on the nightstand and opened it up, searching around inside until I found everything I thought I might need. I had to climb up onto the bed to get to him. Dmitri's bed was a lot bigger than mine, like huge, which made sense considering how big he was.

I carefully peeled back the bandage on his shoulder. Tears welled up in my eyes and slowly slid down my cheeks when I saw the neatly stitched together wound.

It looked so painful.

I grabbed an alcohol swap and gently cleaned the area around the wound before applying an antiseptic ointment with a cotton swab. The last thing I did was reapply a clean bandage over the whole injury.

I was really glad he was resting right now—at least, I hoped he was resting and not knocked out from the pain. If he moved around too much, he'd start bleeding again.

I climbed back up onto the bed and pressed my hand to his forehead. I knew from experience that injuries like this could easily cause a fever, but his brow seemed cool to the touch.

I cleaned up the mess and dropped everything in the garbage before closing up the first aid kit and carrying it back to my bathroom. When I walked back into Dmitri's bedroom, he was in the same position he'd been in before.

I walked over to the chair next to the bed and sat down, staring intently at Dmitri, watching the rise and fall of his chest with each breath that he took.

I didn't understand these feelings of fear that developed just as soon as I heard that Dmitri had been hurt. Despite how kind he had been to me so far, I didn't know this man. I didn't know what he was capable of.

And yet, I couldn't help the concern that welled up inside of me the moment I'd heard he had been injured.

I don't know how long I sat there staring at Dmitri before I heard voices outside the door. I jumped up from my chair to run to the other room, but the doorknob was already turning.

I'd never make it.

I dropped to the floor and slid myself under the bed. I turned so I could see who had come in and then held my breath; praying it wasn't one of the maids there to clean the room.

I recognized the black wing-tipped shoes immediately.

"He's still sleeping," Yasha said. "I want him checked once an hour until he wakes up."

"Yes, sir."

I glanced toward the end of the bed where two more sets of shoes could be seen, these also black dress shoes, just not wing-tipped.

"I also don't want him disturbed unnecessarily. If there's an issue, bring it to me. Dmitri needs all the rest he can get if he's going to heal from this attack."

"Understood, sir."

"Come on, we'd better go before we wake him."

As soon as the door shut behind the three men, I climbed out from under the bed and then climbed onto it, scooting closer to Dmitri. I was now on his left side, but I could clearly see the bandage on his right.

Who had attacked him?

I continued to watch him until my head got heavy and then I laid it down on the mattress where I could still see his chest going up and down as he breathed.

After a while, my eyelids grew heavy as well. I scooted closer to Dmitri for a little warmth and wrapped my hands around his wrist before letting them fall closed. At least if I had a hold of him, I might be able to keep him from moving around too much. I didn't want him hurt anymore than he already was.

That was the thought that followed me into dreamland.

* * * *

~ Dmitri ~

I woke slowly, the events of the day coming back in vivid, painful clarity. I hissed when I tried to sit up, the burning hot agony that flared through my shoulder telling me that quick movement was a big no-no.

When I went to reach for my shoulder, I realized my arm was trapped. For a split second, panic filled me. Had something other than simply being stabbed happened?

Had I been captured?

One quick glance down and I didn't know if I was in shock or if I was dreaming. Eiji was curled up on the bed beside me, holding my wrist with both hands. He had such a tight grip, it looked as if he had no intention of letting go.

I was strangely okay with that.

I just couldn't figure out how he had gotten in here. Eiji didn't leave his room unless I forced him to, and I hated forcing him. I had also given orders that he was not to be told about the attack or my injury.

So, why was he here?

He was also on top of the blankets, shivering.

I reached over to the nightstand and grabbed my cell phone, typing out a message for Yasha to bring me Eiji's fuzzy blanket from his room. I would have preferred to just have Eiji under the covers with me, but I doubted he'd appreciate that.

Yasha knocked on the door between the bedroom suites and then walked in at a fast clip, Eiji's fuzzy blanket in his hands. "Boss, Eiji is mis—"

I held my finger to my lips. "Ssshh."

I pointed to the man curled up beside me.

Yasha's eyebrows lifted for just a moment before he walked over, shook the blanket out, and then spread it over the top of Eiji.

I spoke in a very low tone when I ordered, "See to it that we are not disturbed unless it's an emergency."

"Your bandage, Boss," Yasha said in the same low tone. "Someone will need to change it soon."

I glanced at the crisp white bandage on my shoulder. "I think someone already did."

"He changed your bandage?"

"Someone did and Eiji's the only one in the room." The current bandage was a crisp white color.

"There's a guard posted outside so I know no one came in."

I grinned when all the pieces of the puzzle fell into place. "Then it had to be Eiji." I couldn't even begin to describe how much that elated me. Granted, I wished it hadn't come at the expense of me getting shot, but I'd take what I could get.

Yasha peered down at the white bandage. "It looks like he did a pretty good job."

I chuckled softly as I turned my hand over so I could stroke my fingers along the skin of Eiji's arm. "He probably read a book on first aid."

"He does seem to like to read."

"He does." Speaking of which. "Did anyone bring in those books I bought?"

Yasha shook his head. "I'll have someone go look in the car for them. We were a little more concerned with getting you to the doctor than we were the books."

Oh right, that.

"Any sign of the shooter?"

"One of the guards saw a black sedan driving away right after you were shot, but he wasn't able to get the license plate number. I have our tech guy checking the cameras in the area to see if they recorded anything."

"Keep on it, Yasha. I want whoever did this caught."

"I will."

I waved a hand at him, shooing him away. "Go now before you wake Eiji up."

Yasha shook his head as he started for the door. "I still can't believe he left his room to bandage your shoulder."

Me either. That had been a huge stride in Eiji's recovery. It was almost worth getting shot.

I waited until the door closed behind Yasha before slowly scooting down in the bed so I could wrap an arm around Eiji and pull him closer to me. I didn't know what he'd do or think when he woke up, but I had to chance it.

I had just started to fade off to sleep when I felt Eiji jerk and then his entire body stiffened.

"Ssshh, you're okay, *malen'kiy*. You're safe." I loosened my arm and let it fall back against the mattress so Eiji would know I wasn't trying to keep him here. I wanted him here, but he could leave if he wasn't ready for something like this.

The tension didn't fade from Eiji's body, but he did tilt his head back until he could look into my eyes.

I smiled. "Hi."

There was a small curve to one corner of Eiji's lips before he mouthed, *"Hi."*

When he pointed to the bandage and raised an eyebrow, I groaned. "Someone shot me."

Eiji nodded like he already knew that.

"Yasha is looking for whoever did it."

Eiji's lips pressed thin.

"Eiji, you were told what I do and who I am. I live in a dangerous world. Things like this happen. That's why there are so many guards around all the time. They are not here to keep anyone a prisoner. They are here to keep us safe."

Eiji pointed to my wound.

"Yeah, well, it doesn't always work."

I loved it when his eyes rolled. I just didn't think I was going to get the same reaction when I dropped my next bit of news.

"You have three guards on eight hour rotating shifts while you are inside the house. Their sole duty is to keep you safe. If you leave the house, you will have no less than four guards. You can come and go as you please, but you will be protected."

Eiji huffed.

"Sorry, *malen'kiy*. That's the way it has to be." I slowly reached up and slid my hand over the top of the hood he wore over his head. "I need you to be safe."

Eiji shrugged before looking at me again.

"Why? Is that what you are asking?"

Eiji nodded.

I drew in a breath as I tried to figure out exactly what to tell him. "Did your sister explain to you about the first time I ever saw you?"

Eiji held up his hand, his index finger and his thumb barely an inch apart.

"Okay, so she explained some."

He nodded again.

"I own the Illumination Club. I was there one night when you and your friends were out on the dance floor." I smiled at the memory my words invoked. "I remember standing at my office window watching you down on the dance floor. I'd never seen anyone that glowed as much as you did."

Eiji's eyebrows lifted as he pointed to himself.

I chuckled. "Okay, maybe glowed is the wrong word, but there was a vibrancy about you that fascinated me. Watching you dance was like watching a visual interpretation of joy, and I wanted to feel some of that joy. I don't see much of it in my life. Unfortunately, before Yasha could bring you to my office so I could meet you, your bonehead stepbrothers grabbed you."

Eiji's eyes narrowed.

"Yeah, I wasn't real pleased either. I had Yasha look into you and them, and that's when I discovered Carrie. When she started to tell me about the life you've been leading for the last ten years, I wanted to send my men right out to drown your stepmother in the Hudson River, complete with cement shoes."

Eiji ducked his head, tugging the edges of his hood up around his face. I knew he must have been embarrassed about what Carrie had told me. He didn't need to be. She hadn't gone too much into specifics.

"Carrie didn't tell me everything," I told Eiji. "She just explained that you were basically a prisoner in your own home and she was desperate to get you out. So, after a bit more research, I started making a plan to rescue you. It all started when I learned that Beverly is a gambling addict."

Eiji made the gesture for money by rubbing his thumb over his index finger and then pointed to himself.

"Technically, I guess you could say I bought you, but dowries are a thing in a lot of countries, you know. It just so happens that my dowry for you was the same amount as what your stepmother owed me."

Plus another million dollars.

Eiji didn't say anything for the longest time. He wouldn't even look at me. I wished he would just so I could try and read the emotions on his face. I had no idea what he was thinking.

"Are you upset that we got married?"

Eiji didn't raise his head, but he did shake it back and forth.

I couldn't help smiling as I tried not to let my relief show. "I promise no one will make you do anything you don't want to do, not even me."

This time Eiji did tilt his head back until our eyes met. He didn't say anything, but then he didn't have to.

I smiled a bit wider and pressed my hand to the side of his face. I could still feel the warmth from his skin through the fabric of his hood. "I swear on my life, Eiji. Unless it has to do with your safety, you will never have to do what someone else says again. You can come and go as you please, although I would like to be informed if you leave the house just so I don't worry. But other than that, you get to make the decisions about your life."

Eiji wiggled around, and for a moment, I thought he was trying to get off the bed so he could go back to his room. My heart sank until I saw him pull his cell phone out of his pocket.

He quickly typed something out and then turned the phone toward me so I could read what he wrote.

My eyebrows lifted in surprise. "Yes, of course. If you want to go to school, we can sign you up tomorrow."

Eiji typed something else out and then turned the screen toward me.

"Online school?" I thought about it for a moment, and that made sense considering how much he hated leaving his room. "We can look into that. I'm sure there are some good online schools we can sign you up for. I'll have Yasha look into it."

"Thank you," Eiji mouthed.

"I bought you some books," I said. "Yasha will bring them in from the car later. For right now, I think we could both do with some rest."

Eiji nodded before tucking his phone back in his pocket. When he grabbed his blanket and started to climb off the bed, I grabbed his wrist. He glanced back at me, a bit of apprehension in his eyes.

I instantly released his wrist and then grabbed the edge of my blanket and lifted it up. "You can stay if you want. There's enough room here for both of us."

Eiji pointed to my wound.

"It doesn't hurt." And even if it did, I would never admit it. "You can climb in if you want to. If you don't, that's okay too."

I would never force him.

Eiji stared at me for a moment and then made a hand gesture that made me sputter. "No, no hanky panky. I promise. Just sleep."

He regarded me with narrowed eyes for a moment before pushing his fuzzy blanket to the bottom of the bed and then crawling in beside me. His body was stiff and unyielding for the most part.

He'd never get any rest that way.

I turned partially on my good side and slid my arm under his head before pulling him up against me. I grabbed the blanket and pulled it up over the both of us and then settled my head on the pillow.

"Sleep, *malen'kiy*."

I waited until I felt Eiji's body relax against mine before allowing myself to sleep. I had no idea if he would be here when I awoke, but we had made such strides today that I didn't even care.

Eiji was sleeping in my arms.

That was enough.

Chapter Fourteen

~ Eiji ~

I swallowed down my fear and opened the door. I took a single step out and then nearly jumped out of my skin when the guard at the door turned and looked at me.

I pressed my hand to my chest, trying to keep my racing heart locked behind my ribcage.

"Can I help you, sir?"

I pointed to my mouth and then made the gesture for eating.

"I can have some food delivered to the room for you."

I shook my head. I needed to do this. I wasn't sure why. I just knew it was something I had to do.

Getting to the kitchen, however...

I stepped a little farther out into the hallway, just far enough to close the door behind me. I didn't want anyone waking Dmitri up before he was ready. With an injury like his, he needed all his rest.

Pressing my hand flat against the wall, I started walking down the hallway toward the stairs. Tiny steps. I couldn't seem to make my feet move faster or farther.

Just little baby steps.

A couple of the maids and a guard stared when they saw me, but no one tried to stop me. I had to stop for several minutes when I reached the top of the stairs.

This was like the line of death for me. If I crossed it, I was walking into clear danger. If I stayed upstairs, I could run and hide, but then there would be no food for Dmitri.

Gathering up my courage, I took the first step down, and then the next and the next until I reached the bottom floor. I was still breathing, and no one had attacked me, so that was a major plus.

Now, I just had to find the kitchen.

I cocked my head and listened. When I heard the sounds of pots and pans clanking around, I headed in that direction.

A swinging door opened just as I reached it and a maid with a tray of food stepped out...and ran right into me. The tray and all the food on it went crashing to the floor.

"Watch where you are going, you clumsy oaf." She gestured to the mess on the floor. "Look at what you made me do."

Fear almost paralyzed me, but I still had enough control to drop to the floor and start gathering up the dishes and placing them back on the tray. I wasn't sure what I was going to do about the food.

I picked the tray up and tried to hand it to her, but she knocked it out of my hands and took a threatening step toward me, raising her hand in the air. My fear spiked as I scrambled backward, trying to escape.

I jumped to my feet and took off running. I made it as far as the stairs, but Yasha and one of the guards were coming down them, which meant I couldn't go up. I turned and made a beeline for the next available exit.

I heard Yasha call out my name as I raced into what I assumed was a living room. It took me one quick scan of the room to see that I had made a huge mistake. There was no exit from this room unless I went through a window, and I just might.

I grabbed a heavy black iron poker as I ran past the fireplace, and then over to one of the corners of the room. I couched down to make myself into the smallest target possible and held the poker in front of me with both hands.

Bile rose in my throat when I saw Yasha, the maid, and the other guard standing just inside the entrance. There was no way I could get past all of them. One maybe, but not three.

If they came for me, I was doomed.

Yasha slowly approached me; his hands held out in front of him. "It's okay, Eiji. You're going to be fine."

Tears started to slip from my eyes when I shook my head. I wasn't going to be fine. I could already feel my chest starting to tighten. Any moment now I was going to go into a full-blown panic attack and then they could get me.

"Vasil, go get Dmitri," Yasha ordered, "and hurry." He squatted down several feet from me, not coming any closer. "Do you want your blanket, Eiji?"

I nodded rapidly.

"Vasil, get Eiji's blanket, too."

The guard took off.

The maid stayed. "Mr. Yasha—"

When I stiffened, Yasha held up his hand to her. "Not a word."

"But, sir—"

"Damn it, girl, didn't you hear me? Shut the hell up."

The maid snapped her lips together, not saying another word, but her eyes were shooting daggers at me.

"Can you breathe with me?" Yasha asked right before drawing in a deep breath of air. "Watch my chest, Eiji. Breathe in." He did it again and then slowly let it out. "Breathe out."

I tried, but it didn't work. I clawed at my chest, my grip loosening on the iron poker until it clattered to the floor. I smacked my tight chest several times, unable to draw any air in.

I couldn't breathe.

"I know, Eiji, I know," Yasha said gently as if he was talking to a cornered feral animal. "Dmitri is coming. He'll be here any second now, and he'll take care of you. I just need you to breathe for me until he gets here, okay?"

My eyes flickered to the entryway when I heard the heavy thunder of several sets of feet coming down the stairs. When Dmitri suddenly appeared in the doorway, I slapped the floor, silently telling him to hurry the hell up.

The maid took a step toward him. "Master Dmitri—"

Dmitri barreled right past her as if she wasn't even there and raced across the room to me. As soon as he reached me, he scooped me up in his arms and carried me over to the couch.

Dmitri sat down, cradling me in his arms, and then grabbed my hand and pressed it flat to his bare chest. "Breathe with me, *malen'kiy*."

I could feel the movement of his chest as he breathed, going up and down, up and down. Every time he breathed in, I breathed in. Every time he breathed out, I breathed out.

When the tingling in my limbs faded and the tightness in my chest eased, I slumped against Dmitri. Every ounce of energy I had felt as if it had been drained out of me. I barely even acknowledged the blanket being draped over me and then tucked around my body.

"What happened here?" Dmitri snapped. "Why is Eiji so upset?"

"I'm not exactly sure, Boss," Yasha replied. "I was more concerned with getting him help than figuring out what was going on."

Dmitri's eyes narrowed. "Figure it out."

I reached up and pressed my hand to the side of Dmitri's face, turning his head until he was looking down at me. I slowly made several hand gestures, hoping he would understand what I couldn't verbally tell him.

I wasn't sure what to think when I saw flames of rage ignite in his eyes.

"Yasha!"

"Boss?" Yasha leaned in close.

I didn't mind so much. Yasha was a good guy. He wasn't there to hurt me or Dmitri. He also seemed to understand that Dmitri helped me keep my sanity.

"Get me the security recordings for the first floor," Dmitri said in a near whisper. "Everything for the last thirty minutes. And no one is to leave the house until I say so."

"Right away, Boss." Yasha nodded once and then hurried out of the room.

Dmitri pulled the edge of the blanket back and then stroked a finger down the side of my face. "Better now?"

I nodded.

"Why didn't you wake me up?"

I'm sure my face was fire engine red as I tried to explain that I had wanted to make breakfast for Dmitri myself, not have someone else do it. I still didn't know who had shot him, but I wasn't taking any chances. If I cooked his food, I knew no one could mess with it.

"You braved coming all the way downstairs just so you could cook for me?"

I shrugged as if it was no big deal, but I could still feel the heat in my face.

"Thank you, Eiji," Dmitri said as he stood and started for the entry. "Why don't we go to the kitchen now and you can cook something for me?"

I nodded again before pointing to the white bandage on his shoulder.

"I'm okay. I get a little twinge when I turn the wrong way, but I'm not in any major pain."

That was a relief.

"Master Dmitri—"

I cringed back when the maid stepped forward. I grabbed the edge of my blanket to pull it over my face. I didn't want her looking at me and I certainly didn't want to look at her.

"Sir, if I could just—"

"Who are you?" Dmitri asked.

"Mary Henderson, sir. I was just hired as one of the new maids last week."

"What did you do to my husband?" Dmitri demanded in a harsh tone that probably worried other people. Not me. To me, it sounded like a sword pulled from a scabbard and ready to be used to defend me.

I loved that tone.

I peeked over the edge of the blanket, curious as to what her answer would be.

"I didn't do—" The woman's face turned pale white. "Husband?"

"Yes, this is my husband, Eiji." Dmitri's eyes turned into shards of ice, and I was really glad he wasn't looking at me with them. "What did you do that sent him into a panic attack?"

"I didn't do anything, sir. I swear."

She was lying through her teeth.

I patted Dmitri's chest to get his attention. When he glanced at me, I tried to show him what had happened, but I became agitated all over again. Granted, the woman hadn't actually hit me, but she had intended to.

"Calm down, Eiji," Dmitri directed. "Yasha will get to the bottom of this."

I almost groaned when Dmitri turned and started carrying me back toward the couch. This was not going to get him fed any faster and he needed to eat. He needed the extra boost to help him heal.

I started to pat Dmitri's chest again when he suddenly stumbled forward before falling to his knees, sending me crashing across the floor. I glanced up just in time to see the maid bring another vase down on Dmitri's head.

He slumped to the floor.

If I could have screamed, I would have. Since I couldn't, I searched around for the next best option. My eyes fell on the fireplace poker. I picked it up and jumped up to stand over the top of Dmitri, swinging the poker madly back and forth to keep her away.

My anger at her turned to confusion when the maid let out a scream.

"Oh my god, what are you doing?" she screamed very loudly. "How could you hurt your own husband like that? Master Dmitri has been so nice to you. Why would you hurt him?"

What?

Several people came racing into the room. They all stopped when they saw me standing over the top of Dmitri with the poker held tightly in both hands.

"He's a monster!" the maid wailed as big crocodile tears trailed down her pale cheeks. "He just hit Master Dmitri over the head with that poker. Why would he do that? I thought they were married."

I narrowed my eyes when one of the guards drew his gun. I vaguely remember him standing guard outside my bedroom at night. I did not remember his name.

"Master Eiji, you need to put the poker down."

Yeah, that wasn't going to happen.

I shook my head.

"Sir, I really don't want to have to hurt you." The guard aimed his gun at me. "Please put the poker down."

When he took a step toward me, I raised the poker even more and then mouthed the name of the one man that I knew believed in me. *"Yasha."*

"Someone go get Yasha."

"I'm here," Yasha said as he quickly strode into the room. He gestured to the maid as he passed her. "Detain her."

As soon as Yasha reached me and Dmitri, I handed him the fireplace poker and then dropped down to my knees next to Dmitri so I could check him over. He had a large bump on the back of his head that was trickling blood.

I waved my hand at Yasha before pointing to the injury. I was pretty sure Dmitri had a concussion, and he was definitely going to need more stitches.

"Vasil, call an ambulance for Dmitri, and then call the police. Once you do that, go to the security office and make a recording of everything that just happened in here and the hallway by the kitchen door. The police will want copies."

Someone produced a towel. I grabbed it and pressed it to the back of Dmitri's head, hoping to stop the flow of blood.

"He'll be okay, Eiji."

I wasn't sure I believed that.

Chapter Fifteen

~ Dmitri ~

"How are you feeling, Boss?"

"Like my head is going to explode." I grimaced as I reached back and gingerly fingered my new wound. "What happened?"

"That new maid knocked you over the head with a vase, knocked you out, and then tried to blame it on Eiji."

I glanced down at the man curled up next to me. "Eiji wouldn't hurt me."

I'd bet my life on it.

"He didn't." Yasha let out a low chuckle. "In fact, I'm pretty sure he saved your life."

I glanced up. "What does that mean?"

"I didn't see the whole thing until after the fact, but when I returned to the living room, Eiji was standing over the top of you, swinging a fireplace poker at anyone that got too close. He didn't even waver when one of the guards pulled a gun and pointed it at him."

I growled, my anger instant. "Someone pointed a gun at Eiji?"

Both Yasha and I glanced down when we heard a noise come from the man. Eiji's eyes were still closed, but he was patting my chest and shushing me.

"Did he...?" I know I'd been hit over the head, but I could swear Eiji was making noise. Like, real verbal noise.

"I believe so, Boss."

"Don't say anything to anyone about this. If Eiji can learn to talk again, he'll do it when he's ready. I don't want a bunch of people staring at him, expecting him to do tricks. He hates it when people stare at him."

"I won't say a word."

I stroked my hand over the top of Eiji's head before raising my eyes to Yasha. "About that guard with the gun..."

"I don't think the gun was the important part here, Boss," Yasha stated. "The guard was just doing his job in a situation where no one knew what was going on. The important part is that Eiji protected you and didn't have a panic attack while doing it."

That did seem important, but I still wanted to know which guard had pulled a gun on Eiji. That was absolutely unacceptable.

Yasha held up his cell phone. "You need to watch the security tapes."

I grabbed Yasha's phone and hit the button to watch the recording. I had to watch it twice before I fully understood what I was seeing, and everything Yasha said was right.

Eiji had protected me.

"The other recording shows what happened between Eiji and the maid in the hallway outside the kitchen. Apparently, Eiji was trying to go in there and make you some food when the maid came out and they crashed into each other. That would have been fine because Eiji tried to help clean up the mess, but she went off the rails and tried to hit him. That's when Eiji freaked out."

"Where is she?"

"The police have her. I also gave them a copy of the tapes when they arrested that woman and took her away for assault."

"I want her."

"No, you don't," Yasha replied. "You need to let the police handle this one."

"Yasha—"

"Concentrate on getting better, Boss. We need you back in peak condition. That's twice in as many days that someone has tried to take you out. You need to get better so we can figure out who is after you."

I didn't like it, but I couldn't argue that Yasha was wrong. "Where was his guard?"

"Eiji left through your door, not his. His guard was standing at his door."

"I want Eiji's guards doubled inside and outside the house. I also want a meeting with all of the staff when we get home. That maid seemed to have no idea that he was my husband until I said something to her."

"She was new, and even then Eiji never leaves his room. Very few of our people have seen him."

"I don't care," I snapped. "Everyone needs to be introduced to Eiji so that they know who he is. I don't want him to have to go through another situation like this again."

It wasn't acceptable for Eiji to be frightened in his own home.

"I'll arrange it, Boss. Just get better."

"Any news on the fucker that shot me?"

"No, nothing yet, but we both know who it was."

Sadly, we probably did.

"On the flip side of things, Bev—"

We both turned to look when there was a knock at the door. It opened and Lev stuck his head in. "Sir, Vinnie Borelli is here to see you."

I frowned. "Vinnie?"

"Yes, sir."

Fucking fantastic.

"Yasha, hand me that extra blanket. I want to spread it out over Eiji."

"He's going to know that someone is under that blanket," Yasha said even as he did what I had ordered.

"I don't care about that." I tugged the blanket up until it fully covered the man curled into my side. "Eiji doesn't like strangers looking at him and he doesn't have his blanket with him."

"Maybe we should consider carrying an extra one around in the car in case we have to leave the house in a hurry."

It wasn't a bad idea.

I nodded. "I'll order a new one tomorrow."

"Better order two so there's a backup."

I'd already planned on it.

Once Eiji was fully covered, I nodded to Yasha. "Let him in."

Yasha walked over and pulled the door open and then stood back to allow the other man to enter. "Mr. Borelli."

Vinnie Borelli strolled in as if he owned not only the room, but the whole damn hospital. The man definitely had ego to spare, but I kind of liked that about him. While I instilled fear in most people, Vinnie had always been the charmer.

"Vinnie, to what do I owe the pleasure?" I asked.

Vinnie had an amused smirk on his face as he replied, "Heard you got shot."

"That was a couple of days ago." Not to mention one attack ago.

Vinnie was behind.

Vinnie started to reach into his breast pocket, but stopped when Yasha stiffened. He raised an eyebrow until I shook my head and Yasha took a step back.

"I wanted to bring you this." He pulled out a small silver thumb drive and held it out to me. "It's video surveillance my people got of a black sedan speeding through my territory before crossing over into Queens."

I shot Yasha a quick look. "A black sedan?"

"Yes, I believe you were supposed to think the shooter came from my territory, thus placing the blame on me, but as you will see when you look at that video, my people traced it back to O'Donnell."

My jaw clenched. "I am getting real tired of that man fucking with me."

"You know this won't end until you deal with him, Dmitri. Kirby O'Donnell was a slime bag and his son is an idiot. Michael O'Donnell seems to think the whole world is his for the taking simply because of who his father was."

"I really don't want to go to war over this shit." Especially not now that I had Eiji, not that I would ever admit that to Vinnie. I didn't even want him to know about Eiji.

"You might not have a choice."

"Do you have any idea why it's so damn important for them to have a pathway to Jersey?"

"Drugs would be my bet. While the O'Donnells do run a few brothels, most of their money is tied up in drugs. The Port Authority has been cracking down on ships coming and going out of the port as of late. The only safe avenue for him to ship his drugs is overland."

"Not through my territory." I knew there were a lot of low-level drug dealers in the Bronx, but nothing on the scale of what the O'Donnells put out. They were serious drug dealers.

"I don't want their drugs in my territory either, but I'm not sure we can stop them."

Before I could rebut that statement, I heard a soft inhale of breath and the body beside me stiffened and then started to shake. I immediately dismissed Vinnie from my mind and leaned over Eiji, pressing a hand to the side of his covered head.

"You're okay, *malen'kiy*," I whispered. "I'm right here with you."

I tugged the edge of the blanket down far enough to see Eiji's green eyes. His very frightened green eyes.

"Do you remember me getting hurt?"

He nodded once.

"We're at the hospital right now. The doctor had to put a few stitches in the back of my head where I got hit. I know you don't like leaving your room, but Yasha wasn't comfortable leaving you home without one of us there, so he brought you with us. Lev and Vasil are right outside the door."

Eiji's eyes darted to the side of the blanket, and I knew what—or rather who—he was looking at.

"This man is Vinnie Borelli. He's kind of in the same business as me, but the Italian side of things. He had some information on the guys that shot me and wanted to bring it to me. Since he can't really be seen going to my house, he brought it here to me at the hospital."

Eiji nodded again.

I darted a look at Vinnie. "Would you like to meet him?"

Eiji shook his head, but I hadn't expected any other response out of him. Still, I had to give him the choice.

"Okay, you just rest." I pulled the blanket up over Eiji's head again, but smiled when I felt his hand snake around my arm.

When I glanced at Vinnie, he was staring at the blanket covered figure curled up next to me, a frown pinching the skin between his eyes.

I narrowed my eyes at him. "This is Eiji, my husband."

That right there made him off limits.

"Your husband?" Vinnie asked. "You got married?"

"I did, and I would introduce you, but Eiji doesn't do strangers. I won't force him to, not even for you."

Vinnie shook his head. "No, of course not."

My mouth parted in surprise. I hadn't expected that answer out of Vinnie. I actually thought he'd be pissed.

"You really got married?"

I smirked. "I really did."

"And Eiji is...a man?"

"He is." I knew the danger associated with men in the mafia being involved romantically with other men. There was an even bigger stigma back in my home country.

I just didn't care.

"You have my congratulations then," Vinnie replied, much to my surprise. "I'll make sure all of my people know he's off limits."

I swallowed tightly at the gift Vinnie was handing me. Spouses and children of mafia families were off limits in disputes and Vinnie was stating that he accepted Eiji as my spouse, which made him off limits.

"I'd appreciate it, Vinnie."

"I expect the same for my family."

I nodded. "Of course."

"I will send an appropriate wedding gift after you return from the hospital."

"Don't worry about it."

"It would be disrespectful not to."

Knowing Vinnie would get something that would make me ape-shit crazy, I suggested, "Eiji is currently reading Russian classics." I smiled proudly. "In Russian."

"Bah." Vinnie waved a hand at me. "Italian classics are so much better."

I glanced down when Eiji tugged on my arm and the reached over to lift the blanket so I could see his face. "You wanted to say something?"

As I watched Eiji's hand gestures, my smile grew into a grin. "Eiji says he has read your Italian classics, in English and Italian, and Russian classics are better. They are more..." I frowned until Eiji moved his finger across his throat, and then I turned to Vinnie. "He says Russian classics are more bloodthirsty."

Vinnie sorted out a laugh. "I guess I can't argue with that."

Neither could I.

Eiji tugged on my arm again and then held up his phone so I could see the screen. "Eiji does say that he would accept a hardbound copy of *Il Piacere* by Gabriele D'Annunzio, but only in Italian."

Vinnie's eyebrow rose. "Your Eiji has good taste. *Il Piacere* is a masterpiece." He slid his hands into the pockets of his slacks and took on a casual pose. "He speaks Russian and Italian?"

"English, Russian, Italian, and Thai."

"Thai?"

I just shrugged.

Eiji tugged on my arm, showing me his cell phone screen again.

"English, Russian, Italian, Thai, Korean, Japanese, French, and a smattering of Farsi." My eyebrows climbed up my forehead at that list. It was a long list.

It was a very strange list.

"That's a lot of languages."

I glanced back at Vinnie when he spoke. "Eiji likes to study things that interest him."

Vinnie snickered. "Better hope running the mafia doesn't interest him or you and I will both be out of a job."

Eiji quickly shook his head.

"He says he has no interest in running the mafia."

"Too bad." Vinnie sighed. "I could use a vacation."

Him and me both.

Two days later I chuckled when a hardbound copy of *Il Piacere* by Gabriele D'Annunzio—written in Italian—arrived by special courier, addressed to Eiji Petrov.

Chapter Sixteen
~ Dmitri ~

"Boss!"

My heart froze in my chest at the fear on Lev's face as he came running into my office. The man didn't even knock. Lev was supposed to be on guard duty right now. It was his shift. That panicked look could only mean one thing.

"Where's Eiji?"

"I don't know, Boss. Olav went in to deliver his breakfast and he was gone. I searched the entire room, but there's no sign of him."

"Search the house."

I dropped down into my chair and tapped several buttons on my computer screen to bring up the CCTV set around the mansion and the estate grounds.

I had to search through several screens before I found Eiji and I still almost missed him. I flicked past the screen and then flicked back just as quickly and stared.

I seriously hadn't expected to see him dancing around the ballroom. While the moves might not all be the same, he was dancing like he had at the club, full of life and exuberance as if each movement brought him joy and happiness.

I couldn't look away.

The video was silent from my vantage point, but Eiji seemed to be listening to music. I reached over and typed in the code to get sound and then reared back at the sheer volume of what Eiji was listening to. It must be shaking the windows in the ballroom.

I quickly clicked the button to bring down the sound and then sat there and watched as Eiji danced around the room with stunned amazement. Each step was measured to the beat of the music, not a single one wasted.

There was a part of me—probably a really sadistic part—that was glad whatever trauma he had gone through hadn't taken his hearing but took his ability to speak instead. It would have been a travesty if Eiji couldn't hear the music he danced to.

"Boss!" Yasha shouted as he came running into my office.

I held up my hand to stop him from shouting without even looking away from the screen. Mostly because I couldn't. I was mesmerized just like the first time I'd seen him dance.

A moment later, I felt Yasha's presence at my side. "Is that Eiji?"

"Yep."

"He's in the ballroom."

"Yep."

"How?" Yasha asked. "The ballroom is locked."

"I'm more curious how he got out of his room without Lev seeing him."

Yasha snorted. "He tied bed sheets together and lowered himself down from your balcony."

I chuckled even as my chest puffed up a little. "Of course he did."

I don't know why he simply hadn't walked out the door and made his way down to the ballroom. I'd ask him about that later. I was just thrilled that he had left his room and was enjoying himself.

"What is that music he is playing?"

I shook my head because I really had no idea. It was loud and definitely had a beat to it, but I couldn't even understand the words. It was like heavy rock in a foreign language.

It wasn't Russian.

I jumped to my feet when the doors to the ballroom crashed open and two guards rushed in. If they touched a hair on Eiji's head, I'd remove theirs.

I started for the door.

"Wait," Yasha called out. "You need to see this."

I scowled as I came back around my desk and stared down at the screen. "I need to get..." My words trailed off as I watched the two guards try to grab Eiji, but every time they got close, he simply zipped around them. "What are they doing?"

Eiji was darting all over the place, under the tables lined against the walls, around stacks of chairs. At one point, he even used some of the floor-to-ceiling curtains to swing himself away from one of the guards.

And he was grinning the entire time.

"He's having fun," I whispered.

"He might be," Yasha said, "but they are not."

My eyes narrowed as I watched one of the guards take a swing at Eiji when he managed to get close enough. Eiji effortlessly ducked, but that wasn't the point.

"He dies."

This time, Yasha didn't try to stop me from storming out of my office. He simply hurried along behind me. When we passed Lev and Vasil, I waved to them.

"Follow me."

I had no idea where Boris, Eiji's third guard, was. Maybe sleeping until it was his shift?

I rushed down the hallway to the entrance of the ballroom. We didn't use this room often, hardly at all really, but there were times when we had large get-togethers and a room this size was needed.

"What in the hell is going on in here?"

I don't know what happened between the time I left my office and entered the ballroom, but Eiji had somehow gotten himself up to the top of the curtains and he was clinging to the curtain rod for all his worth. The two guards stood beneath him trying to coax him down.

Eiji was no longer smiling.

The fear on what I could see of his face made me want to hurt someone. I stomped over until I stood right beneath him and then held out my arms.

"Time to come down, *malen'kiy*. I think you've had enough fun for today."

My heart nearly shattered when Eiji simply let go. I leapt forward and caught him in my arms before he could hit the floor. My pulse thundered, my chest aching with how rapidly my heart was beating.

"Lev, get his blanket."

I cradled Eiji to my chest for a moment, basking in the knowledge that he was not hurt. I was also a little astonished at how easily he had given in to my demand and fallen into my arms.

"Were you having a good time, *malen'kiy*?" I asked in a low tone. "I saw you dancing."

Eiji raised an eyebrow.

I turned and pointed to the cameras mounted high on the ceiling in each corner of the room. I chuckled when Eiji's cheeks flushed.

"What was that music you were listening to?"

Eiji wiggled around until he could pull his cell phone out and then typed a message on it before turning the screen toward me.

"Mongolian throat music?" I wasn't sure I'd ever heard of that. "It had a good beat."

Eiji typed something out again before holding the screen up to me.

I chuckled as I read it. "It's good to dance to, huh?"

Eiji nodded.

"Is it also good for escaping your bodyguards?"

Eiji's frown was instant. His fingers snapped as he quickly typed something out. *"You said I could go anywhere in the house I wanted."*

"And you can. You can go anywhere on the entire estate that you want. But you need to tell someone, even if it's just to say that you are going for a walk. You scared a lot of people when we couldn't find you."

"Sorry," Eiji mouthed.

I leaned in close so only Eiji could hear me. "You don't need to use sheets to escape your room. If you want out, simply walk out. No one will stop you."

Eiji shook his head before typing a new message. *"Too many people."*

"I see." I thought about it for a minute before asking, "Would it help if we put a ladder outside your balcony? We could attach it to the side of the house so it would be safe for you to use."

Eiji's eyes rounded before he slowly nodded his head.

"I'll agree to this under one condition. If you decide to go somewhere and don't want to go through the house, you send me a text letting me know so I don't worry about you. Can you do that?"

Eiji nodded again.

I smiled at him and said, "Yasha."

"Yes, Boss?" Yasha asked as he stepped closer.

"Have someone attach a ladder to the side of the house at Eiji's balcony. Make sure it can't come off. I don't want Eiji falling."

"Yes, Boss."

Just then, Lev came running in with Eiji's fuzzy blanket. I took it from him and wrapped it around Eiji as best as I could considering I refused to let go of him. I even made sure to pull it up over his face.

"Better?" I asked.

Eiji smiled, and that was good enough for me.

Now I needed to deal with the other side of this mess.

I kept Eiji held tight to my chest as I turned to face the others in the room. Yasha was beside us with Lev and Vasil standing just off to our left, waiting for Eiji.

That left the other two guards.

My eyes narrowed in on the guard that had tried to take a swing at Eiji. I wanted to hurt him just like he had planned to hurt Eiji, but that would mean putting Eiji down and I wasn't quite ready to do that yet.

"Yasha, I want all the guards called in to the ballroom."

"Yes, Boss."

"Lev, Vasil, you're with me." I started walking, carrying Eiji toward the stage area at the far side of the ballroom. This was usually where we set up the band or put a podium when someone needed to give a speech.

I had a speech to deliver today, but not many people were going to like what I had to say.

Once I reached the stage, I climbed the steps and then turned to survey the room. When my eyes fell on the tables and chairs, a plan began to formulate in my head.

"Lev, Vasil, get some of the guys to help you move the tables and chairs to the middle of the room."

Lev had a deep frown on his face as he glanced out over the open floor and then to me. "Boss?"

"I want an obstacle course set up. Bring in stuff from other rooms if you have to, but I want you to make it as hard as possible for anyone to get from the other side of the room to here. "

"Yes, Boss." Lev still sounded confused, but him and Vasil jumped off the stage and then got the others to help start spreading stuff out.

I stood on the stage and just watched everything get set up. There was a lot of confusion on the faces of the guards that walked into the room.

They'd understand soon.

Strangely enough, this idea came to me when I thought about Eiji hanging from those curtain rods.

"Boss, what are you up to?" Yasha asked as he climbed the steps to the stage and walked over to stand next to me.

"Do you remember watching Eiji evade the guards?"

"Sure."

"He's untrained, so how did he do it?"

Yasha shrugged. "He's smaller."

"Does being smaller explain him hanging from the curtain rods? He had to get up there somehow."

Yasha frowned as he looked from the fuzzy wrapped bundle in my arms to the curtain rods high off the floor. "I'm not sure where you are going with this, Boss."

"You'll see in a moment. Once everyone is here, I want them all lined up at the back of the room."

Yasha nodded and then went off to do what I had ordered.

I turned my attention to the man in my arms. "Eiji, I need you to do something for me. It's going to be scary for you, but it's important to me. Do you think you can do it?"

Eiji shrugged and then moved the blanket off his face so he could look up at me.

"It's nothing major," I promised him, "and you can even play your music if you want." It would probably help. I pointed toward the back of the room to where Yasha was lining up the guards. "See all those bodyguards back there?"

Eiji nodded.

"See all the obstacles between there and here?"

He nodded again.

"The only thing I need you to do is start back by the far wall and get to this stage as fast as you can. You can use any means necessary. Go over the tables, under the tables, whatever works. I just need you to go from one side of the room to the other as quickly as you can."

Eiji stared out over the room for a moment before looking at me and mouthing, *"Why?"*

"You evaded two of my bodyguards, two of my highly trained bodyguards, and that got me to thinking. How did you evade them?"

Eiji shrugged.

"You dance a lot, don't you?"

Eiji nodded.

"They don't."

That frown was back.

"They are highly trained in the art of defense and offense. They know hand-to-hand combat, how to shoot a gun, how to evade capture, and how to protect those they are assigned to protect. But they have no dexterity, not like you do. They can't bend, twist, and turn like you do. I think you get it from all the dancing you do."

Eiji glanced back out over the room. I could practically see the wheels turning in his head. When he glanced at me and pointed to his ear, I nodded.

"You can play your music as loud as you want."

Eiji swallowed tightly and then nodded. *"Okay."*

"No one will touch you and you can keep your hood on. I'll be waiting right here for you. Okay?"

He nodded again.

I carried Eiji off the stage and across the room. I had to do a bit of weaving myself before I reached the far side where all the guards were standing.

When I set Eiji on his feet, I grabbed his blanket before it fell to the floor. "I am going to go stand on the stage now and wait for you. Who do you want to stand here with you?"

"Yasha," was Eiji's instant answer.

I was glad that he trusted my second-in-command. I just wished he trusted his own bodyguards as much.

"Yasha, come stand with Eiji."

Once Yasha was in place, I leaned in and pressed a kiss to Eiji's forehead before he could stop me and then pulled his hood up more securely around his head. "I'll be waiting for you on the stage."

Eiji pointed to his ear.

I smiled as I nodded. "Lev, once I give you the signal, I want you turn on the music."

"Yes, Boss."

"Eiji, you know what to do."

Eiji nodded.

I hated leaving Eiji there, especially knowing how much he hated being around others, but this was important. I was making a point with my bodyguards, one they needed to learn in order to better protect the man that was becoming the most important person in my life.

Once I was on the stage, I turned and faced the crowd of people on the other side of the room. I pulled out my cell phone and brought up the stopwatch app.

I nodded to Lev and then hit the button on the app at the same moment I gestured to Eiji. Watching him start moving across the room was almost as good as watching him dance. He was quick, moving swiftly over the tops of tables, around chairs, sliding down and under more tables.

I should have recorded it so I could watch it in slow motion because he was jumping up on stage and into my arms in a matter of seconds.

I hit the stop button on the stopwatch as I caught him in my arms. I grinned as I glanced down at the app. "Five point six seconds. Very good, *malen'kiy*."

Eiji grinned up at me.

I wrapped the blanket around him before tucking him into my side and facing the crowd of onlookers. I waved my hand at Lev to cut the music and pulled a wad of cash out of my pocket and held it up.

"Eiji just ran this obstacle course in under six seconds. I'll give anyone that can beat his time of five point six seconds a thousand dollars cash right now. You have your choice of music or no music."

It took almost an hour for everyone to run the obstacle course, and by the end, Eiji was cuddled in my arms again, his head resting on my shoulder as he lightly snoozed.

Only one man had beat Eiji's time, and I was kind of surprised considering how big he was. Still, I was glad it was him. I peeled ten one-hundred-dollar bills off the roll and handed them over. "You did very well, Vasil."

The man gave me a bow of his head. "Thank you, Boss."

"Do you dance?" My eyebrows lifted when a flush filled his cheeks. I don't think I'd ever seen him embarrassed before. "Vasil?"

"Ballet, sir," he said in a very low voice. "I wanted to be a professional ballet dancer when I was younger, but I'm too big for anyone to take me seriously. I still dance at a studio once a week, though."

"Good." I smiled again so that he'd know I approved of this. "You should continue this practice. If you need help paying for studio time, let me know."

Vasil blinked at me in surprise. "Yes, sir."

"I'd like you to get together with Eiji and make a workout program for all the guards. Something that will teach them the speed and dexterity the two of you seem to have."

It was kind of sad that none of the other well trained guards had it.

"Yes, Boss."

"They need to be able to move about like Eiji does." I couldn't stress how important that was. "Knowing hand-to-hand combat is all well and good, unless you can't catch the guy you're supposed to be fighting."

"I understand, sir."

"And find out what music Eiji is using. It might help set the tempo."

"I believe it's *The HU*, sir. They are a Mongolian rock band."

"Get some more of it."

Vasil nodded. "I'll see what I can do, sir."

"Yasha, inform everyone that we will be having a mandatory meeting at ten tomorrow. I want everyone there, including the house staff."

Eiji still hadn't been introduced to everyone and that needed to happen sooner rather than later. "I'm taking Eiji upstairs so he can rest. He's had a very eventful day."

"Yes, Boss."

Sometimes it was good to be in charge.

Chapter Seventeen

~ Eiji ~

I opened my eyes when I felt the mattress underneath me and looked up. I don't think Dmitri was aware that I was awake yet. He was trying to slowly pull my shoes off.

I waited until he'd done that and then was pulling the comforter up over me before grabbing his wrist.

Dmitri's eyes snapped to my face.

"Stay," I mouthed silently.

Dmitri's brow furrowed. "Are you sure?"

I nodded.

Dmitri finished tucking the blanket around me before kicking his shoes off and stretching out beside me, rolling until he was facing me. He did leave a bit of space between us, and I appreciated that, but it wasn't what I wanted right now.

One of the tortures of being afraid of people was never being able to touch anyone or get a hug. I missed hugs. I missed being held by someone that cared for me.

I was pretty sure Dmitri cared for me.

I scooted close enough to lay my head on his arm and then grabbed the other one and pulled it around me. I swallowed tightly before tilting my head back to look up at him.

"Okay?"

Dmitri smiled before pulling me closer. I almost shivered in delight at how warm his body was pressed against mine. I hadn't realized just how cold I was until that very moment.

"Thank you for being so brave earlier," Dmitri said. "It was important that my men saw what I wanted them to see in real life. I could explain it until I was blue in the face, but I doubted they would believe me if they didn't see themselves."

I still wasn't quite sure what Dmitri was trying to show them, but I had wanted to help him, especially after all the ways he'd been helping me. I was mute, not stupid. I knew exactly about all of the things Dmitri had been doing to make me feel safe.

I just wished I was brave enough to tell him why I would never be safe. Maybe someday I could tell him, but that day was not here yet.

The man stilled when I reached up and touched his lips. I slid my finger down over to a small scar just under his lip and ran it back and forth across it.

"Motorcycle accident when I was twenty-one," he explained. "When I crashed my bike my two front teeth went through my lip."

I wrinkled my nose at him.

He chuckled. "It was a long time ago, Eiji."

I waved my hand up and down his body.

"Do I have more scars?"

I nodded.

"I have a few. I'm thirty-five years old, Eiji, and I'm in a very dangerous business, as you well know. Injuries happen."

Oh, I was fully aware. In two short days, Dmitri had been shot and knocked unconscious. I couldn't wait to see if he could go the next two days without getting hurt.

I smacked his chest and narrowed my eyes at him.

Dmitri grinned before tightening the arm he had wrapped around my waist. "I promise to try not to get hurt."

I huffed as I settled my head on his arm. I seriously didn't think he was going to be able to keep his word. He seemed a bit accident prone. I understood to some extent that he was in a dangerous business, but he had like a gazillion bodyguards. How did he keep getting hurt?

Maybe that was what this afternoon was all about. Maybe his bodyguards needed more training so they could be better at protecting him. If that was the case, I'd race across the ballroom as many times as he needed.

I was startled when Dmitri leaned forward and pressed a kiss to my forehead. That was the second time he had done that, and it was as strange as the first time. I can't even remember the last time some had kissed me.

Maybe when my father had been alive?

I brushed my fingers over the spot on my forehead where Dmitri had kissed me.

"I'm sorry," he whispered. "I shouldn't have done that without your permission. It won't—"

I stopped him with a finger to his lips. My eyes darted up to his for a moment before falling to his mouth. If someone had asked me in that moment what in the hell I was doing, I couldn't have told them.

I leaned forward and pressed my lips to Dmitri's. It felt so good, so I did it again. I had never willingly kissed anyone in my life. The cute little blonde in second grade didn't count.

This was a real kiss.

I felt as if my entire body had just caught fire.

I looped my arms around Dmitri's shoulders, pulling the man closer. The rough whiskers of his beard scraped across my face. I opened my mouth wider when Dmitri's tongue plunged in, sweeping and exploring.

My body became pliant as Dmitri claimed my mouth, his hands pressing into my back. When our lips parted, Dmitri was staring down at me with intense dark brown eyes.

"Eiji."

I wrapped a hand around the back of his neck and pulled him in for another kiss. I was pretty sure I could go on kissing him for the rest of my days.

Right up until I felt his hard cock brush my leg.

I pushed away from Dmitri and scrambled back, my fear a tangible thing. The hairs on the back of my neck raised and my body started to tremble.

Something flickered in the far back of Dmitri's eyes. When he reached for me, my brain picked that moment to flat line. All I could think about was escape.

My breath burst in and out of my body as I jumped off the bed and raced to the corner where my nest was. I crouched down and pressed myself as far into the corner as I could go.

I closed my eyes and covered my head, wanting the world—and the horrifying memories coming to life in my brain—to just go away.

I felt the weight of a blanket covering me and then a moment later heard the soft snick of a door closing. When I could finally get my heartbeat under control enough to not see spots in front of my eyes, I looked up to find myself alone in the room.

I didn't know whether to be relieved or not. I knew I hadn't wanted him to leave. I just needed a moment or two...or ten.

Maybe I could... I sighed as I shook my head. No, I couldn't. As much as I liked kissing Dmitri—and I really, really did—anything beyond that was quite frankly, beyond me.

I wasn't stupid. I'd read enough to know what a physical relationship was like between two men, but I'd only experienced that one time and I wouldn't wish that on anyone.

So, I'd freaked a little...or a lot. That didn't mean I was opposed to something happening between us exactly. I just needed to work into it, get a little more comfortable being around Dmitri.

He was an imposing man.

I wasn't.

But I also felt as if there was a sweeter side to him that he didn't show to many people. I don't know why he had decided to show it to me, but I would be forever grateful. It made me feel less like I was alone.

I rubbed my hands over my face and then leaned my head against the wall. I needed to fix this. I knew I had upset Dmitri. I needed to talk to him and try and explain why I had freaked out.

It wasn't him.

Well, technically, it had been him, but not for the reasons he was probably thinking. Yes, I had an honest fear of him, but come on. The guy carried a gun, and he wasn't afraid to use it. But at the same time, I wasn't afraid of him, not really. At least not like that.

It was weird, but it made sense in my head.

I dug myself out of my nest, got up, and padded across the floor to the door that went between my room and Dmitri's. I pressed my ear against the door for a moment before softly knocking. When I didn't hear anything, I opened the door and stepped into the room.

It was empty.

I hurried back into my room and ran over to the main door, pulling it open. The guard that stood outside my door immediately turned toward me.

"Dmitri?"

"I'm sorry, sir. The Boss has gone to the club for the evening." He pulled his cell phone out. "Do you want me to call him?"

I shook my head as disappointment swamped me and my shoulders slumped. I mouthed, *"Thank you,"* and then stepped back inside the room and shut the door.

So, that was a bust.

I walked back over to my nest and settled in before digging my cell phone out of my pocket and typing out a text to Dmitri. *"When are you coming home?"*

I stared down at the screen as I waited for him to reply. He almost always replied to me immediately, but he didn't. I waited hours, just staring at my screen, waiting, hoping.

Dmitri never replied.

Night turned into day. Someone brought me a tray of food, but my stomach had too many knots in it to eat anything. I could barely swallow down the orange juice on the tray, but I knew I needed something in my gut.

When day started to turn into night again, and I finally accepted that Dmitri wouldn't reply, I couldn't keep the tears from streaming down my face.

I shouldn't have kissed him. It was that simple, and maybe that complicated. Dmitri had been being nice to me, comforting me, and I had taken it a step too far. I only had myself to blame if he never replied to me again. I had crossed a line I shouldn't have crossed.

I needed to apologize so that things could go back to the way they had been, and then I needed to remember that while we might be married on paper, we were not really married. There was no enduring relationship between us that would last through the ages.

Dmitri had simply felt sorry for me, and he had gone out of his way to save me from an intolerable situation. It was my own damn fault if I had seen something more there than there really was. I hadn't appreciated the things he had done for me and tried to be greedy for more.

I guess I really was the ungrateful little heathen my stepmother always said I was.

Chapter Eighteen

~ Eiji ~

A loud thump jarred me awake. I hadn't even realized I had fallen asleep until that moment. I frowned as I sat up and looked around. It was dark outside the window, but it had been dark earlier, so I had no idea what time it was.

That was easily fixed with a glance at my cell phone.

Three o'clock in the morning.

Still no messages from Dmitri.

I rubbed the sleep out of my eyes and then glanced around for what might have woken me. The tray Olav had brought me earlier still sat beside my nest, the balcony doors were closed, and it was still only me in the room.

So...

My breath caught. I dropped my phone, threw off my blankets, and jumped to my feet and then raced across the floor to open the door between my room and Dmitri's.

A light was on that hadn't been on before, and there was a trail of clothes leading from the door to the bathroom, but no Dmitri.

I followed the trail of clothes to the bathroom. The door was partially open so when I knocked on it, it effortlessly swung the rest of the way open.

And I lost the ability to breathe.

Six foot three inches and two hundred and twenty-five pounds of packed muscle stood under the shower head of a very large walk-in shower, and there wasn't a stitch of clothing in sight.

Just a lot of slick darkly tanned skin.

I swallowed tightly as I let my eyes roam over Dmitri's thick form, from the back of his neck to his wide shoulders and trim waist to the small slope that appeared at the top of what must have been the best ass in the world.

But it didn't end there. Miles upon miles of thick muscular thighs and narrow calves held that magnificent body up and pressed against the shower stall wall.

Yeah, breathing was going to be an issue.

I moved closer, my gaze eating up every inch of Dmitri's luscious body. Just looking at him was enough to make me wish for a really flat surface. No one in the world was as sexy as Dmitri

I grunted as I was grabbed by the wrist and yanked forward. Dmitri's arms wrapped around me, and his hand fisted in my hair. His lips claimed mine. His tongue slid between my lips, plundering, conquering.

I eagerly gave myself up.

He could have me.

I grunted when Dmitri slid his hand under my ass and lifted me up. I don't know when my clothes disappeared, but I groaned as our naked bodies came together, skin on skin. I quickly wrapped my legs around Dmitri's waist.

"Dmitri," I gasped silently when he lifted his head, freeing my lips.

I needed so damn bad. I wasn't sure what I needed, but I knew I needed it.

I closed my eyes and dropped my head back when I felt the hot shower spray hit me. Dmitri must have known I needed a moment, because he just stood there, holding me as I gloried in the feel of clean, hot water beating down on me.

I opened my eyes and looked up at Dmitri. I wasn't sure what emotion I was seeing in his eyes, but it was intense. His brown eyes had darkened to molten lava. I swear there were flames flickering in them.

Dmitri grabbed a bottle off the built-in shelf and popped the top. I wasn't sure what he was going to do so I grunted when he suddenly pinned me against the wall. His mouth came down over mine again, stealing the breath I was about to blow out.

I groaned as I wrapped my arms around his neck and reveled in Dmitri's strength as he held me against the wall, something I had been without my entire life.

I wasn't a weakling, but close enough. My wit was what I was strong at, not holding someone to the wall.

I was really happy Dmitri could hold me against the wall. I was even happier that he knew what to do with those slicked-up fingers of his.

I winced when he pressed a finger into me and started moving it around. It moved in and out of my ass just fast enough to drive my lust to blistering heights, yet not so fast that I was in any pain at all. He took his time, only adding another finger when I was truly ready.

I slid my hands back and grabbed Dmitri's thick hair, fisting my hands in the silky strands. I tightened my legs, bringing him tighter into the apex of my thighs. When I began to move my hips, it rubbed our cocks together as well as impaled me farther on Dmitri's thick fingers.

The third finger took my breath away. I sank into the overwhelming feeling, soaking it up. If I had my way, I would never be empty again.

"You were made for me." As if to prove his point, Dmitri pulled his fingers free and replaced them with his cock, slowly easing inside me as if he was afraid he would hurt me.

I tensed and my heart thudded. I groaned and dropped my head back as Dmitri filled me. It was slow and excruciating and wonderful and oh, god, it felt so damn good.

A shattered gasp left my lips when Dmitri pushed all of his cock inside me, stretching me to the limits. Dmitri's fingers dug into my butt cheeks as he began to move. Thrusting slow and deep.

I moaned as I wiggled my hips to take the swollen shaft deeper inside of me. Dmitri pressed against me, running his lips over my shoulder. My body tingled with a need to come, but I fought against it. I didn't want this to end...ever. I was moments away from coming.

I didn't want to come alone.

Dmitri began to batter my ass, pounding into me with fever. I felt my climax cresting as Dmitri continued to drive into my ass. I was almost there.

"Eiji!" Dmitri shouted my name as his cock began to pulse, hot spurts of seed filling my ass.

I bowed my back, crying out as my release felt as though it was ripped from my body. I jerked, shuddered, and gasped for air as Dmitri's movements became uncoordinated, and then the man finally slowed, slumping against me.

We stayed that way until the water began to cool. I groaned in protest when Dmitri pulled out of me. He just grabbed a clean washcloth and quickly scrubbed me until I was squeaky clean.

By the time he set me on the bathmat outside of the shower, my eyes were drooping. I just stood there and watched as Dmitri did a quick scrub down and then climbed out.

As soon as we were done drying off, Dmitri swung me up in his arms and carried me into his bedroom. He was surprisingly gentle as he laid me down in the middle of the bed and then climbed in after me.

As soon as we were under the covers, Dmitri drew me into his arms. It took a little maneuvering on his part before he had me where he wanted me. My butt notched into his groin, my back to his chest, and his arms wrapped around me.

I sighed happily as I laid my head on one of his arms. I never wanted to leave this spot.

Chapter Nineteen

~ Eiji ~

I awoke with a start, a loud thump jarring me from my sleep. I sucked in a breath and opened my eyes, staring up at the ceiling above me. It was my ceiling which meant I was in my room.

That is not where I remembered going to sleep.

The blankets billowed across me before falling to my waist as I sat up and glanced around. I was definitely back in my room, and I was definitely alone.

So, where was Dmitri?

My eyes snapped to the door between our rooms when I heard another thump. I started to toss back the blankets to get out of bed until I remembered what I had been doing the last time I was awake.

I blew out a breath when I looked down and found myself dressed in my usual silk pajamas. Someone had obviously dressed me before putting to me to bed. I was betting on Dmitri.

I could ask him if I could find him.

I climbed out of bed and padded over to the door. I paused right before grabbing the door handle, wondering if I should get my headscarf. When I heard another thump from inside Dmitri's room, I decided against it.

I had something more important to do.

I turned the handle and pushed open the door. My heart skipped a beat and then thudded faster. What were these people doing? Why were they packing everything up and putting it into boxes? This was Dmitri's private suite. They had no right to be in here.

I ran over to the closest guard and yanked the box out of his hands.

"Hey!" the man shouted as he turned, and then stiffened when he saw me, his face going pale. "Master Eiji, my apologies. I didn't mean to yell at you."

"Dmitri," I mouthed. *"Where is Dmitri?"*

The man frowned at me. "I'm sorry, sir. I don't understand."

I pointed to my wedding ring and then waved my hand around the room. *"Dmitri."*

I didn't expect the man to wince as he glanced away. "You should talk to Yasha, sir."

A sudden fear entered my heart. Had Dmitri been attacked again? Was that why they were packing up his room? Was he lying injured in one of the other rooms? Was he in the hospital again?

Was he even alive?

"Yasha?"

"I'll call him, sir," the guard said as he drew his cell phone from his pocket.

I swallowed tightly and glanced around the room as he made his call. It hurt to see all of Dmitri's stuff being packed up. They were leaving the furniture, but everything that made this Dmitri's room was being taken.

I didn't understand why.

"Master Eiji."

I turned toward the voice, my relief at seeing Yasha walking into the room almost taking me to my knees. Out of everyone—with the exception of Dmitri—I trusted Yasha.

"Dmitri?" I mouthed. *"Where is Dmitri?"*

"My apologies if we gave you a scare, sir. The Boss had to fly to Moscow on some business. Since he plans to be gone for a little while, he asked us to pack up his room and have it made into a dance studio for you. The contractors will be here tomorrow to make the room soundproof and put in an audio system. It should be ready for you within a couple of weeks."

I could have cared less about the dance studio.

"Dmitri is gone?"

Yasha frowned. "Do you have your translator, sir?"

Oh, right.

I spun and then raced back into my room. It took me a moment to locate my cell phone, but it really shouldn't have. Someone had placed it on my nightstand. I assumed it had been Dmitri.

I grabbed it and quickly typed out the question burning in my mind and then held it up to Yasha, who had followed me into the room. *"When will he be back?"*

Yasha smiled when he read what I had written, but there were lines of tension around his mouth that made me wonder if he was lying.

"The Boss will be back as soon as he has completed his business. A few weeks at most."

Dmitri was going to be gone for weeks?

My fingers shook as I typed out my next message. *"I want to talk to him."*

"I will let him know, sir, but he will be fairly busy over the next few weeks. I am unsure of when he can respond to your request."

Why did that sound so cold?

I nodded as if I understood, but I really didn't. It just didn't make sense for Dmitri to leave like he did.

Unless...

I swallowed tightly and turned away from Yasha to hurry to my nest. I quickly sat down and then started typing out a message to Dmitri. *"Please call me."*

I didn't know if he would answer, but I'd wait until he did. I needed to know why he had so suddenly cut me out of his life, and I was positive that was exactly what was happening.

I don't know what was up with the dance studio, but that was a line of shit if I had ever heard one, and I had heard a lot over the years. People had been lying to me for most of my life.

Everyone here was lying, too. I didn't believe they were trying to be malicious about it, but a lie was still a lie. The dance studio was a smoke screen to prevent me from questioning why Dmitri had moved out of his suite.

Even I could figure that out.

Maybe he had even moved out of the mansion. That would explain why Yasha had told me he was going overseas, which had also been a lie.

God, I hated all of this. Why wouldn't someone tell me the truth for once? Good or bad, it was better than knowing the people around me were trying to keep stuff from me.

I really didn't want to think about the real reason Dmitri could have for lying to me or leaving me. It would open up the tightly locked nightmares I held in my soul and free them.

Maybe I should accept the lie I'd been told.

It would be less painful.

Maybe.

I wasn't sure anyone could heal the deep ache I felt in my heart even if they told me the truth.

"Olav will be in with a tray for you soon, Master Eiji," Yasha said. "Please allow the workers to finish packing up the Boss's room before you go in there again. I wouldn't want you to get hurt."

I nodded even as I turned to look out the window beside me. Sometimes, it was really frustrating how much people coddled me. I often wondered if I had been treated just like a normal person—even if I wasn't remotely normal—if my life would be different?

Doubted it.

It hurt to sit there and listen to the workers packing up Dmitri's room. It hurt even worse when he didn't return my text. He didn't return the one I sent the next day or the next, or even the days after that.

By the time Yasha told me the dance studio was ready, two weeks had gone by and there had been no sign of Dmitri. Yasha kept saying that Dmitri was busy with work, but I knew that was a lie. Olav said he didn't know where the boss was. That was also a lie.

Everyone was still lying to me, and I was so damn tired of it. I was tired of everything. I felt exhaustion seeping into my bones, sucking the life out of me. I couldn't even get excited about the snow falling outside my window.

I barely had the energy to lift my head when my bedroom door opened and Yasha walked in.

"Good evening, Master Eiji."

"Dmitri?" I don't know why I asked. Glutton for punishment maybe?

Yasha's wince did not bode well for me.

"The Boss did contact me," Yasha said as he held up some papers in his hands. "He needs you to sign this."

I frowned as I pushed myself up and then held out my hand. I almost didn't want to. Something cold and forbidding sank into my soul as Yasha handed the papers over. I knew whatever they were, I wasn't going to want to sign them.

I knew I was right the moment I saw the first words on the page. I swallowed tightly before raising my eyes to Yasha, praying I could hold back my tears.

"D-Divorce?"

"Yes, sir." Yasha didn't sound happy about it. "I believe Dmitri feels it would be better for you if you were not associated with this life. It's not safe for you." He tried to give me a weak smile, but it turned into more of a grimace. "If you read the rest of the papers, he has outlined everything in the divorce settlement he has arranged for you."

I turned to the next page and carefully read over what Dmitri had outlined. A fully furnished condo complete with guards for my safety, a driver to take me wherever I wanted to go, food delivered once a week, and all of my bills paid, including tuition to the college of my choice.

It was all very neat and tidy.

My anger at his high-handedness warred with my sorrow until I felt numb. Dmitri was getting rid of me, but if he didn't want me, I didn't want to stay.

I also didn't want anything from him.

I glanced over the divorce papers again, finding the part that mentioned the divorce settlement Dmitri had so carefully outlined. I scratched it out with the pen and then signed on the bottom line.

I handed the papers and pen back to Yasha. *"I hope he chokes on it."*

Yasha gave a sad little nod. "Yes, sir."

I waited for Yasha to leave the room before I allowed my tears to fall. My heart ached so much that I could barely breathe. My mother had abandoned me and died when I was born, my father had abandoned me and died when I was six, and now the man that was supposed to be my husband was abandoning me.

I guess I should be grateful he hadn't died as well.

No one ever stuck around. Everyone I cared about, everyone that should have been there for me, had abandoned me. And the people that wanted to keep me, didn't care about me.

Was I that unlovable? Was there something wrong with me that made people not care about me? Made them not want to stick around?

Was I not good enough?

I missed being able to see the snowflakes falling when darkness fell. While there were lights outside to light up the ground, they were not enough to illuminate the falling flakes.

I wrapped my fuzzy blanket tightly around my shoulders before climbing to my feet and walking to the double doors that led to my second-floor balcony. I pushed them open just wide enough to step through.

I stood there for a moment, taking in the darkness and cool night air. Everything was strangely silent. I could hear a few cars off in the distance and a dog barking, but they were far enough away to be mere background noise.

As I stood there leaning against the side of the house, I noticed one of the night guards patrolling the ground beneath my balcony. I watched him until he disappeared from sight around the side of the house.

My mind was blank, my emotions numb. All I wanted to do was see the snow, to look down and see nothing but the white blanket of snow from above.

From my vantage point, I could see the entire back of the estate up until it met the woods. Everything was glistening white. The background noise around me faded away, replaced by sheer blessed silence.

There was something soothing in all of this, the lack of noise and the pristine carpet of white below and hanging on the trees. Not to mention the softly falling snow.

I leaned my head against the side of the house and stared out into the darkness wondering where I was going to go and what I was going to do. I was done trying to rely on other people.

They always let me down.

I needed to learn to stand on my own two feet and that started with getting the hell out of this house. I'd already made huge strides in going to other rooms in the house, but this was just the house, and it was filled with bodyguards.

I needed to brave the world.

I was terrified even thinking about it, but it wasn't like I had much of a choice. Living my life seemed to be at the whims of other people. They were making all the decisions for me. If I wanted my freedom, I had to take that decision-making ability back.

I just had no idea how to do that. I'd spent my entire life a virtual prisoner. What did I know about the outside world? I barely even know how to use a cell phone.

I did know how to sneak out of my room once a month and go dancing. I did not think those were skills that would get me very far. They certainly wouldn't put a roof over my head.

Accepting the divorce settlement Dmitri had arranged for me was a joke that I did not find very funny. It was like hush money. If I accepted, I'd be stuck away somewhere he didn't have to think about. I would no longer be his problem. I doubted I'd even be a bad memory.

No, it was better if I just figured this out on my own.

"Master Eiji."

Wow, I didn't even jump.

I turned to look toward the door to my room. I gave Boris a polite bow of my head. He was one of my three bodyguards after all, although I spent less time with him than I did the other two simply because he was on night shift and I was usually sleeping.

I actually preferred it that way. I knew Boris had just been doing his job when he pointed a gun at me after Dmitri got hurt, but I didn't trust the guy. Call me weird, but I didn't trust anyone that pointed a gun at me.

"I'm here to take you to your new residence."

I gasped in shock. I had just been told about all of this just a few hours ago. How long had Dmitri been planning this if everything was already arranged?

"Your things will be packed and brought to you tomorrow."

I set my cell phone on the nightstand as I walked back into the room. I was an old man. At least, I felt as if I was. Everything ached and I was so tired my eyes burned.

I carefully folded my fuzzy blanket and set it on the end of the bed. I briefly considered taking it with me, but then decided against it.

I wanted nothing from here.

I had gotten a little used to leaving my room and moving around the large mansion, so I didn't have too much difficulty until we reached the front door, and then I stopped cold in my tracks.

I hadn't been outside since I had arrived almost five weeks ago. As much as I wanted to stay and was terrified of stepping a single foot outside, I also knew I couldn't stay.

I wasn't wanted here.

Boris waved his hand toward the open doorway. "This way, sir."

I swallowed tightly as I pulled my hood up over my head and then stepped through the doorway. Something smashed against the back of my head before I took more than a few steps and then blessed darkness took me under.

Chapter Twenty

~ Dmitri ~

I took another sip of the half glass of vodka in my hand even though I heard my office door open and someone walked in. I knew who it was of course. No one else had dared enter my office in the last couple of weeks.

Only Yasha had been brave enough to face the beast within.

"I did as you asked, Boss."

"Did he sign them?"

"Yes," Yasha replied. "But—"

I turned and looked at my second-in-command. "But what?"

"He crossed out the divorce settlement."

I was confused and strangely hurt by that. Despite the fact that we were divorcing, I wanted to provide Eiji with the life he should have had all of this time.

"Did he say why?"

"No, sir." Yasha cleared his throat. "He simply said he hopes you choke on it."

I swallowed down the sharp stab of pain I felt in my chest at those words. I deserved them and worse for what I had done, but hearing Eiji's hate made it all that much more painful.

"How is he?" I asked as I turned and faced the window that overlooked the club once more. I'd been staying here over the last couple of weeks, unable to go home, but unable to move farther away from Eiji.

"The same."

"Is he eating?"

A grimace crossed Yasha's face. "Not as much as he should. Olav has been making different things to whet his appetite, but Master Eiji mostly pushes the food around on his plate. Lately, we've taken to giving him protein shakes so he can keep his strength up."

I closed my eyes at those words. I had brought Eiji to this. He'd been clear about where his boundary was and I had not only stepped over that line, I'd used an atom bomb to blow it up.

I never should have touched him.

I was the monster everyone believed me to be. In my drunken state, I had taken something from him that he hadn't given me permission to take. That sin I could never be absolved of.

Even now, I violated him when I dreamed. No matter how much I tried to drink myself into oblivion, those few hours with Eiji in my bed filled my mind every time I slept.

It was a betrayal, one that could not be forgiven.

"I don't care what he crossed out in the divorce papers," I said as I opened my eyes. "I still want everything arranged for him."

"Yes, Boss."

"Make sure he has everything he needs. I don't care what it is."

"Yes, Boss."

I glanced over my shoulder, my gaze stern and unforgiving. "And make sure he's protected."

Eiji had already been hurt enough in this lifetime.

"I'll see to it personally, Dmitri."

I gave the man a nod of acknowledgement, not just for his acceptance of my orders, but for his personal pledge to see that they were carried out. I knew Yasha wouldn't let me down.

I took another sip of my vodka as I turned back to the window one more time. I heard the door click as it closed and knew I was alone with my thoughts again. I couldn't seem to find enough vodka to make my mind go blank.

If I could find a way to live in that dream with Eiji without him being hurt, I would, but that just wasn't possible. I still shuddered every time I remembered waking up in my bed with a very naked Eiji lying next to me.

At first, I'd been elated, and then I had been horrified as everything I had done to him came back in vivid color. I had treated him no better than a back alley street walker, forcing my lust upon him when he had so clearly rejected me before.

I wasn't even sure if I could blame it on the vodka I had drunk that night. I had wanted Eiji, plain and simple. In my inebriated stated, I somehow thought I could have him.

I was clearly an idiot.

The cold shock of reality had hit me the moment I opened my eyes and realized what I had done. I had carefully cleaned Eiji up, dressed him, and then returned him to his room before running from my shame.

I was still running.

I was just smart enough to know I could never outrun it. What I had done to Eiji would always be with me, my guilt hanging around my throat like a hundred-pound lead weight.

Not that there could be any salvation for what I had done, I still felt as if I had to find a way to rectify my actions. I'd start by making sure Eiji was safely away from me so I couldn't do it again and then follow up by giving him the life he should have had.

I pulled my laptop closer and brought up the accounts for the club. The Illumination Club was one of my legal ventures, kind of like the casino. I wanted to keep it that way, which meant I had to dot all my *Is* and cross all my *Ts*.

The government was funny that way.

I spent the next few hours going over accounts, signing purchase orders, and making sure the employees had all been paid. All things a normal business owner does. By the time I was done, the club was closed, cleaned, and all of the employees had gone home.

I turned off the lights in my office and let myself into the hidden room behind my bookcase. When I bought the club, I'd had this room built just for me. The only people that knew about it or had access to it were me and Yasha.

The most important part of the entire room was the fact that it was totally soundproof. Nothing could be heard from the outside and nothing could be heard from the inside.

It was my space to get away while I was at the club. Unfortunately, I never saw myself living here, which was exactly what I had been doing since leaving Eiji tucked up in his bed.

It wasn't a fancy room, but I didn't need it to be. It was about comfort and exhaustion. It had a bed, a small sitting area, and a television mounted on the wall. I hadn't even hung any pictures.

For me, it was just a room to rest, to get away from the hustle and bustle of the club when I needed a break. Now, it had become my sanctuary away from home.

I shut the door behind me and locked it before tossing my suit jacket on a nearby chair. After cleaning up in the bathroom, I walked over and stretched out on the bed. I knew I should probably shower and change, but I just didn't have the energy.

To be honest, I was exhausted. The last two weeks had been hell. All I wanted to do was see Eiji, to hold him in my arms and beg him to forgive me. I wanted to see his sweet little smile, to watch his joy as he danced.

I doubted I'd ever see any of that again.

I closed my eyes and willed myself to go to sleep, but after a few hours, I gave up. I rolled onto my back, opened my eyes, and stared up at the ceiling.

I sighed heavily as I swung my legs over the side of the bed and sat up. I buried my head in my hands as a sense of desolation came over me. Even awake images of Eiji played through my mind.

Was there no escape from this nightmare?

I groaned when I heard the intercom between my office and my secret room buzz. I didn't want to talk with anyone. Conversing took effort and currently I had none.

I growled when it buzzed again and reached over to the nightstand to push the button. "What?"

"We have a situation, Boss."

Of course we did.

"What is it?" I asked as I stood and reached for my jacket.

"Eiji's missing."

Cold dread swamped my mind, stealing every thought I had except rage and fear. "What do you mean he is missing?"

"During morning shift change, Vasil reported that no one was at Eiji's door. He went in to investigate, but the room was empty. We've searched the mansion, Boss. He's just not here."

"Did you see anything on the security monitors?"

"Someone turned them off."

I growled as I ripped the door between my room and the office open and stormed out. "What do you mean someone turned them off?"

"The first thing I thought of was to check the monitors, but the entire system was shut off, even the alarms."

I ground my teeth together as I tried to rein in the rage taking a hold of me. "This was an inside job."

It wasn't a question.

The only way those monitors could be turned off was if it was an inside job. They were in a secure room. That did lower the pool of suspects because only certain people had access to that room.

The other side of that was that now the mansion was vulnerable. I wished I could say no one would attack us, but I couldn't. Especially not with Eiji missing. I didn't know if this was an all-out attack and Eiji going missing was just the start of things or if it was an isolated event.

"Call up our extra security. I want two teams. One guarding the mansion and one out searching for Eiji. I also need you to get in touch with any informants you might have. I want Eiji found."

"I'll see to it immediately, Boss."

I swallowed down my fear and anger and glanced at Yasha. "Do you think he...left on his own?"

"No." Yasha shook his head without hesitation. "Eiji has issues leaving his room. He wouldn't voluntarily go out into the world."

"I did just present him with divorce papers."

"Yes, but I still don't think he would leave on his own. As much as he might want to be brave, he isn't. Besides, he'd have to get past security in order to leave. The monitors might not have been working, but there were still guards patrolling the grounds. They would have spotted him."

Then how the hell had he been taken?

"Has anyone checked his estate?" I really didn't see Eiji going back there on his own, but he could have easily been taken there. "Find out what his stepmother has been up to. I wouldn't put it past her to take Eiji and hold him for ransom."

"I'll send one of the boys over to see what that old witch is up to and tell them to keep an eye on her."

My brow crinkled as a thought began to fill my mind. "Didn't we put trackers on their cars when we went to get Eiji?"

"I believe so, yes."

"All of them?"

Yasha nodded.

"Find out where they are right now."

Yasha pulled out his tablet and began typing away. It didn't take more than a couple of minutes for him to bring up a map of New York City with four red dots on it.

"Okay, it looks like Beverly is at a casino, one of her sons is at a club in Chelsea, and the rest are at home."

"Is she at my casino?"

"No."

Too bad. If she lost more money to me, maybe I could get her out of Eiji's house. "How do you know which car is which?"

"Oh, the trackers are coded." Yasha pressed his finger to the button on the far side of the screen and a picture of Beverly popped up. "I can't be positive she's the one driving, but the car is registered to her."

"Keep an eye on them. I want to know where they are at all times." I clenched my fist until my knuckles cracked. "If any of them are involved in Eiji's disappearance, I'll slaughter them all."

I'd slaughter anyone that harmed Eiji.

Chapter Twenty-One
~ Eiji ~

I woke up to a splitting headache and total darkness. It took me a moment to realize the darkness came from the hood over my head.

It wasn't my hood.

On the upside, because I wore a hood so often, I knew how to breathe in one. I took a couple of low, shallow breaths and let them out slowly, calming myself.

When I was settled down enough to not freak out, I used my other senses to try and figure out where I was and what the hell was going on. It was dark. I knew that. My head also hurt so I was more than likely injured in some manner.

I was also cold. I couldn't feel a breeze, so I doubted I was outside, but there was definitely no heat wherever I was.

There was a small hissing noise coming from above me, almost like the sound of steam escaping, but considering how cold it was in here, I doubted that was right.

A slow steady drip of water was off in the distance to my left. It sounded kind of like someone had forgotten to turn the faucet off all the way and the water was dropping on something metal.

I'm pretty sure I would never figure out where the smell of cinnamon was coming from. It was strong as if an entire bag of the stuff was sitting right next to me.

None of this gave me a clue as to where I was.

My real panic didn't start until I realized that my hands were tied over my head. It brought back too many horrible memories. At least I wasn't hanging this time—I was sitting on my butt—and I could feel that I had clothes on, but I knew that could change in an instant.

I needed to get out of here before it did.

I felt around with my fingers, trying to figure out what I was tied to and what was tying me to it. The rope was easy enough to figure out. I could feel the coarse fibers under my fingertips.

The round pipe took me a little longer.

The moment I figured it out, the fear that held me in its grip was paralyzing. Black spots appeared in front of my eyes, and I could barely breathe. I thought I was going to die.

The last time I had been tortured I had been tied to a pipe in the basement of one of the privete school buildings. I had been there for two days before anyone found me.

They had been two days of pure hell.

Horrifying images flashed through my mind, each one worse than the other. The beatings that had left me nearly unconscious. The shame and degradation I felt as the men that held me took turns hurting me, taking something from me they had no right to take. The laughter that rang in my ears until I begged to die.

I would never forget those terrifying images, they were burned into my memory, but I realized that their impact had lessened since Dmitri came into my life. I wasn't as frightened as I had been before.

I was pissed.

Maybe still a little frightened.

I slunk down and then patted around the top of my head until I could get a good hold of the hood. It took a little maneuvering on my part to get it pulled off my head considering I was sitting down and my hands were tied just above my head.

Once it was off and I looked around, I almost wished it was back on. I was in a basement again. That much was clear. There were large metal pipes hanging from the ceiling, boxes stacked against the wall, and a large metal furnace. A set of rickety old stairs led to a door at the top.

The room just didn't look to be the size as the basement at the private school I'd been attending back then. This one was much smaller, like a basement for a house.

Not sure if that was better or worse.

I was tied to what I was pretty sure was a water pipe. It would explain the dripping water I heard. Plus, it was smaller around than the pipes hanging from the ceiling.

Still wasn't sure where the cinnamon was coming from.

I tilted my head back and looked at the ropes tied around my wrists. I smirked when I realized I recognized the intricate knot system. I had read everything I could get my hands on to make sure if I was ever taken again, I would not be defenseless. One of those books was on knot tying.

I scooted up onto my knees and moved around until I found the section I wanted and then I bit into it with my teeth and slowly began to unravel the knot.

I had to stop several times to swallow and lick my lips. By the time the rope fell free, I wished I had a gallon of water and a drum of lip balm.

I started to drop the rope onto the floor, but then thought better of it and stuck it in my pocket. Never know when I might need it, especially since there wasn't a sheet in sight.

Now I just needed to figure a way out of here.

It didn't take me too long to cover the entire room, going to all four corners. It was a small basement after all. By the time I was done, I was a bit disheartened.

There were two small windows, but they were very small and very high up on the walls. Even as small as I was, I didn't think I could jump that high or squeeze through the small opening.

That left the door.

I turned to look up at it. It was made of wood, and that was good, but I had no idea what or who was on the other side, and that was bad. It also seemed like the only way in or out of this place unless I could figure out how to fly and make myself into a pancake. Since I didn't see either of those things happening, I made my way up the stairs to the door.

I was so not surprised to find it locked.

I started looking around for something I could use to either break the door handle off or unlock it. I found several cans of paint, some old picture frames and knick-knacks, and a box of books.

None of that was helpful.

I started searching the floor any small bits of metal, anything I could use to break the lock. I searched almost the entire length of the room before I found a metal nail file. I had no idea if it would work, but I had to try. At the very least, maybe I could unscrew the screws holding the door handle in place.

Might work.

I climbed back up the wooden stairs with the nail file clutched tightly in my hands. When I got to the door, I looked the handle over trying to figure out the best possible way to open it, break it, or remove it.

My heart shot into my throat when I heard a scraping noise and then the handle started to turn. I glanced left and right, but all I saw was a solid brick wall on either side of me. The stairs were behind me and there was no way I could get down them and hide before that door opened.

I glanced up.

Might work.

I jumped up and grabbed the top of the door frame. Using my arm strength, I pulled myself up until I could find good leverage with my feet and then heaved myself up to the ceiling, facing down.

Those limber dance moves were suddenly worth every sore muscle I'd ever gotten. I used my arms and legs—pressing them against the old, faded brick—to keep me from falling.

I held my breath as I watched the door handle turn and the door finally push open. A tall dark-haired figure stepped through the opening. It took a single glance for me to figure out it was my nighttime bodyguard, Boris.

The bastard.

I waited until he started down the stairs and I was positive no one was following him before slowly lowering myself to the floor. I thought about turning and running for just a moment before I remembered that this asshole was the one to kidnap me and bring me to wherever in the hell I was.

I kicked him in the backside as hard as I could. As soon as he let out a cry and started tumbling down the stairs, I turned and darted through the doorway, pulling the door closed behind me.

I didn't hear anything from the other side of the door after a moment, so I hoped Boris was suffering the same knocked out headache I had.

I turned the small lock on the handle and then spun around to try and figure out where I was and if I was alone. I was in a hallway, and a shabby looking one at that. The paint on the walls was dirty and faded. There were no pictures, but there were faint outlines where pictures might have been at one point.

There was also no furniture.

This struck me as odd.

I started down the hallway toward the only light I could see. It was a faint light, so I assumed it came from a room or something. When I reached the end of the hallway, there were two archways.

One led to an empty room that looked like it might have been a dining room. It had a large empty cabinet built into the wall that looked as if it might have held fine China at one time.

I crept to the edge of the other archway and peered inside. Going by the single recliner, small table, and television, I was going to assume that it was a living room.

It was a two-story house, and the staircase was near the entrance to the living room and the dining room. I wasn't about to go upstairs to see if anyone was there. My goal was the front door.

I hurried toward it, but just as I reached it, I heard someone talking, their voices becoming louder as they approached the door. I darted into the dining room and then aimed for the open doorway on the far side of the room.

As soon as I realized I was in a kitchen, I started looking for something to protect myself. There wasn't much here. A few dishes, a frying pan, a coffee pot, and some eating utensils.

I picked up the eating utensils. A fork and a butter knife probably wouldn't be of much use, but it was better than nothing.

I cringed in fear when I heard the front door open.

"Boris is probably sleeping, Uncle Mike."

I started shaking when I recognized the female voice. Mary something. She'd been a maid at Dmitri's mansion, the one that had knocked Dmitri over the head with a vase.

What was she doing here?

And who was her uncle?

"Where's the brat?" a deeper, more masculine voice asked.

I did not recognize this voice.

"Boris has him tied up in the basement," Mary replied. "I'll go wake Boris up and then we can go get him. There's coffee in the kitchen if you want to grab a cup."

Damn woman!

I scurried over to the corner next to the entrance of the kitchen and pressed myself back into the corner before squatting down, trying to make myself the smallest possible target.

Being a smaller target was something I excelled at.

As soon as the man passed in front of me, I stabbed him in the back with the fork and knife as hard as I could. I didn't feel an ounce of guilt about it either. The guy obviously knew I had been tied up in the basement, so it wasn't like he was here to save me.

My eyes rounded with shock when the man let out a cry of pain and arched his back, his arms coming back as if to try and grab whatever he had been stabbed with.

That wasn't the shocking part, though.

He tripped and fell, hitting his head on the counter as he went down, and then he just laid there in a growing pool of blood.

I stared at him for a moment, waiting for him to move. When he didn't, my heart started a rapid pace in my chest. I dropped down beside him, checking for his pulse and praying I hadn't killed him.

My relief when I found one made my head swim. I might have been trying to protect myself, but that didn't mean I wanted to kill anyone.

Incapacitating was just fine.

I unwound the scarf around the man's neck and put it on mine. I felt infinitely better when I looped part of it over my head. There was enough length that I would be able to pull it over my face once I escaped.

I started searching the man's pockets. I found a gun in a holster on his side. I stuck that in my pocket. I also found a wallet and a cell phone. I stuck the cell phone in my pocket as well and then opened the wallet.

Michael O'Donnell?

Who the hell was he?

Didn't matter. He obviously wasn't someone I wanted to be friends with. I started to stick the wallet back in his pocket when I heard quick footsteps coming down the stairs.

With it still clutched in my hand, I jumped to my feet and raced for the backdoor. I opened it as quietly as I could, stepped out, and then closed it just as quietly. I had no idea who else might be around and I didn't want anyone to hear me escape.

I was smart enough to know not to head to the front of the house, especially when I heard voices talking casually from that direction. I turned and ran toward the back.

It wasn't easy getting over the back fence, especially as small as I was, but I was halfway across the neighbor's yard before I heard the yelling.

I kept on going.

I don't know how many driveways I ran down or how many yards I ran through before I finally stopped and squatted behind some dumpsters in an alleyway.

My heart seemed to freeze in my chest for just a moment before beating rapidly when I realized I had not panicked this entire time. Not one single debilitating anxiety attack. I had escaped the basement and the ropes keeping me there, dealt with a couple of of my kidnappers, and gotten away, and I'd done it all one my own.

How had that happened?

As much as I'd like to think I was out of the woods, so to speak, I wasn't. I had no idea where I was or where to go, but I knew someone that might.

My hands shook as I pulled out the cell phone I had stolen and started typing out a message to the only number I knew by heart. *"It's Eiji. I need help."*

Chapter Twenty-Two

~ Dmitri ~

Eiji had been missing for nearly twenty-four hours. Well, that we knew of. We still weren't exactly sure when he left his room or the mansion. He'd gone missing sometime last night.

There was simply no sign of him or his night guard. I had my computer guy doing a deep dive into Boris's life. If he was involved in this mess in any way, he was going to pay for it with his life.

I frowned when my phone rang, but reached over to answer it. "What?"

"Dmitri, it's Vinnie Borelli."

Yeah, my frown deepened. "I didn't burn down your warehouse."

"I am aware," Vinnie replied. "That's not why I called."

"Then why did you call?"

I was kind of busy here trying to find my husband. I didn't want to state that because I didn't want too many people knowing Eiji had disappeared.

"Remember that copy of *Il Piacere* by Gabriele D'Annunzio that I loaned you?"

Loaned?

What the fuck?

"Vinnie—"

"The guy I gave it to wants it back."

My breath caught as hope blossomed in my heart.

"I was wondering if you could bring it to me," Vinnie continued.

I had to swallow hard before I could reply. "Yes, of course. Where would you like me to drop it off?"

Vinnie quickly rattled off an address in Manhattan. "I'll give you and three of your men safe passage in and out of the area in order to bring me the book."

"I'll be there in an hour."

"I'll be waiting."

Vinnie hung up before I could say more.

"Yasha!"

My office door flew open, and my right-hand man stumbled in. "Boss?"

"Get Vasil and Lev and have a car brought around front."

"Eiji?"

"I think so."

Yasha's eyebrows lifted. "You think so?"

"Vinnie Borelli called."

Yasha's face clouded instantly, and his fists clenched, which is a surprising response from the man. "If that Italian fuck has Eiji..."

"He just asked for the copy of *Il Piacere* he loaned me back," I explained. "He said the guy he gave it to wanted it back."

Some of the anger fell off of Yasha's face, but it was replaced by confusion. "But...he gave it to Eiji as a wedding present."

"Exactly."

Yasha squinted at me.

"I think Vinnie somehow either knows where Eiji is or he has Eiji. Either way, he didn't feel comfortable talking about it over an open phone line, which was why he asked for the book back."

I grabbed my blazer and pulled it on and then checked the ammo in my gun. Vinnie might have given me safe passage, but I wasn't stupid. I wasn't taking any chances.

I pulled the book off the bookshelf to take with me in case anyone was watching. If they heard the conversation and saw me leave without the book, they'd know something was up.

While we had gotten our security monitors back up and running, I still wasn't positive we didn't have a traitor or a spy in the household. They needed to see what I wanted them to see.

Vasil and Lev were waiting for us at the car when we got outside. We climbed in, me and Yasha in the back, Lev and Vasil in the front, and then I gave them the address to where we were headed.

I felt a little uneasy when we crossed over from the Bronx into Manhattan. While Vinnie and I were on relatively good terms—or at least as good of terms as rival mobsters could be—he was still my enemy. There was a good reason I tended to stay in the Bronx and he stayed in Manhattan.

I was a bit surprised when we pulled up to the address Vinnie had given me. It was a tall apartment building overlooking Central Park. I don't know what I had expected, but this wasn't it.

Lev parked the car in front of the building, and we all climbed out.

"Be on your toes, everyone," I warned as I buttoned my suit jacket and started heading into the building. I was a little surprised when I found Vinnie and one of his men waiting in the lobby for us. There was another taller man standing behind him. "Vinnie."

The Italian mobster raised one eyebrow. "No book?"

"Vinnie."

Vinnie chuckled as he nodded toward the elevator. "I have some people I want you to meet."

I was going to strangle the guy.

"Vinnie, do you—"

"This is Fred," Vinnie said as we climbed on the elevator, interrupting me to introduce me to the tall man. "He works for Jake D'Amato. Have you heard of him?"

Vaguely?

"I think I've heard the name before. How do you know him?"

And why was he being brought up in conversation?

"My grandfather held his husband as collateral for a loan Jai's family took out. Once Jake found out, not only did he pay the loan back with interest, he placed a tracker in my grandfather's pasta and threatened to turn it over to every alphabet agency on the planet if he ever came after Jai again."

My jaw dropped.

"Jake has an interesting circle of friends, most of them from his university days. One of those friends is a man named Lucas Kincaid. I'm sure you've heard of him."

Who hadn't? The man was the very definition of business tycoon.

I nodded.

"Lucas is married to Kyue Kincaid, who is in business with Parker Aetós, one of Eiji's friends."

Now I saw the connection.

"Parker's husband Syros is also the CEO of Seriphap Enterprises, which is owned by Kyue."

That I did not know, and I really didn't care at this point. "Eiji—"

"Is waiting for you upstairs."

I swallowed so hard my throat hurt. "Is he okay?"

"For him, I suppose he is."

"Was he able to tell you what happened?" I asked.

Vinnie shook his head. "He was able to tell Parker some, but he refuses to have anything to do with anyone else to the point of getting quite upset if they even address him."

That sounded like Eiji.

"Eiji doesn't do well with strangers."

I wasn't sure how well he was going to do with me either, especially not after everything we had been through together, not to mention the sins I had committed. If he ran screaming from the room, I would not be surprised.

When the elevator doors open, Fred led us to a large penthouse condo. Voices came from the room in front of us. My heartbeat quickened as I tried not to push past the large man and demand to know where my husband was. That probably wouldn't get me what I wanted.

When we stepped into the living room, there were several people, none of them I recognized.

"This is Dmitri Petrov," Vinnie said. "He runs the Bronx."

I gaped at Vinnie. He was just tossing that out there?

A dark-haired man stood and walked over to shake my hand. "Jake D'Amato." He waved to the strawberry blond standing behind him. "This is my husband, Jai."

"How do you do?" I asked as I shook their hands.

"Lucas Kincaid," the other man said as he waved.

"Syros Aetós," a dark-haired man said as he introduced himself.

"And this is my Nicky," Vinnie said as he wrapped his arm around another man.

"It's a pleasure to meet you all," I said, trying not to demand to know where Eiji was since I hadn't spotted him in the room.

"A few hours ago, my husband, Parker, received a text message from a number he did not recognize," Syros stated. "The message said it was Eiji and he needed help. Parker was able to help him pinpoint where Eiji was because he was lost, and we went to get him."

"Where was he?" I asked.

"Queens."

I growled.

"Once we had him, we were able to piece together most everything that happened, but some of it is spotty. Once Eiji handed me the driver's license he got off the man he knocked out while escaping, I knew there was trouble. I called Lucas, who called Jake, who called Mr. Borelli."

"Please, call me Vinnie."

Syros nodded to him. "Once Vinnie confirmed that it was the same Eiji that was married to you, we called you."

"Whose license was it?" Yasha asked.

"Michael O'Donnell's."

My hands clenched so hard I could feel my nails biting into my skin. "The O'Donnells kidnapped Eiji?"

Why was I not surprised?

"Actually, we believe his bodyguard kidnapped him," Jake said. "Eiji mentioned someone named Boris?"

I nodded. "Boris was his nighttime bodyguard. They both disappeared over twenty-four hours ago. There was no sign of them leaving the house. We're still not sure how that happened as the security monitors were disabled. We've been looking for Eiji since we discovered he was missing."

"My understanding is that Boris kidnapped him and later a woman named Mary showed up with someone she called Uncle Mike, who turned out to be Michael O'Donnell. Eiji did say that Mary used to be a maid in your household, but she was recently turned over to the police after she assaulted you."

"I knew I should have killed her when I had the chance." I glared at Yasha. "You said to let the police handle it."

"I thought they would," Yasha insisted.

I'd have to look into why that hadn't happened later.

"Eiji said Mary called O'Donnell Uncle Mike?"

Syros nodded. "Does that mean something to you?"

"It means O'Donnell has been trying to slip spies into my household for awhile now. Mary came to work for us almost a month ago. It also means our vetting process is not as good as I thought it was."

"Boris recommended her, Boss," Yasha said. "That might explain a few things. He knew the hiring process, knew what we would look into. It's not that hard to fake an identity."

"True, but the question is, was Boris trying to get someone in place before or after I married Eiji? Was it the plan to kidnap him all along, or were they simply looking for information and Eiji fell into their laps?"

"We need to have the house swept for bugs," Yasha said. "There is no telling how long Boris has been a traitor."

"Call the house and see that it is done." My mind was aching with all the possibilities of how things had gone wrong or could still go wrong if we didn't stop this security leak now.

"Do you think this has anything to do with that deal O'Donnell wants with you?" Vinnie asked.

"It has to be," I admitted. "Except for that, I don't have any other deals in place with him."

"You know it is a very bad idea to go into business with any of the O'Donnells. They've been bad blood since before I sent Kirby back to Ireland. Things haven't gotten any better since his son took over."

I nodded. "They should take the entire O'Donnell clan out and just replace them with someone new, someone who understands that no means no."

The O'Donnells certainly didn't understand that.

"Where is Eiji?" I asked, trying not to let my desperation show. Seeing Eiji was the most important thing here.

"He's resting in the guest room with Kyue and Parker," Jake said. "If you want to follow me, I'll take you to him. Oh, and a word of advice. Don't mess with Kyue. He'll burn your entire empire down and laugh while doing it."

I squinted at Jake. "He's that powerful?"

How had I not heard of this man?

Jake snorted. "No, he's that crazy."

Confused, I eagerly followed the man down the hallway, desperate to see Eiji, but also feeling as if I was walking to my doom.

It was a feeling I was getting used to.

Chapter Twenty-Three
~ Eiji ~

I jolted when someone knocked on the door. I didn't want to see anyone. I didn't want to talk to anyone. I just wanted my fuzzy blanket, my corner nest, and to be left alone.

Why couldn't people understand that? There had been so many questions since I called Parker. Some I had answered simply because I knew I must. Others I had not.

The questions kept on coming.

I think that was why Parker and Kyue had taken me to the guest bedroom. They could see how worked up I had been getting. I was on the verge of overloading.

I heard someone answer the door and then voices mumbling, but with the blanket over my head, it was hard to understand what they were saying. I didn't care what they were saying. I just wanted everyone to go away.

"Eiji."

My jaw clenched.

"Eiji, can you talk to me?"

I shook my head.

"Please?"

I shook my head again. Dmitri had made his feelings concerning me very clear, which meant I didn't have to talk to him. He didn't want me, so I didn't want him.

Really.

Swear.

Tears prickled my eyes.

"I'm sorry I didn't protect you, Eiji," Dmitri whispered. "I'm sorry I didn't talk to you. And...And I'm sorry for what I did to you. I had no right to hurt you like that, and if you hate me for it, I understand. You should hate me for it. I do."

Wait...what?

I pulled the blanket down far enough to be able to look into Dmitri's face. I was shocked when I saw the tears in his eyes, some of them dripping down his cheeks.

How could this strong, powerful man be crying?

It looked so wrong.

My fingers trembled as I reached up to wipe the tears from beneath Dmitri's eyes. *"No cry,"* he murmured silently.

Dmitri grabbed my hand with both of his, bringing it to his lips. "I am so sorry, Eiji. I never meant to hurt you. There is no excuse for my actions, but..."

I was so confused.

I patted Dmitri's chest, searching for his cell phone since I had no idea where mine was. When he frowned at me, I gestured to my mouth.

After a moment, Dmitri dug out his phone and handed it to me. I couldn't bring up the speaking app because he didn't have it on his phone. I went to the note pad instead.

"You didn't think divorcing me was going to hurt me?" I typed out with angry hard hits before turning the phone toward Dmitri.

Dmitri stared at my words for a moment, his mouth opening and then snapping shut before opening again. "I thought you'd want the divorce."

I grew even angrier as I typed, *"Why would I want a divorce?"*

"Because of what I did to you."

I squinted at him.

"I practically raped you, Eiji. I got drunk and forced myself on you. Why wouldn't you want a divorce after what I did?"

Dmitri's face paled when I just sat there and stared at him. I don't think he understood my shock. He dropped his head down and his shoulders began to shake.

"I am so sorry, Eiji."

I couldn't stand the sorrow and remorse I could hear in Dmitri's voice. It was something that should never be there.

I tossed my blanket aside and reached out to wrap my arms around his broad shoulders, resting my head against him. I couldn't very well tell him to stop crying, but I could rub his back and try and comfort him.

I didn't know what to think when he froze in my arms.

"Eiji?"

I wiped at the tears on his cheeks with the pad of my thumb. *"No cry."*

"Eiji—"

I pressed my fingers to Dmitri's lips before pointing to him. *"You"*—I shook my head—*"No hurt"*—I pointed to myself—*"Me."*

"But, I..." Dmitri shook his head as if he didn't believe me. "After what I did, how can you—"

I pressed my fingers to his lips again. *"You no hurt me."*

I didn't know how to get that through Dmitri's thick skull. He hadn't hurt me. Yes, I had been a little resistant in the beginning simply because of the fact that I hadn't thought Dmitri saw me that way. Once I knew he did, I had been all in.

I had enjoyed every second of what we had done together, which had been a bit of a shock for me. After what had happened in my past. I had never expected to enjoy the physical aspects of our marriage.

Boy, had I been wrong.

I grabbed Dmitri's face, pressing his cheeks between my hands and then slowly brought our lips together. I kept my gaze on his eyes and was rewarded by their slight widening when our lips met.

"You. No. Hurt. Me." I made sure to express each word as clearly as I could. *"I want you."*

Dmitri's breath caught and the darkness in his eyes lightened, becoming molten brown. My name was a whisper on his lips, "Eiji."

I kissed him again.

When I leaned back this time, there was a slight curve to the corners of his lips.

"You want me?" he asked with a hint of wonder in his voice.

I nodded.

"And you're okay with what we did before?"

I nodded again.

"Then..." Dmitri swallowed hard. "Can we not get divorced?"

I was all for that.

"No divorce."

Dmitri's arms wrapped around me, almost crushing me. Seriously, the man did not know his own strength.

"I love you, Eiji."

I forgot to breathe.

"I promise I'll protect you from now on. I won't let anything happen to you. I swear I'll never hurt you again. Please don't leave me."

Huh?

I tried to lean back so I could see Dmitri's face, but he had it buried in my neck, and it didn't seem like he planned on moving it any time soon. I threaded my fingers through his hair and just held him to me, rubbing his upper back with my other hand.

"I'm selfish, and I know that."

I yanked on his hair until he lifted his head and then frowned at him. *"Not selfish."*

"I am, though. I should let you go. If I was a stronger man...but I'm not. I know it's wrong, but I want you here at my side. I want you where I can see you and keep you safe, even from me."

I smacked his shoulder. *"Dmitri."*

"I'm so afraid of you," he whispered, stroking a finger down my cheek. "You could break me."

I frowned as I pointed to myself. *"Me?"*

I couldn't fight a noodle.

"If I ever hurt you, even by mistake, I couldn't live with myself."

My brow flickered as I considered Dmitri's words. He was a very large man, even by other people's standards. He did have the potential to hurt me, even kill me.

But would he? Would he really?

I thought back to everything he had done for me and all the ways he had made me safe and kept others from hurting me, the ways he had cared for me when I had been a frightened little bird, and I knew he didn't have it in him to harm me.

Other people, yes.

Me, no.

I pointed to Dmitri and then to myself. *"You won't hurt me."*

"You don't know that. Look at what I did to you already."

I smacked Dmitri on the chest. *"I do know that."*

I reached for his hand, but he swung it away from me before shooting to his feet and taking several steps back.

"Don't you understand? I want to lock you up where no one can see you or take you from me. I want to surround you with armed guards so no one can harm you. I don't want you stepping one single foot outside the house without me there by your side."

I tilted my head just a little as I regarded Dmitri with curiosity and a bit of confusion. This time I grabbed the cell phone and typed my response out because I didn't want there to be any mistakes in what I said. *"You seem to think I have a problem with that."*

Dmitri froze in place and just stared at me. I wasn't even sure if he was breathing.

I smirked as I typed again. *"In case you're wondering, I don't."*

Something like that would make me feel even safer.

"You'd be okay with me placing more guards on you?"

"Not Boris."

Dmitri growled as he grabbed me and pulled me to my feet, his arms tightening around me again. "I'll kill Boris if I ever get my hands on him."

I smirked as I typed out my next message. *"I pushed him down the basement stairs and then locked him in."*

"Good," Dmitri replied. "Vinnie and the others explained to me that you ran into Michael O'Donnell."

"Mary called him Uncle Mike." I winced as I remembered what I had done to him. *"I stabbed him in the back with a set of eating utensils. When he fell, he hit his head on the counter. He had a pulse when I checked it, but there was a lot of blood."*

"He's lucky I wasn't there."

I cocked my head. *"Who is he?"*

"Michael O'Donnell is the head of the Irish mob in Queens."

Oh crap!

"I beat up the head of the Irish mob?"

Dmitri grinned. "Yeah."

I was going to die.

Chapter Twenty-Four

~ Dmitri ~

I sighed as I buried my face in Eiji's throat again, sniffing his unique scent. I couldn't believe he was going to let me keep him. I had been so sure that my actions had destroyed any chance I had with him.

I still wasn't sure I believed him.

"Will you let me take you home?"

Eiji leaned back and typed away on my phone again before turning it toward me. *"Are you going to divorce me again?"*

"What?" My eyebrows snapped together. "No!"

"Are you sure?"

"Yes."

"Then I'll go home with you."

My relief was so great, I had trouble catching my breath. I hugged Eiji close to me so that he wouldn't witness just how much his agreement meant to me.

"Thank you, Eiji."

I leaned down to press a kiss to Eiji's lips, but I was not expecting him to throw himself into it with such enthusiasm that my toes curled. It was almost as if he was touched starved, and he probably was. He trusted me to touch him, and very few others.

I would not abuse that trust, not again.

Eiji silently murmured something after he broke the kiss and leaned back. I frowned, not quite able to make the words out. "What?"

Eyes rolling, Eiji quickly typed something out and then turned the phone so I could see it again. *"Lock the door."*

My eyebrows shot up. "Eiji."

His eyes dropped and he was a little slower typing this time. *"Unless you don't want to."*

I wasn't stupid.

I turned and stormed across the room like a man on a mission, and I was. I didn't care if there was a room full of people just on the other side. If Eiji wanted me to lock the door, I was locking the fucking door.

As soon as I was done, I turned...and nearly tripped over my own damn feet at the sight before me. Eiji was smiling and holding his arms out to me.

Again, I wasn't stupid.

I hurried back across the room and drew him into my arms before leaning down to rub my nose against Eiji's warm skin. "I love the way you smell."

I started alternating between sniffing Eiji's skin and licking it. Eiji tasted as good as he smelled. I wanted to start at the top and lick my way down to the bottom, and then maybe lick my way back up to the top.

I gently edged Eiji down onto his back on the bed and started to pull his shirt up his stomach. I wanted more skin. When Eiji's shirt was up around his armpits, I moved from the man's neck to his chest. I latched my lips onto one of Eiji's dark-hued nipples.

The small shudder that shook Eiji's body made my cock rock hard. I had done that. I had made him feel that good.

Had anything ever felt so powerful?

"Arms up, *malen'kiy*," I said as I tugged the shirt up even more. I definitely needed more skin, preferably naked skin from head to toe. Once Eiji lifted his arms, I whipped the shirt off over his head and tossed it on the floor.

I started to reach for the waistband on Eiji's pajama bottoms when I noticed the lower lip caught between Eiji's teeth. I instantly stopped what I was doing and cupped the side of Eiji's pale face.

"Are you okay, Eiji? Do you want me to stop?"

Eiji's face flushed as he shook his head. I grinned as I reached down and edged down his pants. Moving over to stand next to the bed, I grabbed the legs of Eiji's pants and pulled them down his legs.

I could feel Eiji watching me as I stripped off my clothes. I slowed down, taking my time. I was horny as hell and just wanted to get to the fucking part of things, but Eiji seemed to be enjoying the show if his hard cock and the need in his eyes were any indication.

Once I was naked—and Eiji was panting—I climbed up on the end of the bed between Eiji's thighs. I stroked my hand down one of Eiji's legs, awed at how smooth his skin always felt.

As smooth as silk.

I pushed myself up Eiji's body until I reached the hard cock jutting out from Eiji's groin. I grabbed his thighs and pushed them up so I could get a better angle and then made one long lick with my tongue from Eiji's perineum to the top of his cock.

The man really did taste fantastic. I could lick Eiji all day long and be a very happy man. I used my tongue to bathe Eiji's body, moving back and forth between his ass and his cock.

After a few moments, I licked my fingers and then started applying pressure, slowly inserting them into Eiji's ass, one at a time. By the time Eiji was humping into the air, his head thrashing about on the pillows, I was about ready to explode.

I was ready to plow right into him when a sudden horrid thought hit me. I raised my head to look up at Eiji. "We have no lube or condoms."

It wasn't like I carried that stuff in my pocket, although maybe I should start.

Eiji grinned before rolling to the side of the bed. I watched with avid curiosity as he opened the nightstand drawer and searched around in it before circling the bed and doing the same for the other nightstand.

I wanted to crow with relief when he held up a single use packet of lube and a condom. I also wanted to question why they were there and how he knew they were there.

"Eiji?" I asked when he climbed back on the bed and then handed them to me before laying back down in the same position he had been in before.

"Jai," he murmured silently.

I had no idea what that meant.

He pointed to the items he had given me. "Everywhere."

Still confused, but whatever. I had what I needed.

I tore open the lube packet and poured some of the lube out onto my fingers before dribbling a little between his ass cheeks. I watched his face carefully as I slowly inserted one finger and began to move it around, stretching him and making him ready for me.

Eiji was the most responsive man I'd had ever met. I knew exactly when I hit a sensitive spot and when I didn't. Eiji's cries and moans, and the shivers that racked his body, told me everything.

Eiji was a dream.

My dream.

I finally sat up to kneel between Eiji's thighs. The sight of Eiji lying naked on the mattress with his legs spread, his skin flushed with arousal, and his mouth slightly parted as he panted, was the most erotic thing I had ever seen.

I stared for a moment, drinking the sight in, and then leaned over Eiji.

"Come for me, *malen'kiy*," I whispered as I wrapped my fingers around Eiji's hard cock and quickly jerked him off. "I need you to come for me."

I could see the edge of an orgasm riding Eiji hard in the widening of his beautiful green eyes. Eiji was close. I quickly leaned over and covered Eiji's lips with my own, thrusting my tongue into his mouth, swallowing his cry as hot spunk shot all over my hand.

Before Eiji could come down from his high, I rolled the condom on and then smoothed the rest of the lube over Eiji's hole, pushing some deep inside of him.

Once we were both ready to go, I grabbed Eiji by his hips and encouraged him to roll over onto his hands and knees. I yanked Eiji's ass up into the air and lined my cock up.

I took my time pushing into Eiji's ass. My eyes nearly crossed as I watched myself sink into the man's tight hole. Eiji rippled around me, cradling my cock, holding me as if we were made to be together instead of apart. My cock felt like it was sinking into a vise grip as I thrust into Eiji's tight ass.

When my balls rested against Eiji's ass, I stopped and took several deep breaths. If I didn't, the show would be over before it began. It was always like this with Eiji. Our passion burned hot and burned fast, consuming both of us.

"So beautiful, *malen'kiy*," I whispered, more to myself than to Eiji. I pulled out until just the head of my cock remained in Eiji's tight grasp, then watched myself sink in again.

The image was too perfect to not watch a few times. I nearly swallowed my tongue as I watched my cock move out of Eiji's ass then sink back in. I had thought seeing Eiji all laid out on the mattress was hot.

This was hotter.

The need to feel Eiji come apart in my arms was overwhelming. I started thrusting harder, faster, and deeper. Sweat started to build up between my shoulder blades.

My level of arousal seemed to be tied into Eiji's. The more pleasure Eiji felt, the more filled me. Eiji's body seemed to swallow me up every time I thrust into the man, squeezing me and massaging me as if that alone could get me off.

It just might.

I had never felt anything like it in my life. The more I moved, the more Eiji panted. There seemed to be a direct connection to Eiji's breathing and the force of my thrusts.

I went with it, grabbing Eiji's hips and pounding into the man as fast and as hard as I could. The sounds of Eiji's heavy breathes mingled with the sound of our flesh slapping together.

It was heaven to my ears.

"Spread your legs, Eiji."

I swallowed hard as Eiji did just as I commanded. The man's knees spread apart, displaying Eiji's balls beautifully. I reached under Eiji and wrapped my hand around his cock. I started stroking the man with each thrust of my hips. The faster I pounded into Eiji's tight ass, the faster I stroked the man's cock.

"Come for me, *malen'kiy*."

The tight, inner muscles wrapped around my cock rippled and dragged me to the edge, but I'd be damned if I'd blow before Eiji did.

Eiji suddenly groaned and shot all over my hand. The scent of Eiji's spunk wafted into the air, filling my senses. I growled and thrust into Eiji's tight ass one last time.

My orgasm hit me with the force of a freight train. I felt as if my entire body had gone up in flames as I filled Eiji's ass with my release. My skin prickled with sensation, the very air around me seeming to caress me as if trying to draw out my climax until my legs shook.

Fuck!

I leaned over Eiji's body as I tried to regain my control of my pounding heart. I could feel Eiji's heart beating against me as I planted small kisses along Eiji's collarbone.

"Are you okay, Eiji?" I asked.

Eiji blinked several times and then smiled as he nodded. *"I'm good."*

I grinned as I carefully pulled free of Eiji's body then reached down onto the floor to grab Eiji's shirt. I cleaned Eiji up and then myself before dropping the shirt back to the floor. I collapsed down on the bed next to Eiji and curved myself around him.

This was the most perfect place in the world.

I was still reeling from the orgasm that had racked my body, hitting every nerve and taking me to heights of ecstasy I only ever felt with Eiji. My muscles felt like I had just run a marathon.

I wanted to lie there with Eiji wrapped up in my arms and pretend the rest of the world didn't exist. Just for a little while.

Chapter Twenty-Five

~ Eiji ~

So, the walk of shame was a thing, but I wasn't ashamed. I was a little embarrassed for using my friend's guestroom to have sex, but hey, I was married, damn it. It was allowed.

Besides, he told me he loved me.

Oh, my god, the man I was married to loved me. How in the hell had that happened? Granted, I'd fantasized about it more times than I could count, but to actually hear the words come out of Dmitri's mouth wasn't something I ever thought I'd hear.

The sex wasn't bad either.

I knew at some point I'd have to tell Dmitri the truth about my past, but I was kind of putting it off for right now. Getting kidnapped, knocking out a dangerous mafia boss, and finding out my husband loved me seemed like a bigger deal.

Could be wrong.

"So, you're really married?" Kyue pointed a finger to me and Dmitri. "You and the mob boss?"

I nodded at Kyue. I'd already tried to explain it once, but writing it all down on a piece of paper had kind of taken the wind out of my sails and I'd overloaded.

"We've been married for almost six weeks now," Dmitri explained.

I moved a little closer to Dmitri when Kyue's eyes narrowed. I didn't know if I was looking for protection from him or to protect him, but it was never a good thing when Kyue got pissed.

I patted Dmitri's chest until he handed me his cell phone, and then I started typing. *"Dmitri made a deal with my stepmother to get me away from her. Part of that deal was for us to get married so he could protect me legally."* I shot Dmitri a quick glance. *"We just fell in love along the way."*

I smiled and ducked my head when his arm tightened around me. This was not the way I wanted to tell him how I felt about him. I'd have to come up with a plan that didn't involve a room full of people.

A room full of people...My jaw dropped as I turned to look at Dmitri, tugging on his shirt.

He frowned as he looked down at me. "What is it?"

I quickly typed out what I wanted to say and then held the phone out to him. A smile started to spread across Dmitri's lips before he glanced at me. "Not a single panic attack while you were escaping?"

I shook my head. I had been shocked when I realized it just now. I had freed myself, taken down the people that kidnapped me, and ran away to get help...all without panicking. Granted, I had panicked afterward, but still. That was a big feat for me.

Dmitri pressed a kiss to my forehead. "Good job, *malen'kiy*."

Yeah, I was beaming.

The guy sitting next to Vinnie chuckled. "Falling in love like that seems to happen that way with these mafia types."

"No, Nicky, it happens with a lot of types." Kyue snickered. "Mr. Kincaid and I were an arranged marriage."

"Us, too," Parker added. "Syros and I had been betrothed since I was like six or something, but we didn't actually fall in love until after we ended the betrothal agreement."

Huh?

"Jake and I got married to save me from my family," Jai said.

"A lot of our friends have ended up married and in love due to arranged marriages or betrothals," Jake said with a vast amount of amusement in his tone of voice. "I think it's a pattern. I'll need to get Dr. Teller on researching that."

I had no idea who that was.

Didn't care.

"I'm really not sure if they are related," Dmitri said, "but it is an interesting theory."

Why were we talking about this?

I tugged on Dmitri's blazer to get his attention. Even though he'd been speaking to Jake mere moments before, his gaze zeroed in on me like I was the most important thing in his universe.

I could live with that.

"Home?" I asked silently.

Thankfully, he nodded.

"I need to get Eiji home," Dmitri said. "Thank you for your assistance tonight."

Parker shot Yasha, Vasil, and Lev a hard glare. "Is it safe for him to be going home?"

"I'm having the house swept for bugs as we speak, and we will be going over all of our personnel." Dmitri nodded to our three bodyguards. "I trust these three men with our lives."

"You might have to," Vinnie said. "Until you know if Boris was working alone or not, I would hesitate to trust anyone that hasn't been fully vetted. The O'Donnells are going to be looking to blame someone for assaulting their boss."

"Michael O'Donnell is getting off easy after kidnapping my husband," Dmitri snarled. "The entire O'Donnell family is fucking lucky I'm not burying every damn one of them six feet under."

"It might come to that," Vinnie warned. "Are you ready for it if it does?"

"I'll do whatever I have to do to keep Eiji safe."

I scooted a little closer to Dmitri for that statement. I just hoped it was true or my goose was cooked. I had no doubt that there was a price on my head for what I'd done. Dmitri might be the only thing standing between me and a very painful death.

"I can lend you some of my bodyguards," Vinnie offered.

Dmitri shook his head. "No, that probably wouldn't go over well with a great many people."

Vinnie chuckled. "Maybe not, but who cares?"

"Your grandfather?"

Vinnie shook his head. "I doubt it. He understands things like this. You might want to send word out to the other families that you've married Eiji so that he falls under the family veil. Once they know you are married, that makes him untouchable."

"I don't think the O'Donnells will care."

"No, but the other families will, including mine. Nicky falls under the family veil. There might be those out there that don't like the fact that I married another man, but that does not negate the fact that we are legally married. If they want to keep me from going after their family members, they need to not come after mine."

"I would never go after Nicky, even if you weren't married."

"I know that, Dmitri. You've done a lot of things to piss me off, but you've never crossed that line, not even with the people working for me."

"And I never will," Dmitri said. "Business is business, but family is family."

"Then let me make a few phone calls, Dmitri. I can put a bug in people's ear about O'Donnell and let them know Eiji falls under the family and spouse veil. It might give you the time you need to make sure he's safe."

Dmitri gave a nod, but it seemed like a reluctant nod. I was trying really hard to understand the dynamics of what was going on here, but none of it made sense.

Vinnie and Nicky seemed like perfectly nice people. Why was I supposed to be so wary of them? Because Vinnie was Italian and Dmitri was Russian? My mother had been Irish and my father Japanese. Did that mean I was even lower on the totem pole than them?

It was all very confusing.

I tugged on Dmitri's arm again. *"Home please."*

I wanted my snuggle nest. As much as I was thrilled that I hadn't freaked out while escaping, my tolerance for other people was thinning fast. I needed peace and quiet, and Dmitri.

He was included in my plans.

"Okay, *malen'kiy*." Dmitri patted my hand before returning his attention to Vinnie. "Call whoever you like. I'll do the same on my end. Maybe we can nip this in the bud before it becomes an all-out war."

"If things get too out of control," Jake said, "we do have someone on the police force we can talk to. He's a stickler for the rules, but he does understand that sometimes they need to be bent a little. If we're trying to prevent a mob war, he'd be willing to help."

"While I appreciate the sentiment," Dmitri replied, "let's hold off on that for now. I'd rather not get the police involved if we can help it."

"I agree," Vinnie added. "Just because they might be willing to work with us on something like this, doesn't mean once they get their foot in the door, they wouldn't try for more. It's best to leave the authorities out of it if at all possible."

Jack gave a sharp nod. "I'll leave it in your hands then."

"Thank you again for what you did for Eiji."

"There's one more thing I'd like to do for him, but we can't do it until the office opens up tomorrow."

Dmitri cocked his head. "What's that?"

Jake quickly explained about the tracking device he had implanted in his hand and how it worked. He also explained that they had used it track down Parker when he had been kidnapped.

"If you are agreeable, you can bring Eiji by my office tomorrow and we'll get one put in. It's relatively painless."

"And what do you want in exchange?" Dmitri asked.

I thought it was rather rude to ask that until Jake chuckled.

"One favor to be named later."

"Done," Dmitri agreed. "We'll come by your office tomorrow. What time?"

"Ten?"

"Ten o'clock it is."

Dmitri nodded to everyone—I gave a little wave—before steering me toward the front door and the elevator. Once we were inside the elevator, he grabbed the scarf around my neck and pulled it up over my head, looping the ends around my neck.

"This isn't your normal head cover."

I shook my head and then mouthed, *"Stole it from O'Donnell."*

Dmitri's jaw clenched. "I believe we have a spare one in the car."

He really didn't want O'Donnell anywhere around me, not even his stuff. I was so okay with that. The only reason I was even using the scarf was because they had taken my head cover. I'd be thrilled to trade it for mine.

The car was waiting for us right outside the door and as soon as we walked out, we were hustled into it before the doors were shut tight, locked, and we were on the road.

Yasha was sitting in the back with us. Lev and Vasil were in the front seats. I typed out a question to Dmitri and then showed him the screen. *"You turned your bedroom into my dance studio. Does that mean you will be sleeping with me?"*

Dmitri smiled when he read what I had written and then nodded. "It does."

"Does that mean I get to keep the dance studio?"

He nodded again.

Nothing in the world could have kept the smile off my face. *"You dance?"*

"Me?" Dmitri's eyebrows lifted. "I can dance a little, but nothing like you."

"I'll teach you."

"I actually wanted to talk to you about that. I'd like you to teach my guards to dance."

I squinted at him.

"I talked to you about this, remember?"

I shook my head.

"My guards know how defend themselves in a fight, but they don't have your dexterity. They can't move like you do, which means they are vulnerable. It also means they are not fully equipped to protect us because they do not use their full potential."

That made a weird sort of sense.

"Okay." If he wanted me to teach them to dance, I'd teach them to dance. *"They laugh, they in trouble."*

Dmitri's jaw firmed as he read my message. "They laugh and they can look for another line of work."

My jaw didn't firm. It dropped. My fingers flew over the keypad. *"You'd fire them if they laughed at me?"*

"I would," Dmitri admitted. "You are my husband. You belong to me. That means they need to respect you. If they don't then I don't want them working for me."

I didn't know what to say to that, so I said nothing.

No one had ever been so defensive of me before. Hell, no one had ever protected me before, not since my father passed away.

No one had cared.

Now, for the first time since I lost my father, it felt as if someone cared if I lived or died, if I was happy or sad. My wants and needs were important to Dmitri, and not because he wanted to bribe me or convince me to do something, but because he cared about me.

I didn't know how to express to Dmitri how much that meant to me, so I just held his hand and snuggled into his side. It was the best I had to offer at this point.

It was all I had.

Chapter Twenty-Six
~ Dmitri ~

"He's asleep."

I glanced down to find Eiji's eyes closed, his head resting against my shoulder. I raised my arm and turned in my seat slightly so he could rest against my chest instead.

"He needs it," I said as said as I stroked my fingers down the side of his face. "We still haven't fully talked about what happened to him beyond him telling me he got out of his restraints and then pushed Boris down the basement stairs of wherever he was being held. All that before he stabbed O'Donnell in the back with a fork and knife and escaped."

I still didn't know exactly where he had been held other than the fact that it was somewhere in Queens. That was a lot of area. Queens was the biggest borough in New York City. It was the second most populated county in New York State, behind Brooklyn, and also the second most populated of the five New York City boroughs.

Finding where Eiji had been held would be hampered by the fact that I needed permission from the O'Donnells to be in their territory. Since I suspected they were behind Eiji's kidnapping, I doubted I'd get it.

"Has there been any word on Boris?" I asked as I glanced up and looked at Yasha.

Yasha shook his head. "No, but everyone is looking for him. If he steps a single foot in the Bronx, we'll find him."

I snorted. "He'd be stupid to come back here."

I'd kill him the first chance I got.

"He was stupid to take Eiji in the first place," Yasha pointed out.

"There's still something off about that." I just couldn't figure out what it was. "Mary was brought in on Boris's recommendation. She started working at the house less than two weeks after Eiji and I got married. That's not enough time to plan something like this. How did they even know about him?"

I hadn't exactly advertised the fact that I had gotten married. I wasn't ashamed of Eiji or anything. I just hadn't wanted him to be in danger.

"Are you sure it wasn't a crime of opportunity?" Yasha asked.

"Maybe, but that doesn't explain why Boris vouched for an O'Donnell and helped her get inside our house. You know she was there to spy on us."

Yasha nodded. "I know which is why I ordered the entire house swept for listening devices. It would be stupid to think she was just there to keep an eye on us and report back to O'Donnell."

Stupidity like that got people killed, but it also might be our ace in the hole.

"If you find any, don't destroy them all. Leave one active."

Yasha's eyebrows hit his hairline. "You want me to leave an active listening device in the house?"

"Yes, I do. We might be able to use it to trap O'Donnell."

When Yasha started to chuckle, I grinned and held a finger to my lips. Eiji was still sleeping, and I wanted him to get his rest.

"I do like the way you think, Boss."

"Just make sure all these are removed, and I don't want any in the master suite, Eiji's dance studio, or my study." We needed some place to be where we didn't need to worry about the words we spoke.

"Make sure our electronics are cleared, too," I stated. "Mary was only there for a week, but Boris has been there a lot longer. If the two of them were working together with O'Donnell, there's no telling what kind of mischief they were up to."

The list of things we needed to check and double check was growing by the second. This was a dangerous life and I'd always known that, but it was frustrating when the people that were supposed to be protecting us were the ones we had to look out for.

There were very few people on the planet that I trusted fully. I could count them all on one hand. But I had always had some level of trust in the people that worked with me simply because I had to. They helped keep me alive. It was disconcerting to know one of those people had betrayed me.

"I also want a deep background done on everyone at the house." I think I mentioned this before, but I couldn't remember. My mind was too filled with keeping Eiji safe. "I need to know if anyone else was involved with this mess."

If there were more traitors in my organization, they weren't going to last long once I got my hands on them.

"I'm already working on that, Boss. Our computer guru should have a preliminary report for us by morning. Anything deeper than that might take a few days."

I wasn't sure we had a few days.

"Have one of our guys check around Queens and find out what happened to O'Donnell and Boris after Eiji escaped. If we can locate where they were holding Eiji, we might be able to get some CCTV footage. I also want to know where they are right now."

"Why CCTV footage, Boss?" Yasha asked.

"If this goes before the heads of the other families, I need to have evidence and a valid reason for taking O'Donnell out. Footage of him kidnapping my husband should be enough."

I hoped anyway. Considering the general stance on gay men in the mafia, I could be wrong. I was hoping the fact that Eiji was my legal spouse—man or not—would be enough.

"A complete background on that maid wouldn't hurt either." If I could prove that she was working for O'Donnell when she came into my house and assaulted me, that would be just one more piece of evidence in my favor.

Murder attempts on the heads of families happened all the time and were an accepted part of being in the mafia. I didn't like it, but it was what it was.

Kidnapping also happened. Kidnappings of spouses was a completely different animal. Like Vinnie had pointed out, spouses fell under the veil of protection.

If other mafia groups wanted their families and spouses to be off limits, they had to respect the fact that my family and spouse were off limits as well, even if my spouse was a man.

"Call the house and have Olav ready a tray for Eiji. I have no idea when the last time was that he ate. Once we know the master bedroom has been cleared, we can take him up so he can eat and then rest."

Pretty sure there was a snuggle nest in my future.

Yasha pulled out his cell phone and dialed. After a moment, he frowned and then dialed again. "Sir, I think we might have a problem. There is no answer at the house."

"Pull over, Vasil." I wasn't about to take Eiji into a possible hostile situation. "Keep trying to get through, Yasha."

I dug my phone out and starting dialing. When I couldn't reach a single person at the house, I knew Yasha was right. We did have a problem.

I glanced at Eiji. He was still passed out cold, and I wanted him to stay that way. I pulled my gun out and checked the clip before slamming it back into place and putting the gun back in my shoulder holster.

I needed to be ready in case there was trouble.

"Vasil, how far are we from the house?"

"About four blocks, Boss," Vasil replied.

I really didn't like the idea of walking four blocks, but taking Eiji with me wasn't an option. I had no idea what kind of situation I might be walking into.

"Yasha, I need you to—"

The rest of my words were lost in the horrifying sound of bullets hitting the side of the car. I threw myself over Eiji, taking him down to the seat and pinning him beneath me.

"Get us out of here!"

I felt the car jerk as it took off, but more bullets hit. One of them shattered the back window, raining glass down on top of me and Eiji. I heard a grunt as if someone had been hurt and for a moment, pure panic seized me.

I ran my hands over Eiji, checking to make sure he hadn't been the one that had been shot. When I found nothing but a set of fear filled green eyes staring back at me, I cupped the side of his face to reassure him.

"You're fine, Eiji. Just stay down, okay? I'll get us out of this."

One way or another.

"Who got hit?" I asked as I sat up.

"Me, sir," Lev replied from the front seat. "It's just a flesh wound on the arm. I'll be fine."

"Can you still shoot?"

"Yes, Boss."

"Tie something around your arm to stop the bleeding. We'll get you to a doctor just as soon as we can."

"I'm fine, Boss."

"Vasil, take us to the club." As much as I wanted to go to the house and find out what was going on there, getting Eiji somewhere safe was more important.

"We have a tail, Boss," Vasil called out. "Two cars coming up fast."

"Don't let them catch us." I searched around until I found the cell phone I had dropped when the shooting started and dialed a number I really didn't want to dial. "Vinnie..." God, this was going to hurt. "I need a favor."

"You need a favor from me?" Pure doubt laced his deep voice.

"Someone just shot out the windows of my car and there's no answer at my house. I need to find out what is going on, but I—"

"Do I have your permission to send a team in to assist you?" Vinnie asked.

I swallowed hard. "Yes."

"Stay alive. We'll be there soon."

"We?"

Vinnie chuckled, which seemed totally out of place considering the situation, but I understood why he chuckled. "We'll be there soon."

"I'm taking Eiji to my club." It was the safest place I could think of to take him. "Meet me there."

"Thirty minutes."

"Just hurry."

I wasn't sure we'd be alive in thirty minutes.

Vinnie hung up before I could say anything more. I was kind of glad he did. I was reeling from the fact that I had asked another mob boss for a favor and he had readily agreed.

Maybe—for the sake of our husbands—we needed to consider some sort of non-aggression treaty between our two territories. I wasn't going to let him do business in my area, but I could agree to not try and take out any of his people if they came into the Bronx.

"Vasil, get us to the club. Vinnie and some of his guys are going to meet us there."

The car swerved for a moment before Vasil glanced over his shoulder. "Is that a good idea, Boss?"

"Probably not, but it's the only one I have at the moment." I grimaced as an acidic taste filled my mouth. "Someone is shooting at us; we don't know what is going on at the house so we can't call up any of our people. At the moment, it's just us."

I didn't like asking for help, especially not from another mafia boss, but we were really flying blind here. I had no idea what was going on, what had happened to my people, or who was after us. Most importantly, Eiji was in danger.

For him, I could swallow my pride.

Chapter Twenty-Seven
~ Eiji ~

I was petrified.

I didn't know whether to sit up or stay where I was. I wasn't even sure what was going on beyond the fact that someone was shooting at us, and we were driving through the city at a rate of speed that would surely kill us.

I tugged on Dmitri's sleeve until he glanced down at me. The furrowed brow did not help my fear level at all. *"What's happening?"*

"It's fine, Eiji. You're fine. I won't let anything happen to you. Just stay down."

I guess that answered that question, but it left me with a lot more. *"What's happening?"*

Dmitri's lips twisted into a grimace. "Someone is shooting at us and there might be a problem at the house, so I am taking you to the club instead of going home. Vinnie Borelli and some of his men are going to meet us there."

I curled my fingers tighter around Dmitri's shirt. *"Are we going to die?"*

"No, *malen'kiy*. I won't let anything happen to you."

I wasn't worried about me. I knew Dmitri would keep me safe. I was worried about him because he would stand between me and whatever danger there was. He would shield me with his life.

I held out my hand. *"Gun."*

Dmitri blinked at me.

I wiggled my fingers in a "give me" gesture. *"Gun."*

Yeah, I was pretty shocked when Dmitri reached into the center console between the two seats in front of us and grabbed a gun before holding it out to me.

"Do you know how to shoot a gun?"

Sort of.

I nodded anyway.

So, okay, I had never shot a real gun before, but I'd played first-person shooter games a lot before my laptop had been taken away from me. There hadn't been a lot else to do when I'd been locked up besides read.

I checked the clip as I'd seen Dmitri do and then slid the gun into my pocket. I didn't have a holster, but maybe I needed to consider getting one. I doubted this would be the last time someone was shooting at me.

"Try not to shoot me."

I narrowed my eyes at the man only to watch him chuckle. While that was a good look on him, I was not going to shoot him. But I might consider it if he didn't stop laughing at me.

"We're here, Boss," Vasil called out from the front seat.

Dmitri suddenly lost all amusement on his face as he glanced out the shattered back window and then toward the front of the vehicle. "Pull as close to the front entrance as you can, Vasil. Once we stop, everyone needs to get inside immediately. I want Eiji taken to the hidden room off my office as soon as we get inside."

I clutched at Dmitri's shirt in protest, shaking my head.

"It's just until Vinnie gets here, Eiji," Dmitri explained. "I refuse to put you in the line of fire."

My nostrils flared as anger burned around the edges of my consciousness. I jabbed my finger into Dmitri's chest. *"You no danger!"*

"I wish I could say I wasn't in danger, but I refuse to lie to you, Eiji. We are all in danger right now and I am doing everything I can to get us out of it. I need you to do what I say so I can concentrate on that. Can you do that for me?"

I didn't like it, but I would be stupid to refuse. Dmitri had more experience at this high intensity danger stuff than I did. Besides, I didn't want to put him in more danger because I was being hard-headed.

I nodded before pointing my finger at him. *"Be careful."*

Dmitri's grin made my heart skip a beat. "I will, *malen'kiy*. I promise."

My heart climbed into my throat when the car screeched to a stop. Yasha threw open the passenger side door and climbed out. A moment later, Dmitri grabbed my wrist and pulled me out of the car with him.

I was escorted inside the club so fast I could barely keep up. With Dmitri's arm wrapped around me, I was pretty much floating alongside of him anyway.

Once we got inside, it wasn't any better. I was quickly ushered up the stairs to Dmitri's office. My jaw dropped when he walked over and pressed something on the wall-to-wall bookcase, and then a portion of the bookcase simply opened up.

"In here, Eiji. Quick."

I scurried in after him like the flames of hell were licking at my heels...and then I stopped and stared. It was like a studio apartment without a kitchen, although there was a small fridge and microwave.

It was also very "lived-in". The bedding was ruffled as if someone had slept there recently, and there was a small pile of clothes on one of the chairs. A coffee cup sat on the nightstand along with an open book lying face down.

"You live here?"

"I was staying here, yes." Dmitri nodded. "I was trying to give you space, but now that we're no longer getting divorced, I'll be moving back to the house with you." His eyebrows lifted a little making his eyes seem wider. "If that's okay with you."

I nodded quickly, not wanting him to get the wrong impression. Him moving home was more than okay with me. I'd missed him every second that he was gone.

"Boss!" Yasha rushed into the room, a panicked look paling his face. "Three carloads of men just pulled up in front of the club."

"Vinnie's guys?"

"I don't think so, Boss. Boris and O'Donnell were in the lead."

"Damn it!" Dmitri grabbed me by the arms. "I need you to stay here, Eiji. This room is soundproof so no one will hear you and only me, Yasha, and now Vasil and Lev know that it is here. You should be safe as long as you don't leave this room."

I stabbed a finger at Dmitri. *"You."* I pointed to myself. *"Come back to me."*

A small, yet sad smile spread across Dmitri's lips. "I will."

I noticed he didn't promise this time, and as much as I hated that, I was grateful for it to. He wasn't going to try and make me feel better by lying to me. I'd prefer the truth over a lie, even if I hated what that truth was.

Dmitri pressed a kiss to my lips that went much faster than I would have liked, and then him and Yasha were out the door, closing it behind them and locking me in this luxury soundproof room.

I stood there in the middle of the room for a moment, or two or three, and then I began to pace. I chewed on my thumbnail as I glanced at the door, wanting it to open, aching for it to open.

I had just gotten Dmitri back. I couldn't lose him now. Not knowing what was going on, if he was hurt, if he was alive or dead...It was driving me insane. I needed to know.

Surely one little peek wouldn't hurt.

I started for the door, but stopped halfway there, turned and paced back the other way. I walked back and forth for a few minutes before storming over to the door once again.

This was a really bad idea.

My hand shook as I grabbed the door handle. I still turned it and pulled the door open just an inch, just far enough for me to see out of the little crack between the door and the door frame.

When I saw the scene before me, I sucked in a quick, painful breath, and then quickly slapped my hand over my mouth to keep from making any noise. I didn't want anyone to know I was there.

I knew Dmitri was going to be pissed at me for leaving the secret room, but what else was I supposed to do? Yasha lay on the floor a few feet away in a pool of blood. I didn't know if he was alive or dead.

I had no idea where Vasil and Lev were.

Dmitri, however, he was the one that most concerned me. He was kneeling on the floor with his fingers laced together behind his head. The guy I had stabbed with a fork and knife stood in front of him pointing a gun at Dmitri's head.

How had it come to this?

I pushed the door open just enough to slip out and then carefully closed it behind me before dropping down close to the floor. I slid across the floor until I could hide myself beneath Dmitri's desk.

Before I did anything, I needed to know just how many people were in the room. One wrong move and Dmitri could end up with a bullet in him, and I couldn't allow that.

Once I was scrunched under his desk, I pulled the gun Dmitri had given me out of my pocket. I wasn't sure I was going to be able to use it, but maybe I could get it into Dmitri's hands. I had no idea where his gun was.

My head snapped up I heard a voice that sent chills down my spine.

"I know he's here somewhere. I tracked the cell phone he stole from me. Just tell me where he is and this can all be over."

The phone?

I quickly patted down my pockets until I found the cell phone I had taken off of O'Donnell after stabbing him. I stared at it for a moment before turning it off and then flipping it over to pull the battery out. I had no idea how he was using it to track me, but I wasn't taking any chances.

"You're insane if you think I'll tell you anything, O'Donnell," Dmitri spit out. I could tell from the cold tone of voice that he used that he was pissed. "You've crossed the line this time."

O'Donnell let out a laugh. "So the fuck what? No one cares. Not even the police. That's the nature of this business, Petrov. If you can't handle it, I suggest you run back to Russia to your mommy."

"You kidnapped my husband. You know he falls under the family and spouses veil agreed upon by all the heads of the five major families. You violated that agreement."

O'Donnell snorted out another laugh. "You ain't married to that little whore. You can't be."

"Oh, I assure you I am."

"He's a guy."

"So am I," Dmitri stated. "What's your point?"

"No one in our world is going to accept two guys being together. It's just not done, which means they ain't going to give a shit if something happens to your little boy toy."

"Vinnie Borelli might have a problem with it considering he's married to a man, and it was a marriage that received Carlos Borelli's blessing. I imagine the other heads of the families will care as well. Not because Eiji is a man, but because he is my spouse. It's as simple as that. Man or not, he is married to me, and that means he falls under the agreement we all made."

"You made the agreement," O'Donnell protested. "I had nothing to do with it."

"Your father was part of that agreement. It's why your stupid ass was never taken out."

I heard a smack and a grunt and had a fairly good idea what had happened. Dmitri really needed to learn not to poke the bear when he was armed.

"My father is no longer in charge," O'Donnell snapped. "I am."

"With as much trouble as you are causing, I doubt you will be in charge for very long. Sooner or later your superiors in Ireland are going to figure out what a fuck-up you are, and they will send someone to replace you."

"I am never going to be replaced. Never! And do you know why? Because I'm smarter than all you idiots. I know where the real money is, and once I start raking it in, my superiors will be thrilled with me. Hell, they'll probably give me a promotion. Maybe they'll even give me the Bronx."

"That's never going to happen."

I heard a gun click.

"Are you so sure of that?" O'Donnell asked.

I knew it was now or never.

I crawled out from under the desk and scooted my way around the side until I could see Dmitri and O'Donnell again. O'Donnell was still pointing the gun at Dmitri.

I gripped my own gun and brought it up, pointing it at O'Donnell, but I couldn't get a good angle. I was too afraid I would end up shooting Dmitri by mistake. I shoved it back into my pocket and then thrust a hand through my hair.

I had to come up with something else, but what?

As soon as O'Donnell started pacing again, I knew what I had to do. I watched him for a moment, and the second he spun and started walking away from me, I jumped to my feet and rushed him.

I heard a startled yell when the glass window that overlooked the dance floor shattered as O'Donnell and I crashed through it.

Having spent many a night at this club, I knew where we were headed. As we sailed through the air, I scrambled to reach out with my hands, trying to grab the decorative gold accent piece that ran along the length of the upper wall around the bar.

As soon as my fingers grazed it, I tightened my grip and held on. My body jerked and then was suddenly lighter as I separated from O'Donnell and he fell to the hard marble flooring below.

"Eiji!"

A bullet whizzed past my head.

I glanced behind me to see two men come running into the club with guns. My gaze fell to the bar top below. I made a split-second decision and let go, swinging my body inward as I did.

I landed on the bar top with a hard—and very painful—thud and immediately rolled off to hide behind the bar. When several bullets slammed into the shelves of liquor above me, I jumped to my feet and ran to the far end away from all the breaking glass.

I couldn't stay here. I needed to keep on moving. A stationary target was a dead target. Being at the hands of my cruel stepmother and my vicious stepbrothers for all those years had taught me that. Movement didn't necessarily mean pain free, but it could keep me from death's door.

I waited until the shooting had stopped and then darted from behind the bar across the floor to the DJ's booth. Like I said, I'd been here a few times. I happened to know that there was a trapdoor in the floor of the DJ's booth. It was used so technicians could get underneath the booth to deal with the wiring.

It also made a great hiding spot.

As soon as I reached the booth, I pulled open the small door in the floor and shimmied down through it, pulling the door closed over the top of me. There wasn't a lot of room down here, but I was small. I easily fit.

Now, I just had to wait for Dmitri to come save me.

I really wish he'd hurry up.

Chapter Twenty-Eight
~ Dmitri ~

My life came to a freezing halt as I watched Eiji run past me, slam into O'Donnell, and then the both of them went crashing through the glass window, disappearing from sight.

Fear held me immobile for a moment as a deep cold darkness threatened to take me under. Had I just seen Eiji fly out a window?

Was he even alive?

I jumped to my feet and raced over to the edge. I could see O'Donnell lying at an odd angle on the floor below, his sightless eyes staring up at me. Pretty sure his neck was broken.

There was no sign of my husband.

"Eiji!" I screamed in desperation.

I ducked down when the front doors slammed open and two armed men came running inside. They started shooting at anything and everything.

I hurried back to my desk where O'Donnell had put the gun he'd taken off of me. I still couldn't believe the bastard had gotten the drop on me after shooting Yasha.

Yasha!

I ran around the desk to the far side and dropped down beside my second-in-command. I admit I had to swallow my fear before searching for a pulse. While there was one, it was weak. If Yasha didn't get to a hospital soon, he wasn't going to make it.

I quickly ran my hands over Yasha's body, looking for a bullet wound. When I found one on his upper chest, I grimaced. It looked too high to do any real damage, but it was still bleeding pretty heavily.

I pulled my jacket off and pressed it down over the wound before reaching over to lightly smack him on the face. "Yasha, wake up."

I didn't have a lot of time.

I smacked him again a little harder. "Yasha!"

When I couldn't wake him up, I untied my tie and used it to anchor my suit jacket to the wound. It wouldn't do much, but it was all I had at the moment.

I needed to call an ambulance, but I needed to secure the place first. The paramedics would not enter an active shooter area.

And I really needed to find Eiji.

I swung my gun up when my office door crashed open, only lowering it when I realized Vasil stood in the doorway. "Where's Lev?"

"He's holding them off at the bottom of the stairs."

"Come help me with Yasha," I ordered. "He's been shot in the upper chest." As soon as Vasil reached me, I stood. "I need to go find Eiji."

"But isn't he—"

I gestured toward the broken window as I checked my gun. "He went through the window with O'Donnell. I think the bastard broke his neck when he fell, but there's no sign of Eiji. I have to find him."

"I'll stay here with Yasha."

"Call Borelli and let him know what's going on. Tell him Yasha is going to need a doctor as soon as possible."

"Yes, Boss."

"I'm going to lock this door when I go out, but I doubt that will stop anyone determined to get in here. If you think it's safe to move him, you might want to take Yasha to the hidden room. No one can find you in there."

"I'll take care of it, Boss."

"Stay alive," I said as I headed for the door.

I had my gun ready as I stepped out into the hallway. Despite how much I wanted to run downstairs and scream for Eiji, I moved slowly and carefully toward the top of the stairs. If I got shot, I'd never have a chance to find him.

As soon as I spotted a couple of men I didn't know coming up the stairs, I took them out. I took out anyone that didn't belong to me. Since Vinnie and his men hadn't arrived yet, I felt safe in doing that.

When I reached the bottom of the stairs, I quickly scanned the large open space of the first floor. This was a dance club. There weren't a lot of places to hide here, so where had Eiji gone?

If he was taken again...

I started toward the front door only to be brought up short when Boris walked through them. This was the man that I wanted dead almost as much as O'Donnell, and since O'Donnell was already dead, Boris was next on my list.

I raised my gun and pointed it at him. "I hope betraying the family was worth it because you are going to die."

Boris also had his gun pointed at me. "Like I believe that."

"Oh, it's true. People who betray me die. Happens all the time." Not really, but Boris didn't know that. "Why would you do that, Boris? You've worked for me for a long time and I trusted you." Sort of. "Why would you betray me like that?"

"Fuck you!"

That was not an answer.

"Do you think I wanted to spend the rest of my life as some glorified babysitter for your little freak?" Boris shouted. "O'Donnell was going to give me my own crew."

"O'Donnell was going to put a bullet in your head the moment your usefulness ran out."

Boris snorted. "See, that's where you are wrong. O'Donnell wasn't going to do anything to me. His favorite niece, and my fiancée, would be upset if he did."

My eyes narrowed. "Mary?"

"I'm not stupid," Boris said. "The only way to stay alive in this business is to marry into one of the families, the stronger the better, and there is no one stronger than the O'Donnells."

This guy was an idiot.

"Oh, don't worry," I said. "She's next on my list."

I had just enough time to see the rage in Boris's eyes before I put a bullet between them.

"Boss!"

I swung around, gun raised. I only lowered it when I saw Lev coming from the back of the club. "How many are left?"

Lev shook his head. "I think we got all of them, but I'd feel more confident in that statement once we search the place."

"I need to find Eiji."

Lev's brow flickered. "Isn't he upstairs?"

My stomach clenched as I gestured to O'Donnell's body again. "He took O'Donnell out through the window of my office. He was gone by the time I was able to look." I glanced around, a little frantic. "He has to be here somewhere."

I prayed he was here and he hadn't been taken again.

Before I can even start looking for him, more armed men begin to pour into the club. Lev and I dove for cover before lifting our guns to start shooting.

Man, this was going to be a mess.

My eyes snapped to the ceiling when the lights started flashing and then darted toward the DJ booth at the side of the room. The amount of pride I felt when I saw Eiji effortlessly working the light controls warred with my fear of him being shot.

I shot one of the men that aimed at Eiji and then jumped from my hiding spot behind a pillar and raced across the dance floor. I felt the heat as a few bullets whizzed past my head and the white-hot agony as one hit its mark.

My arm went numb almost immediately.

I was kind of glad it did when I had to dive into the DJ booth, catching Eiji around the waist and taking him to the floor with me.

It hurt less.

Until Eiji landed on it and then it hurt a whole lot more than I ever thought it could. I grunted at the blistering pain and rolled so that my body covered Eiji, and my arm was free of his weight.

"Are you hurt?" I asked in a panicked tone. "Are you hit anywhere?"

Eiji's eyes were as wide as saucers as he shook his head.

I wanted to berate him for leaving the safety of the hidden room, but I couldn't. I knew why he did it. I just wished he had chosen to stay where I could protect him.

I doubt I'd ever forget him falling through that window.

I glanced toward the dance floor, but I couldn't see anything from my vantage point. Too many wires and electronics in the way. I lifted up enough to peer over the glass partition, which surprisingly hadn't been shattered yet.

I could still see a couple of guys hunkered down by the door, one was shooting toward the DJ booth and the other one was shooting at Lev. I needed to take these guys out so I could get Eiji to safety.

"Stay down!"

Eiji nodded rapidly again.

I got up on my hands and knees and started to crawl toward the edge of the booth, but Eiji tugged on my arm sleeve. I frowned as I glanced toward him until he pointed to a lever on the floor.

Eiji grabbed it and pulled the hatch open.

I felt like smacking myself. How had I forgotten this? I'd designed the damn club. I knew this was here.

I pointed my finger at Eiji. "Get down on the floor and cover your head."

We were stuck in a freaking booth. There was really nowhere for him to go at the moment, at least not until I cleared a path for him.

As soon as Eiji laid down flat on the floor and covered his head, I hopped down into the small access area and squatted down. I quickly scanned the small space before going to my hands and knees and crawling toward the front edge of the booth.

There was a row of small circular openings used for electrical cords, but they were big enough for what I needed. I scooted as close as I could get and then stuck the barrel of my gun through one of the holes. From there, it was fairly easy to pick off the remaining goons attacking us. They had no idea where the bullets were coming from.

I waited a few minutes after the last one fell just to make sure no more were hiding and waiting for us to step out so they could shoot us. When no one else appeared, I scooted back to the hatch opening and climbed out.

Eiji was still lying on the floor with his arms over his head. He jumped when I grabbed him and picked him up, his eyes impossibly wide. I pulled him into a tight hug.

"You're okay," I whispered into his ear. "You're safe now."

I hoped.

Eiji's body slumped against mine.

For a brief moment, I felt as if my world had settled and calmed. It wasn't a feeling I was very familiar with. Being who I was and having the job I did, calm wasn't something I felt very often.

I wanted to simply stand there and bask in the feeling for a moment, but our situation was still pretty fluid. We weren't safe yet, Yasha was hurt, and I needed to find the rest of these fuckers and take them out.

The Russian mafia had gone to war with the Irish mafia.

"Come on," I said to Eiji as I put him down on his feet. "I need to get you back upstairs."

Eiji nodded, but latched onto my arm.

I was fine with that.

I led Eiji to the entrance of the booth and then stopped. "Lev?"

"Yeah, Boss," the man called out from the other side of the room.

"Do you see any more?"

"No, Boss."

I stepped out of the booth, pulling Eiji with me, and then hurried across the floor to where Lev was standing next to O'Donnell's body. Eiji cringed when I kicked at the body just to make sure and then pressed his face to my arm.

Yeah, he was dead.

"Kirby O'Donnell only had the one kid, right?" I asked. It would be nice to know if more were going to come after us.

"Yeah, I think so," Lev replied. "There are a few cousins, but no one that can take over. Ireland is going to need to send someone if they want to retain control of Queens."

Well, I didn't want it.

"Let's get upstairs." It was safer up there. "I need to call Borelli and let him know the situation. We need to get Yasha to a hospital before we can head home."

Before we could take a single step, the front doors burst open again and several men poured in. My heart slammed into my throat before I spotted Vinnie walking in.

Oddly enough, he had Jake D'Amato with him.

The jaws of both of them slowly started to drop as they glanced around the ravaged club interior. Yeah, it was going to take a lot of work to get this place up and running again. Bullet holes and bodies littered the place.

"Glad to see you are still alive," Vinnie said as he strode toward us.

I nodded toward the body at my feet. "He isn't."

Vinnie's eyebrows lifted as he glanced down. "O'Donnell?"

I nodded before pointing up. "I pushed him out the window after he shot Yasha."

I felt Eiji stiffen when I lied, but I wasn't about to let him take the rap for killing the current head of the Irish mob. He didn't need that kind of thing hanging over his head.

"Sounds to me like he got what was coming to him," Vinnie replied. "Between him kidnapping your husband and attacking you, no one is going to question why you took him out."

I hoped not.

I grimaced as I glanced around the club. "I have no idea how I am going to explain this to the police."

That's when Jake spoke up. "I have a guy, a detective. I've already put in a call to him. He should be here soon."

I blinked at the guy for a moment before asking, "You have a detective on your payroll?"

Jake wasn't even mafia.

"No." Jake chuckled as if what I had said was vastly amusing. "I doubt anyone could buy off Detective Waterston, but he's a good guy. He understands that there is a gray area between right and wrong."

Was there?

I had no idea.

"Yasha needs a doctor."

Vinnie nodded. "Your man called me. I have a vehicle waiting outside to take him to the hospital."

"Lev, can you get a couple of Vinnie's guys and go up and get Yasha. You can escort him to the hospital so you can get your arm treated. I need Vasil to stay here."

"Sure thing, Boss."

I glanced at Lev when his phone rang before he could walk away. I didn't like the grimace that crossed his face when he answered and spoke to whoever had called, especially when it turned into a scowl.

"What?" I asked when he looked at me.

"It's Olav, sir. The mansion was attacked."

We knew this. It was why we came to the club.

"And?"

"It's on fire, sir. We lost five men, but everyone else was able to get out before it burned down. Olav took them to a safe house."

Christ on a cracker.

"Okay." I rubbed the bridge of my nose. I was starting to get a steady ache right between my eyes. "Tell Olav to send five guys to us, but have everyone else stay there for now. Once I figure out where we are going to stay, I'll let him know."

I had more than one safe house around the city. If we couldn't all fit in one place, we could spread out between them, but I hesitated to do that. I wasn't positive this was over.

"You don't want them to come here?" Lev asked.

"Hell, no."

I didn't want to be here.

I glanced down at Eiji when he tugged on my sleeve. My brow flickered when his lips started moving. It took me a minute to figure out what he was saying and then my eyebrows tried to become one with my hairline.

"Are you sure?"

Eiji nodded.

"You know we'll have to deal with your stepmother and stepbrothers first, right?"

He paled, but nodded again.

It was a good idea.

My lips pressed thin as I glanced up. "Eiji says we can use his place, but we have to clear it out first."

"His place?" Vinnie asked.

I quickly gave Vinnie and Jake a rundown of what had happened with Fiji's stepfamily and inheritance. "Technically, the entire estate belongs to Eiji. We just have to take it back from his stepmother, and she's not going to give it up without a fight."

"I might be able to help you with that," Jake said. "Do you have the papers that say it's Eiji's?"

"Yes, of course. I had my lawyer get them all straightened out when we got married, but why?"

"I have a couple of lawyers that work for me, good lawyers. I say we simply file the paperwork and serve Eiji's stepmother with an eviction notice. We can even have the police escort her off the premises since we'll have the paperwork that makes this all legal."

My jaw dropped when I heard Eiji snort. When I glanced down, I could see the smile Eiji was trying to hide spreading across his lips. It made an answering smile spread across mine.

"Do you like that idea, *malen'kiy*?"

Eiji made grabby hands, so I reached into my pocket and pulled out my phone, handing it over.

He quickly typed out a message and then showed me the phone screen. *"I'd love to see the look on that bitch's face when the cops legally kick her out."*

I snickered as I read it. Yeah, okay, I could see where he was coming from. It would be amusing to see Beverly's face when she was legally served an eviction notice and escorted off the property.

"If I get you the paperwork, can you help me make it happen?" I asked as I glanced back at Jake.

"It might take a couple of days, but I think so. Miles and Joe would know more about this stuff than I do, but if that place is legally Eiji's, I don't see how she can keep him from living there."

"I just want to make sure she can't continue to live there if we move in. I'd also like to make sure she doesn't leave with anything that doesn't belong to her. She's already taken enough from Eiji."

Jake smirked. "I think we can do that."

"Where are you going to stay in the meantime?" Vinnie asked. "I don't think you can stay here. Jake's guy might be understanding, but this is still a crime scene."

"I'll book us a suite at the Opera House Hotel. We can stay there until your lawyer gets all the paperwork ready to go."

I guess a few nights wouldn't matter one way or another.

As long as Eiji was safe.

Chapter Twenty-Nine
~ Eiji ~

Eiji felt as if he was seriously dragging ass by the time they walked into the hotel suite Dmitri had rented for them. It was already early afternoon. We had spent hours giving statements to the police and then waiting at the hospital to hear about Yasha and for Lev to be treated.

"Vasil, once you've had a chance to get something to eat and rest, go to our tailors and buy new clothing for Eiji and me...and maybe for yourself as well. We're all a little gross right now."

"Yes, Boss."

"Have someone relieve Lev as well. He needs to come here and get some rest, but I don't want Yasha left unprotected until this is over."

"I'll let him know, Boss," Vasil replied. "I'll call Olav and have him send two guys to the hospital to keep watch over Yasha."

"*Is he really going to be okay?*" I asked.

I was so glad to have use of a phone again. Dmitri had sent one of his men out to buy me a brand new one since I had no idea where mine was. I'd lost it after Boris took me.

"The doctor said he'll make a full recovery," Dmitri said. "He just needs to stay in the hospital for a couple of weeks. He'll enjoy the time off."

"Can we go see him?"

Dmitri smiled. "After we get some rest."

I smiled and nodded before turning to face the room, and then my jaw dropped. This place was amazing. Thick cream-colored carpet, overstuffed couches, colorful paintings on the wall. Even a large screen television and a wet bar.

This place had it all.

Did it have a bedroom?

I walked over to a set of double doors on the left side of the room.

Yes, there was a bedroom, and a rather large one at that. Pretty sure the bed was bigger than the one I'd had back at the mansion. It was covered by a thick cream-colored comforter with a darker tan blanket folded across the bottom of the bed.

This room also had a large television mounted on the wall opposite of the bed...and a bathroom I wanted to be buried in.

The huge walk-in shower was beyond anything I had ever seen. It had shower heads on two of the walls, opposite of each other and a large round showered head hanging from the middle of the shower.

There was also a double vanity, the biggest jetted soaking tub probably ever made, and a small room that housed the toilet. I had no idea what kind of tile it was other than white. Didn't matter. It still looked great.

I wanted something like this for my own bathroom.

"I'm sorry we couldn't go home, Eiji."

I glanced over my shoulder to find Dmitri leaning against the door frame, his hands in his pockets and a deep frown marring his lips.

I shrugged as I turned and walked toward him. Home wasn't a building for me. I'd grown up in a mansion and hated it every second. I'd been forced to live in another mansion when I married Dmitri, but I'd been too terrified to appreciate the freedoms I had there.

As safe and as comforted as I was by Dmitri's mere presence, I was starting to think that home wasn't a wooden or brick structure, but the man before me.

I pointed to Dmitri and then to myself and then made the shape of a rooftop with my hands before pressing both hands to my heart. The smile that blossomed across Dmitri's lips at my silent gesture was one I doubted I'd ever forget. It matched the joy in his eyes.

"I love you, too, Eiji."

That wasn't exactly what I said, but the premise was the same. Dmitri loved me and I loved him. I didn't need a brick and mortar building to be my home. I had one in the tall sexy Russian holding me in his arms.

This might be the one time in my life that I truly regretted not being able to verbalize what I was feeling. I wanted to tell Dmitri how I felt, to have him hear my words, and yet nothing came out of my mouth.

The most I could do was move my lips. *"I love you."*

Dmitri's smile brightened even more, becoming wider. His dark brown eyes began to twinkle with unshed tears. "I never thought I'd hear you say that, especially after everything that has happened."

He hadn't actually heard me say it, but...

My eyes widened lifted when Dmitri pulled a condom and a packet of lube out of his pocket as he started backing into the bedroom area.

He smirked when I lifted an eyebrow. "I stole them." He shrugged when I stared at him. "I'm a mafia boss. That's what I do."

Yeah, I couldn't argue with that.

I fingered the collar of Dmitri's shirt and then slowly unbuttoned it. I'd seen Dmitri without a shirt before, but not like this. Not when I could touch. I licked my lips as I trailed my hand down the front of Dmitri's chest.

I could almost smell the man's growing arousal, Dmitri's dark brown eyes flickered with hunger as he watched the tiny movement of my tongue.

I pushed Dmitri back onto the bed and straddled his thighs. From the desire I could see burning in Dmitri's eyes, no words were needed. Dmitri knew exactly what I wanted. I could feel it in the hard cock pressing up against my ass.

An involuntary shiver raced through my body when Dmitri's large hands closed around my waist.

I pulled my shirt over my head and sent it sailing across the room. It was a little disconcerting to be half naked in front of this man. That uncertainty faded away when I felt Dmitri's delicious hands move over my naked chest, settling on my nipples to pluck and pull at them.

I dropped my head back on my shoulders and groaned. It was unintelligible sound, but crystal clear in its volume. A deep groan of need, my need. Dmitri seemed to know just how much to tug, to pull, how much pressure to use to bring me to the very edge of bliss.

"I'm going to give you everything you've ever dreamed of, Eiji."

Oh, that deserved a reward.

I couldn't help grinning as I scooted back. I quickly lowered the man's zipper and reached in to pull his cock out. My heart skipped a beat before my hand had fully pulled Dmitri's cock free from his pants.

I remember feeling it before, but I hadn't seen it.

Damn.

The man was hung like a fucking horse.

His thickly veined shaft was so thick that my hand wouldn't even fully close around it and I seriously doubted I could cover every inch of his length if I had four hands. Dmitri had to be at least ten inches long.

I was going to have so much fun with this.

When I glanced up, Dmitri's dark eyebrow was arched as if he were challenging me. I grinned, almost feeling sorry for the man. I'd read enough books over the years, and experimented with a few carrots and cucumbers out of curiosity to know he was in for a big surprise.

I had no gag reflex.

Keeping my eyes locked with tall, handsome mob boss, I carefully lowered my mouth and swallowed just the tip of the man's cock. My lips burned as they stretched around Dmitri's wide girth.

The drops of pre-cum pooling on the head of Dmitri's cock trickled over my tongue, bathing me in the most exotic flavors I had ever tasted in my life. I could seriously get addicted to sucking this guy off on a regular basis. I might even beg for the chance.

I stroked my tongue over the head of Dmitri's cock as I waited for my lips to get used to the burn as they stretched enough to swallow him. It was obvious that it was going to take a little more effort than normal for me to suck Dmitri off.

Once my mouth had adjusted to Dmitri's size, I licked a long path from the tip of Dmitri's cock down to the root and then down just a bit further. I felt Dmitri's hand fist in my hair when I sucked one of his balls into my mouth.

Oh yeah, he liked that.

I could tell.

I took the time to suck the other ball into my mouth, rolling it around with my tongue before licking a line back up the thickly veined sides. By the time I reached the slit on the head of Dmitri's cock, another pool of pre-cum had gathered and started dripping down the sides. I eagerly licked at each drop.

A deep groan fell from Dmitri's lips as I slowly sucked his shaft down my throat. I got about halfway down the man's impressive erection before I had to pause and draw in a deep breath through my nose.

Once I had more air in my lungs, I continued.

The lust that flared in Dmitri's dark brown eyes as I swallowed him down until my nose was nestled in pubic hair was the biggest ego boost I had ever received. It made me feel as if I could conquer the world.

I wanted more.

I slowly started to bob my head, sucking in my cheeks as I moved my mouth over Dmitri's thick cock. I wanted to savor every last inch. The more I moved up and down, the easier it became to swallow Dmitri down. I could still feel drops of luscious tasting pre-cum splattering over my tongue every time I swallowed, and god, it was fucking fantastic.

When Dmitri's balls started to pull up tight to his body, I increased the speed of my movements, sucking Dmitri's length down my throat faster and faster each time, hollowing my cheeks out as I moved back up to the tip.

I knew Dmitri was getting close and I wanted him to remember this blowjob as the best one he'd ever received. I breathed through my nose, but it was buried in Dmitri's pubic hair as Dmitri shoved his cock all of the way down my throat and came with a low rumble.

Load after load of cum shot down my throat. I swallowed as fast as I was able to, but I could still feel drops of it slide out of the edges of my mouth. I ached to swallow every drop, but I just couldn't. There was just too much of it.

When the pressure on the back of my head released, I lifted my head, Dmitri's cock falling from my mouth with a loud plop, and went about licking up every drop of cum I could find.

My eyebrows rose when I realized he was still hard. I was suddenly rolled over onto my back, Dmitri coming over the top of me.

"My turn," Dmitri growled.

My pants were yanked down and tossed away and then my legs were pushed apart. Dmitri tossed the lube packet and a condom onto the bed next to me.

Dmitri chuckled as he tore the lube packet open and poured a sufficient amount of slick out onto his fingers. My high-pitched grunt as Dmitri's fingers pushed into my ass echoed through the room. I stiffened for a moment and then shuddered.

My heart thundered against my chest when Dmitri started thrusting his fingers into my ass over and over again, until I felt the little ring of muscles stretch and pulse against Dmitri's fingers.

"Need you, Eiji," Dmitri whispered. "Can I have you like this, or do you need to be on your hands and knees? I want you to be able to see my face."

It was sweet that he asked.

I smiled at him.

Dmitri pulled his fingers free and scooted up between my thighs. I watched as he tore the condom package open and rolled the condom on. and

A moment later that big thick cock was pushed into my ass. The burning was so intense that for a moment, I thought I might pass out. I was pretty sure my ass was being speared in two as Dmitri slowly pushed forward, sinking his huge cock into my tight hole.

By the time I felt Dmitri's thighs brush up against my ass I thought I might be able to taste the man's cock in my throat. I gripped the sheets and tried not to wince when Dmitri stilled inside of me. I might have needed just a bit more stretching.

I breathed for several moments, and then nodded.

"I'm okay," I mouthed.

My legs were spread until they draped over Dmitri's arms. As Dmitri's body settled over mine, the cock in my ass slid in even further, which surprised the hell out of me. I didn't think Dmitri could sink any further inside of me.

When the man started to move, a loud grunt of ecstasy flew out of my throat as I curled my fingers in the sheets. Every inch of Dmitri's massive cock dragged across my sweet spot as the man pulled out and pushed back in.

For one crazy second, I wondered if Dmitri's cock had been specifically designed just for my ass. It felt as if he filled every inch of me, as if Dmitri was supposed to ignite every nerve in my ass.

It was fucking fantastic, better than I had even hoped.

My ass was being pummeled as the man pounded into me at a rate that was, frankly, very astonishing. I could barely register the fact that Dmitri had pulled out before he was pushing back in.

All thoughts and breathing in general faded from my mind when I felt a hand close around my cock. I was so sensitive; I swore I could feel a tickling on my balls as Dmitri started to stroke me.

Maybe it was sweat.

I didn't care.

Really.

I just needed that magnificent cock to not stop filling me. I was so close I could practically taste it. I needed so fucking bad. Every inch of my skin tingled. I was flushed with heat and getting hotter.

"Dmitri!"

No one had ever fucked me like this, making me want and need more than my next breath. Blood pounded through my body as I was impaled on Dmitri's cock over and over again.

It felt so damn good.

My eyes rolled back in my head as my release filled Dmitri's hand. Dmitri's roar filled my ears as the man shoved his thick cock as deep into my ass as he could possibly go.

He'd never come out if I had my way.

Dmitri's hand stroked down my chest as my rapid panting slowed to a low rise and fall. I smiled when Dmitri reached up and brushed the sweat dampened hair back from my face.

"I love you, Eiji."

More satisfied than I ever remember feeling, I smiled up at the man. *"I love you, too."*

Chapter Thirty
~ Dmitri ~

I could feel Eiji sitting rigidly beside me and I couldn't blame him for being anxious. As far as he was concerned, we were headed back into the den of the demon that had tortured him for years.

I'd be anxious, too.

I gave a gentle squeeze to the hand I held with my own, trying to reassure him. "It's going to be okay, Eiji. We have plenty of men with us."

Not to mention a lawyer and a couple of police officers.

The police officers were the ones that got me. I was actually relying on the cops to assist me. *Me.* If that didn't mean my life was bizarre, I didn't know what did.

Eiji pulled out his phone and typed something before showing me the screen. *"I just don't think this is going to be as simple as serving her some paperwork and asking her to leave."*

Oh, I was aware.

"That's why I brought extra men."

"How's that going to go over with the police?"

I hadn't worked that part out yet.

"I'm hoping we can simply serve her with papers without involving the police." It would be great if they just stayed in their cars. "If things go sideways, I'll take care of it."

Eiji nodded.

"Lev is going to stay with you at all times. You are not to leave his side. His only duty is your protection. If Beverly or her brats try anything, he will get you to safety. You are to do what he says."

Eiji frowned, but nodded. I knew he didn't like what I had said, but I needed to not have to worry about Eiji while I dealt with Beverly. I needed to know he was safe for my own peace of mind.

I actually wished he could have stayed home, but our home was in rubbles. I considered having him stay back at the hotel, but that was even worse than having him walk into a potentially dangerous situation with me.

My heart still ached every time I thought about him being kidnapped. It had happened under my watch, whether I had been there or not. I had been tasked with protecting Eiji and I had failed.

I would not fail again.

"We're here," I said as the car slowed and we started to pull into a gated driveway. I darted a look at Lev. "You know what to do."

"I do, sir."

"Don't mess up," I growled harshly, putting as much force behind my tone as I could. "You won't enjoy my response if you do."

Lev gulped, his eyes going saucer size. "No, sir."

I kept a tight hold of Eiji's hand once the car came to a stop. I waited until Lev and a few of the other bodyguards got out before joining them.

Thankfully, the police officers would wait in their vehicles unless we needed them. They had been ordered not to interfere unless there was trouble. I prayed they stayed there. I really did not need the authorities all up in my business even if this time it was legal.

I stayed down at the bottom of the steps while Miles Cranston, the lawyer Jake had set me up with, walked to the door and knocked. Vasil stood behind him like a silent warrior, his hands clasped casually in front of him as if he was simply an observer to what was going on.

I knew better.

"Do you recognize him?" I asked Eiji when a man in a butler's outfit answered the door. "Wasn't he here before? I think I recognize him from when we got married."

Eiji quickly typed a message out and then held up his phone. *"He's been my stepmother's minion for several years."*

Minion?

Fantastic.

Maybe I'd get to shoot someone after all.

I returned my attention to the front door when it closed, leaving all of us outside.

Miles glanced over his shoulder at us. "The butler is going to see if Mrs. Yamada is receiving visitors." He rolled his eyes before turning back toward the door.

It opened a few minutes later, the butler standing there once again. "My apologies, sir, but Madam is unavailable at this time."

"Make her available," Miles stated firmly.

The butler glared with indignation in his eyes. "Sir—"

Miles pointed to the two police cars sitting in the driveway. "Make her available or get arrested."

The butler's eyes darted to the two vehicles before he slowly stepped back and opened the door. Miles gestured to us and then stepped inside. I could feel Eiji shaking, so I wrapped my arm around his waist and pulled him tightly to my side.

"You're safe, *malen'kiy*. I won't let anyone hurt you."

Eiji didn't respond, but I could feel him shake a little less. I knew no matter what I did or said, he was still going to be frightened. He did not have good memories of this place.

I hoped to change that.

I kept a tight hold of Eiji as we followed Miles into the mansion. Miles was in the lead here simply because this all needed to be legal like. I would have preferred just to throw that bitch out on the streets, but if I did, Eiji could lose everything. I couldn't allow that to happen.

The butler led us into the same living room I'd been in the last time I was here before clasping his hands behind him.

"Can I offer you some coffee?"

Miles shook his head. "No, coffee, thank you, but we do need to speak with Mrs. Yamada immediately."

"Of course, sir. I will inform her right now. Please wait here."

While the butler might have said those polite words, I could tell that was the last thing he wanted to do.

I carefully pulled the hood up over Eiji's head before stating, "Eiji, stay here with Lev. I think Miles and I need to help the butler inform your stepmother we are here."

I had this uneasy feeling that Beverly was going to try something. I just didn't know what that something was, and I wasn't taking any chances with Eiji's safety.

I gestured to Miles and then started walking in the direction the butler had gone in. I wasn't surprised to find him heading toward the study where I had met with Beverly once before. I was surprised to hear Beverly ranting through the closed door.

"What do you mean he's unavailable?" she screeched. "We had a deal, damn it. I gave him information and he gets that little brat to sign the papers before he kills him. If he can't follow through on his end of the bargain, I'll tell Petrov everything. Now, get him on the phone right this instant."

My eyes narrowed as anger ignited in my gut faster than a match to a barrel of gasoline. I wanted to ask who "him" was, but I was pretty sure I already knew, which meant Beverly had been working with O'Donnell.

Question was, how long had they been working together? I distinctly remember Konstantin telling me that the O'Donnells had been behind the troubles I had at the casino.

When the butler opened the door and stepped into the room, Miles and I stepped in behind him.

"Hang up the phone."

Beverly's eyes rounded and she slowly hung up the phone. "Dmitri, I wasn't expecting you. You should have called first. I would have arranged lunch."

"This isn't a social visit, Beverly." I wouldn't eat with this woman if she was serving imported caviar. I probably imported better anyway.

"Mrs. Beverly Yamada," Miles started as he held a piece of paper out to her. He waited until she took it to continue. "You've been officially served. You must leave the premises immediately. Your belongings will be packed for you and shipped to the address of your choosing."

I had no idea how Miles had gotten the judge to evict her from the estate so quickly. From what I knew, it took weeks if not months to evict someone.

Beverly gasped as she looked over the papers Miles had handed her. "You can't do this."

"We can and we have," I stated. "It's time for you to go."

Rage glared in her eyes when her head snapped up. "You said I could stay in the mansion."

"I did, but I never stated how long you'd get to stay. You've been here almost six weeks since I married Eiji. That's long enough. Now it's time for you and your little minions to go."

There was no way in hell we were keeping the butler, or anyone else that had worked here when Eiji was here. They were lucky they got to continue breathing.

"You can't make me leave." Beverly tossed the papers back in Miles's face. "This has been my home for twenty years. I won't leave. You can't make me."

"We can actually." Miles gathered up the papers and stuck them back in his briefcase. "The Ninth Circuit Court of New York has deemed you a squatter in this residence. They have ordered your immediate eviction along with that of your sons. If you do not leave immediately, the nice police officers waiting outside will escort you off the property."

"No!" Beverly snapped. "This is my home. I won't give it up."

"It was your—"

The scream from down the hallway was unexpected because I'd never heard it before. It was also loud and terrified.

I knew it was Eiji.

I raced out of the study and down the hallway to the living room. The scene I found sent my temper roaring to the surface. Three men had Eiji surrounded and they were tugging at his head hood.

"Let him go!"

Everyone froze.

"Let him go now!"

I did not like having to repeat myself.

As soon as they released him, Eiji started racing across the room. He tripped and fell to his knees halfway there, but instead of climbing to his feet again, he just scrambled across the floor on his hands and knees until he reached me.

I dropped down to my knees to catch him, lifting him up against me. "It's okay, Eiji," I whispered as soon as I had him in my arms. "I've got you."

I kept one arm wrapped tightly around him, keeping him pinned to me. I used the other to run my hand over his body, looking for any signs of injury or something that might explain the terrified scream I had heard.

I didn't find anything, which made me worry even more. That frightened sound should never come out of Eiji's mouth. I wanted to know why it had, but I needed to comfort my baby first.

I threaded my fingers through Eiji's hair before grabbing a fistful and forcing his head back. The tear stains on his pale cheeks were too numerous to count.

"What happened, *malen'kiy*?"

More tears slid down Eiji's cheeks as he grabbed my hand and brought it up to his chest, sliding it just under the edge of his shirt and then pressing my fingers against his warm skin.

I frowned as I lifted the material out of the way. As soon as I saw the scratches on his chest I knew. I lifted my head and glared at the three individuals standing across the room from me.

"Were they bullying you?"

Eiji sucked in a breath so hard, I worried about him. He started slapping his hand against my chest. His wide eyes dominated his face. His chest moved rapidly up and down as he frantically tried to draw in more air.

"Ssshh, ssshh, ssshh." I threaded my fingers through his hair again, trying to calm him. "You're okay. You're safe now. I've got you, and I won't let you go."

Eiji slapped my chest again before curling his fingers around the fabric of my shirt.

"I know, I know. Take a deep breath for me." I breathed in deep and then slowly let it out, directing him on what to do. "Match your breathing to mine. Come on, deep breath and then slowly release it." I smiled down at Eiji, watching as he did as I directed. "That's it, slow and easy, *malen'kiy*."

When Eiji loosened his grip on my shirt, not fully releasing it, just easing up a bit, I knew he was going to be okay.

"Miles, would you get me the fuzzy blanket from the back of the car," I ordered without looking away from Eiji's face.

As soon as Miles handed it to me, I wrapped the blanket around Eiji. Thankfully, it wasn't a large blanket. I was still able to wrap it fully around him before tucking him against my chest again.

When I stood, I had Eiji wrapped in my arms, his head resting on my shoulder and partially hidden by the edge of the blanket. I knew Eiji liked it that way. He didn't like others looking at him.

I pinned my anger on the three men standing across the room, glaring at them. "Explain yourselves."

Tom snorted. "Seriously, Dmitri? You're treating him like a fucking sissy. He needs to grow the fuck up." Tom waved his hand toward me and Eiji. "I mean, look at him. You have him wrapped up like a baby burrito."

I felt Eiji shudder in my arms and wished I could have him taken anywhere else but here. I also knew if I did that, the damage would be worse. "My relationship with Eiji or how I treat him is none of your concern."

When would these idiots get it through their thick skulls that Eiji belonged to me now?

"He's our brother," Dick said. "Of course we have a right to be concerned."

"Stepbrother," I corrected, "and what you were doing to him was not being concerned. You were bullying him."

"We were not!"

"You were, actually. What other reason could Eiji have for being so upset?" I smiled down at the vivid green eyes staring up at me. "Besides, he told me exactly what you did to him."

"Bullshit!" Tom shouted. "Eiji can't talk. He's mute."

"Eiji can talk and he talks quite well. You're just too stupid to understand him." I nodded my head toward the door. "Lev, Vasil, please see that these three and their mother leave the estate. They are not allowed back."

"Uh, sir?"

I glanced at Vasil. "What is it?"

"I can't find Lev."

Come to think of it, I hadn't seen him when I entered the room either, but all of my attention had been on Eiji so...

Eiji patted my chest again and then made grabby hands. I handed over my phone.

"Lev went to get my jacket from the car," Eiji typed out. *"These three showed up before he came back."*

"I didn't see him when I went out to get Eiji's blanket," Miles said.

I sighed. "Vasil, have the other guards find Lev."

What the hell was going on here?

Chapter Thirty-One

~ Eiji ~

Even with my face buried in Dmitri's neck, I could feel all three of my stepbrothers glaring at me. That was par for the course with them. I wasn't even sure they knew how to do anything except glare.

Well, that wasn't totally true. I knew what they looked like when they were inflicting pain. I knew what they sounded like, too. That almost gleeful laugh that haunted my dreams even when I was awake.

I peeked up at Dmitri for a moment wondering if I should say anything or just let it go. Life had gotten pretty good for me as of late and I kind of didn't want to upset that. If I spoke out, I knew it would, but what would happen if I didn't speak out?

I wasn't sure I wanted to know.

I started slowly typing out what I wanted to say to Dmitri, but my fingers moved faster the more I typed. They also started to tremble a little.

"When I was fifteen years old, three men kidnapped me and tied me up in the basement of one of the buildings where I attended private school. They had me for two days. They beat me, humiliated me, and did...other stuff. They also threatened me that if I ever told anyone what happened, they would kill me. That's when I lost my voice."

Dmitri's brow flickered with unease as he read what I had typed. His dark eyes were filled with rage when they lifted to mine.

I typed out the one truth that had lived with me every single day I had been held prisoner in this mansion, the one that kept me silent. *"It was my stepbrothers that hurt me."*

I had been blindfolded when I'd woken up in that basement, but there was no way I could have missed their voices. They didn't even try and disguise themselves.

Considering the things they had said to me then and again over the years—sometimes the exact same things—it hadn't been too hard to figure out it had been them.

I had always feared that they would come after me again. Sure, they had beaten me on numerous occasions, but that was it. I'd take that any day over what else they had done to me.

My anxiety, fear of other people, and the loss of my voice could all be laid at the feet of my dear stepbrothers, and I hated them to the depths of my soul.

Dmitri's eyes narrowed as he turned to look at my stepbrothers. I knew that look. He wanted to eviscerate them where they stood and then dance in their blood.

I couldn't say I had a real problem with it.

Except for the police waiting outside. I'd rather have my husband here at my side rather than kill the three men that had made the last ten years a living hell.

"Dmitri, the police are outside. You can't do anything to them. There is no evidence of their crimes beyond my word, and I doubt it would hold up in a court of law."

Especially considering I couldn't speak.

My eyes rounded when Dmitri took my phone from me and typed something out instead of just saying it. I could only assume he didn't want my stepbrothers to know what he was saying.

"Is there some place here we can hold them until the police leave?"

I quickly read the message and then grinned. *"My old bedroom on the third floor. The door has a lock, and the windows are nailed shut the last time I escaped. It's high enough up that no one will see them or hear them."*

I spoke from experience.

"Go stand with Miles," he said out loud as he set me on my feet.

I quickly complied, curious as to what he was going to do. His hands were kind of tied at the moment due to the officers outside.

My jaw dropped when he pulled out his gun and pointed it at my stepbrothers and then ordered his men to escort them upstairs to my old bedroom.

"Once you get them upstairs, I want them stripped down to their underwear. They take nothing with them inside that room. I want the door locked and two men guarding it until further notice. If they try and escape, shoot them."

"You can't do this!" Tom shouted as he tried to evade the guard coming after him, running around to put a chair between them.

"As I told your mother, I can and I am. Now go with my guards or I will just shoot you here where you stand." Dmitri smirked as he cocked his head. "Personally, after what you and your brothers did to my husband, I kind of hope you try and escape."

A flash of fear went over Tom's face. "We didn't do anything to him."

"Really?" Dmitri rubbed his jaw with his free hand. The other one was still pointing a gun at the three men. "You didn't kidnap Eiji, tie him up in a basement of that fancy private school, and torture him for two days? You didn't threaten to kill him if he told? You didn't continue your abuse for the last ten years?"

"There's no evidence that we did anything!"

Evidence or not, that kind of sounded like an admission of guilt to me.

"You're right, there is no evidence. Just Eiji's word against yours. Sadly for you, I believe him, not you." Dmitri waved his gun. "Take them away. Gag them and tie them up if you have to, but only after you strip them down to their underwear."

I kind of wanted to ask for a picture of that scene, but figured it was really out of place at the moment.

Maybe later.

As soon as my stepbrothers were led out of the room—struggling the entire time—I hurried over to Dmitri's side.

"What now?" I mouthed.

"Once we get your stepmother out of here, I'll take care of them." Dmitri's arm wrapped around me, holding me close. "You'll never have to deal with them again."

That was a dream I'd long had. It had just never been realized before. I had the impression from the tight clench of Dmitri's jaw that that might have just changed.

Dmitri jerked me closer when the front door slammed open. Pressed as close as I was, it was all I could do to turn my head to see who it was.

Lev stormed inside with Vasil right on his heels. Neither man looked happy. Lev's nostrils were flaring, and he looked as if he wanted to start shouting but was holding himself back.

"What happened?" Dmitri asked. "Where were you?"

"Fucking cops," Lev snapped. "I went out to get Eiji's jacket and they cornered me, started asking me all sorts of questions about you. When I tried to come back into the house, they threatened to arrest me."

"Where are they now?" Dmitri asked.

Lev grimaced. "When Vasil came out to get me, they jumped in their cars and took off."

"I don't think they are here to evict Mrs. Yamada, Boss," Vasil said. "From what Lev said and what I overheard when I went outside, they were just a little too interested in what we were doing here."

Freaking fantastic. We hadn't even moved in yet and the local authorities were already trying to get all up in my business.

This did not bode well for the future.

"I want two guards on the door," Dmitri ordered. "Call in more if you need them. I need to finish dealing with Beverly."

Nothing could have prevented my shudder.

"Do you want to stay here with Miles and Lev?"

I rapidly shook my head, desperate as I latched onto Dmitri's arm. It wasn't that I didn't trust the other two men, but they weren't the strong imposing mountain of a man standing next to me. The only time I knew I was truly safe was when I was with Dmitri.

"She's going to be vicious. Are you prepared for that?"

Not really, but I nodded anyway.

Dmitri didn't seem to mind the tight hold I had on his arm as we walked down the hallway toward the study. Nothing good had ever come from entering this room, although I had a few good memories from before my father passed away. Only pain after that.

A gust of breath shot through my mouth when Dmitri suddenly pushed me away and then raced across the room.

"Going somewhere, Beverly?" Dmitri asked as he pulled her back in the window she had been attempting to climb out of.

"Get your hands off me!"

"Drop the bag," Dmitri countered.

"No, it's mine!" Beverly clutched the large lavender colored bag to her chest. It was bigger than a purse, but smaller than a duffle bag, so I wasn't quite sure what it was.

I did know she didn't want to let it go.

"You're not leaving here with anything that you can't prove is yours," Dmitri said. "Mr. Cranston is here to make sure you don't take anything that doesn't belong to you."

"No!"

Dmitri held out his hand. "Hand it over."

"No!" she screamed again.

Dmitri stepped over and forcefully pulled the bag out of her hands. When my stepmother tried to take it back, Dmitri gestured to Vasil, who hurried over and grabbed her and forced her to sit in one of the chairs in front of the desk.

"What was so important, Beverly? Huh?"

I walked a little closer when Dmitri grabbed the bottom of the bag and turned it upside down. A gasp flew from my lips when I saw all the coins, jewelry, and stacks of cash.

I didn't care about the cash, but...I quickly typed out a message to Dmitri. *"That's my mother's jewelry, and I'm pretty sure those coins belong to my father's coin collection. I was willed all of this when my parents passed away."*

Dmitri's jaw clenched as he lifted his head to glare at Beverly. "I figured as much."

"It's mine," Beverly spit out. "I earned it."

Dmitri snorted. "You married Jiro Yamada. That made you his wife, not his whore. You are only entitled to what he gave you. Nothing more, nothing less."

"That's not true," Beverly shouted as she leapt to her feet. When she pointed in my direction, I edged behind Dmitri. "I had to take care of that useless brat every day for the last twenty years. I deserve all of this."

I felt Dmitri stiffen.

"You never took care of Eiji," Dmitri snapped. "You abused him and used him to take everything his father left him away from him. I wouldn't be surprised if you were the one that ordered your sons to kidnap him all those years ago."

When Beverly paled, I knew Dmitri was right.

"You did, didn't you?" Dmitri's hands clenched into fists. "Did you just order them to beat him up, or did you order them to rape him, too?"

"I would never!"

"Yeah, I don't believe you, Beverly." Dmitri nodded his head toward the door. "Take her upstairs and lock her up with the others until I can figure out what to do with them, and strip her down to her underwear just like those three bastards."

As Lev and Vasil grabbed Beverly and started dragging her out of the room, I edged around Dmitri so he remained between me and her. Guards or not, I didn't trust her not to try something. Her empire of evil was crumbling, and she was trying to claw her way out of it.

Once I had worked my way around in front of Dmitri, I buried my face in his chest. My trembling slowed as he rubbed his hands up and down my back.

"She won't ever hurt you again, *malen'kiy*. I swear it."

I believed him.

I hugged him tight and then tilted my head back so I could see his face. I swallowed hard before uttering words I never thought I'd say, let alone out loud.

"I love you."

They were croaked out by a throat unused to using those muscles, and it was a bit painful, but the grin that spread across Dmitri's face made it all worth it.

"I love you, too," Dmitri stated.

Yep, worth it.

Chapter Thirty-Two

~ Dmitri ~

It had only been two months since we moved into Eiji's estate, but already the place was starting to feel like home. I knew a large part of that was due to Eiji.

Since finding his voice, he'd been talking a lot more. He still used his phone—usually when he was tired—but those times were becoming fewer and fewer.

"Konstantin just called, Boss," Yasha said as he walked into my new home office. "He's landed in Ireland. Once he gets a little rest, he'll start his search. He'll call when he finds something."

"Good."

Mary had fled back to Ireland when word got out that I was looking for her. I wasn't about to let her get away with what she had done so I'd sent Konstantin to hunt her down. If she came willingly, she wouldn't die. If she didn't, she died on the spot.

"What did he do with Clausen?"

"I don't know." Yasha shrugged. "Left him with some friends or something."

"Any word on Beverly's guards?" I wanted each and every guard that had ever laid a hand on Eiji dealt with. It was unfortunate that Beverly had fired them the moment Eiji and I got married. It meant I had to hunt them down as well.

I glanced toward the office door when someone knocked. "Come."

Olav opened the door. "Mr. Vinnie Borelli is here to see you, sir."

"Show him in."

I stood as soon as Vinnie strolled into the room and then shook the man's hand before sitting down. I gestured to the chair in front of my desk. "Please, sit."

Once Vinnie sat down, I smiled at him. I really did owe this man, as much as that grieved me. "How can I help you today, Vinnie?"

"I thought I'd bring you a little news," Vinnie replied. "My grandfather received word that Ireland is sending someone new to take over Queens."

My eyebrows lifted. "Did they say who?"

"His name is Angus King," Vinnie replied. "That's all the information I received. I don't know much about him, although I have heard his name here and there. My understanding is that he's a ball-buster that they send in to clean up messes."

"Do you think he's going to be a problem?" I had just cleaned up one mess. I didn't want to fall into another one.

"Ireland is trying desperately to smooth things over with us. They are more than aware that what the O'Donnells did was out of line and violated pretty much every agreement you or I had with them. I doubt they want to rock the boat now by sending us another O'Donnell."

"Let's hope not or I'll put him in a cell next to Eiji's stepbrothers."

"So it's true." Vinnie snorted.

"What's true?"

"You shipped those three asshats back to a Russian prison in Siberia."

"Oh, yes, that's true." It had been one of my brighter ideas. "It's only a ten-year sentence for each of them, but those will be ten very long years."

Only the hearty made it out alive.

"What about his stepmother?"

I was pretty sure my feelings on that woman came through when Vinnie's eyes widened. "Beverly likes to gamble. She's so addicted to it that she made Eiji's life a living hell. I merely returned the favor."

Vinnie cocked an eyebrow.

"She will spend the next ten years as a cocktail waitress in a casino my family owns in Russia. She must earn enough in tips to pay for her food, lodging, and any extras. It's up to her how she earns it."

"She could start gambling again."

I grinned evilly. "I hope she does."

Beverly was a lousy gambler, and the casino was rigged in favor of the house. She didn't stand a chance in hell of making a big score. If she got too in debt, I had no doubt that my family would put her to work in a brothel somewhere until she paid off what she owed.

Either way, she was out of Eiji's life for good.

I glanced at my cell phone when it chimed, and then smiled as I lifted my head and looked across my desk to my guest. "Would you like to join me for coffee out on the veranda? It's time for morning calisthenics."

Vinnie lifted an eyebrow. "Morning calisthenics?"

"It's something I treat myself to every morning at ten. After the fire, we lost a few men. We had to hire new people and get all settled into Eiji's mansion. This is one of the ways our new men train."

Vinnie looked skeptical.

I chuckled as I got up from my desk. "I promise you'll enjoy it."

I led Vinnie out through the patio doors and around to the back of the house where we had a full view of the backyard. A small table and a couple of chairs had already been set up near the railing next to the stairs.

I gestured to one of them before sitting down. "Coffee?"

"Please," Vinnie replied.

I gestured to the maid standing by. "Two coffees."

While we waited for our coffee, Vinnie glanced around, the frown on his face becoming even deeper. "Why am I out here, Dmitri?"

"Just wait."

Vinnie stiffened when two lines of bodyguards walked out of the house and then down the stairs to the lawn. They spread out evenly spaced with each man having enough room to move about.

"What are they doing?"

"As I am sure you are fully aware, in order to have adequate protection, your bodyguards must be in good physical condition."

"Yes, of course, but—"

"What I didn't realize until recently is that while they are strong and muscular, they don't tend to be all that flexible. Their dexterity is not where it should be. I didn't discover this until Eiji escaped two of my guards."

"Your husband?"

I pointed to the man currently walking out of the patio doors followed closely by the Black Russian Terrier I'd gifted him when we moved into the mansion. He might be small, but he was a trained guard dog and he was vicious. He was also totally devoted to Eiji and went everywhere with him.

"Him?"

I understood Vinnie's doubt. I'd had the very same thing until I saw Eiji in motion. It didn't help Vinnie's confusion that Eiji was dressed in flower print leggings with a pink long-sleeved shirt that hung down to mid-thigh.

He must have known we had a guest because he also wore his head cover, although he did match it with the flower print leggings. It hid his hair and most of his face.

"He's not very big and he certainly isn't as strong as my guards," I said, "but he's fast, flexible, and ferocious in tense situations."

Vinnie jumped when loud music began blaring through the speakers we had set up. I leaned forward; my gaze riveted on the man at the front of the crowd of guards as he began to move.

My guards had been reluctant to join in with morning calisthenics until they saw the way Eiji moved and the things he had been able to do simply because he was more limber than them, and then they had jumped at the chance.

"They are dancing."

"They are," I agreed. "But watch how they move, the way they are able to stretch, twist, and turn. Now, imagine they are protecting you. Picture that in a fight."

It didn't take long for Vinnie to nod his head. "I see your point."

"I thought you might."

"I can also see why you come out here for your coffee break every morning. That is quite the view."

Yes, it was.

I smirked as I picked up my cup of coffee and watched my husband lead my bodyguards through their training session. Even with his head covering still on, he looked glorious.

And he was all mine.

~ The End ~

Also Available By Aja Foxx

AN EAGLE CREEK RANCH STORY
Cowboy's City Slicker
Cowboy's Tender Touch

GALEAZZI TRILOGY
That One Time
One More Time

GUARDIANS OF THE PACK
Protecting His Own

Mafia Mayhem
The Capo's Boy
The Boss's Boy

Marriage Mayhem
The Marriage Contract
The Marriage Runaway
The Marriage Switch
The Marriage Betrothal
The Marriage Merger

SHIFTER KINGS
Alpha Knows Best
Savage Bite

SOLDIERS OF FORTUNE
Forgiveness
Reckoning
Absolution

SINGLE TITLES
The Rising
Human ~~Vampire~~ Prince
Prince Charming NOT!
How To Summon A Boyfriend
The Art of Seduction

Also Available From Aja Foxx & Ciena Foxx

WILDE WOLVES
His Unconventional Omega
Denying His Alpha
Lone Wolf
Cry Wolf

THE CAPO'S BOY

~ *Nicky* ~
I never intended to be a mobster's secret lover, but somehow I found myself in that position. It's been two years now and I can't say I hate it. It only becomes a problem when Vinnie's family tries to marry him off to someone else. I may be his little secret, but I refuse to be his side-piece.

When I find myself on the run, fearing for my life, I'm not sure who I can turn to, especially when I'm not positive Vinnie isn't behind the threats to my life. I was his dirty little secret and if he wants to get married, it made sense for him to get rid of me first. I just don't think I can take the fact that the man I love wants me dead.

~ *Vinnie* ~
He was supposed to be a one-night stand, but that turned into a week, and then a month, and then two years. Before I knew it, Nicky was engrained in my very soul. I would do anything for him, protect him from anyone, even the dangerous life I live.

When he ran from me, I knew I should let him go for his sake, but I can't. Being the *caporegime* of my mafia crime family means nothing to me without Nicky at my side. If I can figure out who is trying to kill him, I just might be able to bring him home. I just have to find him first.

https://www.amazon.com/Capos-Boy-Romance-Marriage-Mayhem-ebook/dp/B0C4K8Y3VD

STORY EXCERPT

"What do you want?"

"Let me in, Nicky."

I rolled my eyes and moved away from my front door. There was no point in closing it. Vinnie would just go through it. As soon as I was in the middle of my living room, I spun around and crossed my arms, pinning my angry gaze on him.

Vinnie was dressed in his usual black Armani suit...crisp white dress shirt open at the collar, pressed slacks, suit jacket hiding the gun in a shoulder holster. He had another one hidden in his ankle high boots.

To say he looked hot was the understatement of the millennia. He was sex on two legs, and I wanted to lick him.

Damn it.

"You get that I am not going to do this with you, don't you?"

"Nicky—"

"No!" I shouted as all the anger and hurt I'd been feeling for the last week welled up inside of me. "You made your choice, Vinnie. I'm done."

I'd been on the verge of tears since the moment I heard Vinnie was engaged to get married to some woman his grandfather had picked out for him.

"The hell you are!" Vinnie shouted right back to me. "You belong to me. You will always belong to me."

"I used to belong to you, but you gave me away."

"I did not give you away."

"Fine, you decided you didn't want me anymore and tossed me away. Same damn thing."

It was hard looking at him, knowing that he didn't want me as much as I wanted him. I had been stupid. So stupid. I had made him the center of my world...and he had not.

To Vinnie, I was a toy to be taken off the shelf occasionally and played with. I was not the love of his life.

Too bad he was mine.

"You need to go," I whispered, wanting him to leave before the tears flooding my eyes spilled down my cheeks. I didn't need that humiliation on top of all the rest.

"This is still my apartment, Nicky."

I refused to acknowledge how much those words hurt. Yes, Vinnie paid for the apartment, but he didn't need to remind me I was a kept whore who only had a roof over my head because I warmed his bed.

I really had been stupid.

I walked over and grabbed my jacket, pulling it on, and then made sure I had my wallet in my pocket. Pretty sure I was going to need it. I thought about taking my cell phone, but Vinnie paid for that, too.

I picked up the house keys and stared at them for a moment before tossing them at Vinnie. They hit him in the middle of his chest before falling to the floor.

"It's all yours, Mr. Borelli. Hope you can get your deposit back."

I walked out the door and slid between the two bodyguards standing right outside before they could stop me. I heard Vinnie shouting my name, ordering me to come back, but I just kept on walking. When I heard the squeal of tires behind me, I started running and I didn't stop.

I probably should have packed my belongings before leaving, but once again, almost everything I had had been paid for by Vinnie, from my apartment right down to the clothes on my back and the food on my table.

I had thought there was something special between me and Vinnie, but he had proved that theory wrong when he tossed me away like yesterday's trash when he agreed to marry the woman his family had picked out for him.

I would never hold a special place in his heart. I would always be a booty call for him, his side piece while he built a family with some woman I didn't even know the name of. I would never be anything more than his whore.

I wanted to smack myself for even thinking there could be something special between us or that what we had would last a lifetime.

I should have known better.

Vinnie was a *caporegime* in the Borelli crime family, and I was his dirty little secret. He could never acknowledge me in public and he certainly couldn't marry me or even live with me on a fulltime basis. People didn't do "gay" in the mafia.

It was a death sentence.

When I slipped in the snow and almost kissed the pavement, I slowed down and started walking at a normal pace. I had probably looked like a crazy person running down the sidewalk the way I was.

I slid my hands into the pockets of my jacket, wishing I had thought to grab my gloves. They were fur lined and very nice, but they were yet one more thing that Vinnie had bought for me.

I stopped suddenly right there in the middle of the sidewalk and let out a laugh that for sure made me seem crazy. I had nothing. I'd spent the last two years living off of Vinnie, and with the exception of a small box of personal items shoved in the back of my closet, I had nothing that Vinnie hadn't provided for me.

I had just lost everything.

Well, maybe not.

I started down the sidewalk again, walking a little faster as I headed for the nearest ATM. Vinnie provided me with an allowance once a week, play money he called it, but we both knew what it was.

I had been a very well-paid whore.

If I was lucky, he hadn't cleared out my bank account. The last time I checked, there had been a little over three thousand dollars in there. If I could get to it fast enough, I might be able to pull it out.

It would keep me from sleeping on a park bench. Considering there was snow on the ground, I'd rather avoid that scene. That didn't mean I wasn't going to pay back every single penny of the three thousand dollars.

The apartment and everything he had provided for me before was on him. It had started out as a business deal. My body for him taking care of me. I'd been the stupid one to bring emotions into it.

Anything I took after I left had to be repaid. I might be a mafia man's whore, but I did have my pride. I would pay Vinnie back if it was the last thing I did.

I was lucky. I spotted a bank branch down the street. I walked directly to the ATM to check my balance. As soon as I saw the balance, tears sprang to my eyes.

It was all there.

I quickly walked into the bank and pulled everything out and then closed the account. I wouldn't need it anymore. Well, once I got a job, I would need one, but I wouldn't be using the same account. Vinnie had access to this one.

After putting the cash into my wallet, I pulled out the debit card and credit card Vinnie had given me. I smiled at the woman behind the counter. "Do you have a pair of scissors I can use?"

As soon as she handed the scissors to me, I cut up both cards into as many pieces as I could manage. I smiled again when I handed them back. "Do you have a garbage can?"

Her eyes were a little wide as she reached down and grabbed her garbage can. I took it and swept all the tiny pieces into the can and handed it back. "Thank you."

"Man troubles?"

I nodded. "Big time."

"You should have maxed out his card first."

I shook my head. "I just want it to be over."

I didn't want another thing from Vincenzo Borelli.

Aja Foxx

MM ROMANCE WITH FIERY PASSION

The vicious bite of an enemy, a shout, a cry in the dark. A lover's touch, the whisper of a kiss. A sigh, a groan, heart beating faster, desire surging through a body. Love words spoken in the shadows. The yearning for a soft caress. I'm a writer of fiery passion in all its glorious forms. Paranormal, Contemporary, Sci-Fi, Fantasy, MM Romance books. There is no limit to my imagination.

https://ajafoxx.com/
https://www.facebook.com/aja.foxx.69
https://www.amazon.com/Aja-Foxx/e/B07VX6TYJ4

Made in the USA
Las Vegas, NV
04 December 2023